Out of Left Field:
A Small-Town Sports Romance
Book One in the North Bay Series

By Stephanie Giese

ISBN-13: 9781737206842

Cover design by: Rachel Howard
Interior illustrations by: Abigail Giese

Published by Binkies and Briefcases, LLC

Printed in the United States of America

Dedication:
To Eddie, who is both my Mike and my Jake.

And to my great-grandmother, Bessie Armstrong, who raised the generations of women who melded together into my inspiration for Honey and also had the largest collection of romance novels I have ever seen in one place.

Content Warning

The reader should be aware that this book contains adult content and is recommended for readers over the age of eighteen. The following pages contain strong language and on-page consensual sexual encounters as well as alcohol, prescription drug use, gambling, non-lethal automobile accidents, and smoking. Human and animal deaths are also referenced but occur off-page. Mike and Danielle's book is a love story with themes of addiction, abandonment, and grief. I promise there is a happy ending.

Chapter 1

Danielle

A bell dings in the open window that separates the kitchen from the indoor dining area of The Blue Crab, and our cook lays a plate of crab cakes on the rustic wooden counter. When he sets a pitcher of Coke down next to it with a thud, some of the sugary brown liquid sloshes over the side, creating a puddle.

"Order up." Jackson's deep voice booms from the belly of the restaurant, and he slaps the counter twice.

I rush to grab the food, but footsteps behind me, along with the unmistakable tinkling of a dozen metal bracelets, cause me to swivel and face our boss.

"I'll take this one, Dee. Go ahead and get out of here," Edna offers, stepping around me. She removes a rag from her back pocket to wipe up the spilled soda. "You've been in every day this week. I'm sure you've got studying to do, and Honey is going to let me have it if your grades start to slip."

"You're daggone right, I will," my grandma yells from the corner booth where she is eating her dinner and eavesdropping on everyone, as always. I'd like to say she's here to visit me, but it's more likely that she's trying to get the scoop on our regulars.

"Thanks, Edna. I'll head out now if you don't mind. Regina should be here soon."

After delivering the crab cakes and soda to their rightful owners, Edna slides across from her favorite partner-in-crime and steals a french fry from Honey's plate. Honey swats her friend's hand away, causing her own reading glasses to sway on the beaded chain where they hang around her neck. A second pair is perched on top of her head.

"You're scheduling her too much, Edna. How is Danielle supposed to keep up with school?" Honey takes a long sip of her margarita, and a drop falls on her neon green cotton dress. It blends seamlessly with the dots of melted wax from her candle-making endeavors.

"She's my best server. What do you want me to do?" Edna asks as she takes another fry.

"I'm a full-grown adult woman," I remind them. "If there's a problem with my classes or the schedule, I'll let you know. Now I really am leaving."

"Sure ya are." Honey offers a half-hearted wave while she focuses on protecting her plate.

I only have a month left to go before I finish my associate's degree at the community college. You would think my grandmother and my boss have no business discussing my grades. Yet, because this is North Bay, you would be wrong. In this town, everyone's business is everyone else's business. That should probably be the North Bay motto. It's a great philosophy when people need help and the whole neighborhood rallies around them in hard times. Edna and Honey are exactly the gals you want on the phone tree when there's a hurricane headed our way or the school needs to raise money to install a new water heater. Not so great when it comes to gossiping about my social life.

When Steve ended our relationship last Fall, it took three months for me to be able to make it through a shift without customers shaking their heads and asking how I was doing. I was fine, by the way. Eventually. If I've learned anything in my life, it's that people rarely stick around. Men almost never do. That's okay. I don't need them. I'm secure being single. I just don't want to talk about my self-centered ex every time someone orders a crab pretzel. Is that so much to ask?

I choose to ignore the rest of their discussion about my grades. I'm going to get out of here soon. Really, I am, but Regina is late and I don't want to leave my tables without a server for long.

I turn back to Edna. "I'll just check and see if Table Three has their crab dip first. You said you can give Honey a ride back to the house, right? Don't let Jackson serve her any more drinks. You promised. We don't need a repeat of last week."

Honey mooned the sheriff last Tuesday and she came home in the back of his squad car. He let her off with a warning and a roll of his eyes because he didn't feel like doing the paperwork it would have taken to book her. Good thing, because we can't afford to pay another two-hundred-dollar fine for Honey's shenanigans.

Edna nods and shoos me off with the rag that is still in her hand. She will definitely be sneaking Honey another frozen margarita right alongside that crab imperial.

North Bay, Virginia is known for three things: blue crabs, the Blue Crabs, and The Blue Crab. I promise those are three different things. The shellfish are self-explanatory. There are crabs here. A lot of them. Thanks to our location on the Chesapeake Bay, we are a prime habitat for the crustaceans that mate in brackish areas along the East Coast. Plus, our crabs really are blue before you cook them.

That's why they named our minor league baseball team the Blue Crabs, and it's also why Edna Plum dubbed her restaurant The Blue Crab when she opened it in 1987. I don't think anyone would be surprised to discover what's on the menu. Spoiler alert: It's ninety percent crab.

Also not surprising is The Blue Crab restaurant being my place of employment. It's not like there are many choices. When I'm not in school, I'm here. I need the money for tuition, and a girl only has so many options when the population of our entire county couldn't fill half a shopping mall. I'm not exaggerating. When I say I live in a small town, we are talking only two traffic lights within a ten-mile radius. We have to drive almost thirty minutes to Marnock to find a McDonald's. We share one high school with three other towns, and even if we had a football team, there would hardly be enough athletes to make a roster. North Bay Community College might not be a big school either, but at least it does offer a few teams, so their events can fill our social calendars. Sports are a big deal around here. When there is nothing else to do for miles, games tend to be the main events of the week.

Thanks to the Blue Crabs baseball team and their minor league stadium about twenty minutes outside of town, we also have a steady supply of professional baseball players, most of whom are in their twenties and passing through on the way to bigger opportunities. Praise be for that revolving door of testosterone (not that any of it is directed my way). Otherwise, the only option for us single folks would be to cycle through the handful of guys who have known us since we were in diapers. As my BFF Alice would say, *a hearty no thank you to that.*

My shift ended twenty minutes ago, but I'm still a little bit reluctant to leave before another server gets here to take over. I don't want to leave my regulars to suffer the wrath of Edna and Honey, so I'm refilling their drinks and keeping their bread baskets stocked until Regina arrives. At least when she runs late I get to collect the extra tips. A vibration in my pocket causes me to pull out my phone, wondering if Regina has to bail on her shift and needs me to stay on. I know it can be hard for her when there is a childcare change at the last minute.

Nope, that's not it. I shake my head as I read the latest message from North Bay's biggest gossip. The one sitting three feet away from me.

Honey: *You're still here. I also noticed you never made it home last night. You forget how the car works or did my favorite granddaughter finally get lucky?*

The text is followed by three winky faces and, for some inexplicable reason, a penguin.

"I'm right here." I roll my eyes. "You don't have to text me." Honey's flattery isn't fooling anybody, I'm only her favorite because I'm also her only granddaughter.

"Yeah, but the messages have those fun little pictures. And when things are written down, I can go back and look at what you wrote. Sometimes I can't remember what you said." She uses her fist to knock lightly on the top of her head.

Add my sex life to the list of *Things I'm Not Discussing with My Grandmother*. It's a long list. Even if she is the woman who raised me, my current roommate, and –fine I'll admit it– one of my three closest friends, I'm not sharing any details with Honey Daniels. Mostly because there's nothing to discuss, but also because she's got the loudest mouth this side of the Potomac, and whatever I told her wouldn't stay between us for long.

"Don't pretend for one second you aren't still as sharp as a tack. You just want to copy and paste what I tell you, then share it with your nosy friends. And for the last time, there's nothing to tell. I was with Alice."

Case in point: Edna Plum apparently already knows I'm walking the line between a B minus and a C in British Lit. Who knows what else Honey would share? I don't need half of the North Bay senior citizen population offering their opinions about my lackluster dating life as I wait their tables.

Honey feigns innocence and bats her false eyelashes, making a big show of taking a bite of her crab imperial.

That reminds me.

"Table Three is still waiting on that crab dip," I call to Jackson through the service window before I make a final sweep around the empty tables, wiping down the red vinyl cloths and refilling ketchup bottles and salt and pepper shakers.

It may be true that I didn't make it home last night, but that has nothing to do with a hookup. In reality, I had a coffee date at Brew-Ha-Ha with Alice. Our only local coffee shop also offers open mic nights twice a week. People perform poetry, sing, or attempt stand-up comedy, hence the "ha ha" part of their name. We stayed for two acts, but it was underwhelming. A fifth grader read a few haikus, which was brave of her, and then one of the baseball guys was on stage attempting to play guitar in public for the first time. I know he was just learning because that's what he told everyone, and also because he was terrible.

It didn't matter. It was sort of fun to watch. There was a table full of other muscular men clapping and hollering for him. They sang along, loudly, as he did his best to strum through a few of Ed Sheeran's bigger hits. At least he had a lot of support.

We sat at our own table and kept to ourselves for about an hour while Alice had her usual oat milk latte and I had a cup of chai. We had a few laughs before ducking out early. Then we went back to Alice's apartment, where we watched reruns of *Gilmore Girls* until I was too tired to drive and fell asleep on her couch. That was the extent of my big night out.

"Here. I'm here." Regina is out of breath as she hurries through the door. "So sorry. The babysitter was late again." She smooths her hair in place with one hand, then ties her red half-apron around her waist. The white polo shirt she's wearing won't stay clean for long. Mine is already stained with smears of Old Bay and soaked with mystery liquids.

Regina is a single mom to a very sweet little girl named Emily. The two of them remind me of what it felt like growing up with my own mom. Before we moved to North Bay to be near Honey, it was always the two of us against the world. Plus, just like my mom, Regina is also chronically late.

My phone pings again with another text from Honey. This time it's an eggplant emoji. I already regret telling her what that means.

"You're fine. Table Nine needs ketchup, and we're running low on fries, so push the potato salad. Good luck." I smile at Regina, trying to hide how close I am to losing my patience, which, surprisingly, has nothing to do with how late she is.

I know my grandmother means well with her texts. Her heart is even bigger than her mouth, and that's saying something. That's why when I was a toddler and started calling her Honey, it stuck. But for crying out loud.

"It's weird that you're so much more concerned about my dry spell than I am. You know that, right?" I say, still facing her as I walk backwards toward the kitchen.

"Dry spell? Sugar, at this point it's a full-blown drought." I can hear Honey's musical laugh and throaty voice still teasing me as I push my way through the swinging doors and into the back area of the restaurant.

As a child, I was supposed to call her Grams, but every time she saw me she'd say, "Hi, honey. How are ya?" I started saying it back and associating that phrase with her face. I guess my two-year-old brain thought Honey was her actual name. Now, nineteen years later, that's what everyone calls her. It suits her better than Grams would have anyway. Honey is the sweetest, loudest, and most colorful woman I know. She's had her fair share of time being the one up on stage performing at Brew-Ha-Ha, margarita in hand, especially if Edna Plum is there egging her on.

Honey retired from the library a few years ago. Now she sells her homemade candles at the farmer's market every Wednesday and runs her book club each month, between said margaritas. She has also recently discovered how much she loves to text, so I find myself on the receiving end of messages like these quite a bit. Lucky me.

"Here, I made you a seafood club to go. Don't forget we are hosting that crab feast after the game tomorrow." Jackson hands me a foam take-out box that contains my favorite item on the menu. Our club sandwich is layers of crab cake and shrimp salad, separated by toasted bread and three pieces of bacon. He always puts extra bacon on mine.

"Thank you. You're my favorite. And you can count on me tomorrow. We've got this." Jackson and I are in charge of running the first large event of the year. He grunts and turns his attention back to the flattop grill.

I can see that Honey and Edna are still watching me through the circular window in the swinging doors, so I stick out my tongue. *Oh hush.* I balance the take-out box in the crook of my arm and type my two-word response to the eggplant with one hand, as I use the other to untie my apron and fling the red fabric over my shoulder. I grab my purse from the shelf behind the counter, waving to Jackson on my way out. As I'm deleting Honey's messages, I notice I missed another text during my shift. Even though I'm tired from work and a little irritated with Honey's prying, I can't help my smile when I see the notification came from Jake, the friend I have saved in my contacts as the "Boy Next Door."

BND: *Hey. Let me know when it's a good time for a quick call.*
Me: *Free now if you are, College Boy.*

He is the one guy I've always been able to count on. Although, technically, Jacob Gibson did not live next door. He lived in his parents' house across the street. We met back before either of us could walk or talk, but we became real friends somewhere around age five when my grandfather passed away and mom and I started spending more time in North Bay to be near Honey. Jake's family owns the waterfront land across from Honey's property on Pinecrest Avenue, which makes them our closest neighbors. Besides his annual return for a few weeks each summer, Jake hasn't lived with his parents for three years. He got himself a scholarship to Virginia Tech and now he's at school full-time, three hours away.

My phone rings and his photo appears on the screen as I slide into the driver's seat of the old gray Honda that Honey and I share, so I sit in the parking lot a few minutes longer to talk to him.

"Hello?" I adjust the vent to blow cold air directly onto my face and scan my surroundings to make sure no one can see me before I unhook my jeans and let my muffin top free. That button has been digging into my stomach for the last three hours, and I almost moan in relief.

"Hi, Dan-Dan."

I roll my eyes as Jake greets me. He insists on calling me that just because he knows the nickname irritates me. Why my mom named me Danielle Daniels, I do not understand. But then again, there are a lot of things about my mother I will never understand. When I got to college, I started introducing myself as Danielle, and my full name is printed on the metal nametag pinned to my Blue Crab polo shirt at the moment, but those who know me from home still always call me some version of Dan, Dani, Dee, D.D., et cetera. There were even a painful few months in the fifth grade when some of the more popular girls started taunting me with the nickname Double D, ironically in reference to my then-non-existent chest. Thankfully, I've filled out quite a bit since then. Jake is the only person on the planet who calls me Dan-Dan.

"What's up, Jake?"

"Hey, so listen. We're hosting this philanthropy event to raise money for charity, and I thought maybe you'd be into it. It's actually kind of several events, a full weekend of different activities. There's a bonfire, a hotdog eating contest, and a bunch of other stuff. Then Saturday night there's a formal gala, which is basically a dance with a silent auction at the end."

"Um, cool, I guess. So, are you looking for sponsors to send you donations or something?" I glance over at the seat next to me, where the thirty-seven dollars in cash tips I made during today's slow lunch shift is poking out of my apron pocket. I could probably send him ten bucks, but that feels lame. Honestly, I'd rather just send a donation straight to whatever charity it is than pay some drunk dudes to watch each other puke after eating one too many hot dogs. Plus, then Jake would never have to know how pathetically small my contribution was. Maybe I can ask Edna Plum if the restaurant would be a sponsor.

"No, Dan," he scoffs. "I'm not asking you for money." He pauses and his voice gets a bit softer. "I'm asking if you'll come out and be my plus one for this stupid dance. It's next weekend. I know it's a long drive and short notice. Plus, I'm asking you to, you know, get out of the house and talk to strangers while you wear a dress." I make a gagging sound into the phone and he laughs. "But I thought maybe you'd do it for me? Pretty please?"

My phone buzzes with a new text. He sent a selfie. Jake's making a puppy dog face with a pouty lower lip. The word "please" is flashing in the corner in a neon cartoon font.

"Does that help you make a decision?"

"Your parents must hate that you are so into frat life now." I'm aware that's not an answer. It's true, though. The Gibsons have always made their feelings clear about drinking, smoking, tattoos, piercings, and pretty much any kind of fun. Their views about all of those things can be summed up in one word: don't. They had a conniption when Jake got his first tattoo. Obviously, they don't get along with Honey at all.

"Of course they hate it, but don't try to change the subject. Will you come?"

He's playing it cool, but I know Jake well enough to hear the embarrassment in his voice. I know he's disappointed to not have a date locked in yet, and I can imagine him fidgeting, shifting from one foot to the other as he waits for my answer. I stay quiet, thinking about the logistics of rearranging my shifts at work and if I would need to skip my Friday morning psychology class, before I give him an answer.

He continues, "I know it's kind of a big ask, but I'm supposed to bring a date. I thought it would be cool to see you. If I have to wear a suit and be miserable kissing up to alumni donors, I'd rather do it with you. I know we'll find a way to have fun. Otherwise, I'm going to have to deal with the added pressure of carrying on small talk all night with some hot sorority girl I barely know."

"You'd rather take me than a girl who is actually attractive? Um, ouch, but fair I guess." I keep my voice light, but I'm only half-kidding. I know he doesn't look at me that way. I'm not delusional. I glance at myself in the rearview mirror. There are several strands of dull brown hair falling loose from the bun I hastily managed before work, and I sweat off the majority of my makeup while I was running in and out of the steamy kitchen for the past few hours. There are bags under my eyes and pit stains under my arms. "Hot" is not the first word I would use to describe me either, unless we're talking about the temperature in this car.

"That's not what I said, and you know it. Look, I'll sleep on the floor and you can take my bed Friday and Saturday nights. Please? You'd really be doing me a solid. Otherwise, since I'm single and most of the brothers are already matched up, they are going to make me go with this chick from our sister sorority who hasn't found a date yet either."

"Sounds like a real hardship for you."

"To be honest, she's incredibly annoying." He lowers his voice to near a whisper. "I've heard her say 'pacifically' instead of 'specifically' more than once. Plus, I don't think she remembers my name. She refers to me as, and I quote, 'the tall one obsessed with *Lord of the Flies.*'"

"Yikes. Okay, that is annoying." Jake's entire left arm is covered in *The Lord of the Rings* tattoos. It's his favorite book. Mixing up the two is a cardinal sin in his eyes. "But if she's so hot, surely you can overlook these tiny flaws in your future bride. What's the big deal about mistaking an ocean for an adverb?" I tease.

He doesn't take the bait. "Come on, please? Don't make a man beg."

"Ugh, fine. As long as Regina can take my shifts." I know she will. She's been asking around, trying to pick up more hours so she can put Emily in ballet classes.

"Cool. Thanks, Dan-Dan. Looking forward to it."

"Text me when you have some more information about the events, please. And don't call me Dan-Dan."

"Sure thing, Dan-Dan."

Click.

I shift the car into gear and pull out of The Blue Crab's unpaved lot. I know absolutely nothing romantic is going to come out of a night with Jacob Gibson, but at least now I can tell Honey I have a date and maybe she'll get off my back. I'm ready to get home and eat my sandwich in peace.

Chapter 2

Mike

We're down by an absurd amount, and it's killing me not to be out there. I lean so far forward on the metal bench in the dugout that my chin is almost touching my knees. The afternoon sun is brutal, and I need to adjust the brim of my hat to shade my vision so I can see the field.

"Let's do this, Crabs." I clap a few times and bounce my knee, trying to rein in some of the adrenaline that has nowhere to go when I'm not in the game.

One of my teammates tosses a red Starburst at me, and I catch it without looking, unwrap the candy, and pop it into my mouth. As I start to chew, the next Chesapeake batter steps up to the plate. All I can do is watch as he hits a pop-up right down the center of the field.

"Got it," our pitcher, Lincoln, calls because the ball is coming right to him. This should be an easy out. We run this drill at every practice. Of course, our shortstop, Davis, wants to be a hero and calls for it at the same time, so Lincoln backs off, and the ball lands on the ground between them and rolls just out of easy reach. Ridiculous

15

mistake. There's not a high school coach in the country who would stand for it, and we are supposed to be professionals.

"Christ. What the hell was that?" Coach Johnson drops his clipboard in the dirt and puts his hands on his hips, sticking his large gut out a bit further while muttering the same profanities I want to scream at my teammates.

"Come on," I yell from the dugout, throwing my arms up in frustration, then immediately clamping my mouth shut. I'm not stupid. I know cussing out our starters won't be the thing that finally gets me into the game. But I do fully support Coach swearing at them all he wants while I sit here and bite my tongue, because that play was trash. So instead, I focus intensely on sucking the life out of this piece of candy while he reams them out.

Lincoln recovers quickly and throws the ball to Smithy at home plate, but the Cheetah player on third is too fast. His foot hits home and it's another run for the visiting team. 13-2. Pathetic.

Jordan, my roommate, is playing first base. I can see him wiping his right hand down his face in frustration and looking up toward the sky. I know it's taking everything he has not to scream at Davis, too. Instead, he breathes deeply and punches his free hand into his glove twice.

"Okay Crabs, let's turn this around," he calls out in an effort to encourage everyone, as if there is any coming back from this one.

The most frustrating part of being benched is knowing that if I could be out there these errors wouldn't keep happening. I don't mean to sound ungrateful, I know I'm damn lucky to even be alive after all of the stunts I pulled on my way to get here. I just didn't realize achieving my childhood dream was going to involve quite so much sitting on my ass. It's not like I was expecting a multi-million-dollar deal and cereal commercials right off the bat (pun intended). The fact that I have a steady, albeit small, paycheck coming in regularly from playing baseball still boggles my mind.

Things might have been different if it weren't for that shoulder injury sophomore year and all the drama that came after, but I'm not a man for what-ifs. I'll put in my time on the field, I'll keep going to meetings, and I'll get to the majors eventually. It's a solid plan. In the meantime, playing for a few dozen fans in the stands as the rookie shortstop on the minor league team in North Bay is still playing pro ball. Or at least it would be, if I were playing. That's the problem, though. I'm not.

"We're going to need to fly your old man out here to perform our funeral, because they are killing us," Rodriguez says. He's my fellow bench-rider and the other rookie on our team.

I only grunt because he's not wrong about the game, but he doesn't know how long it's been since I spoke to my dad.

I'd take playing ball any day of the week over going back to Idaho to work in the family business, which is selling caskets and urns. My great-grandfather turned death into a profit-steady business, and we've been feeding our family off of other people's misery for generations since. We offer full "celebration of life" services at the Miller Family Funeral Home from start to finish. "Death is recession-proof" is what my old man likes to say. Or at least that's the kind of thing he used to say before he stopped talking to me. If the baseball thing doesn't work out, there's a Plan B waiting, assuming my dad might forgive me eventually for everything that happened before I left. At this point that's not a guarantee, so I need baseball to work out.

Unfortunately, the Cheetahs just hit a triple, and they are already leading us by almost a dozen runs. I wish I could say it's a fluke, but we lost our last four games with similar scores.

I look out to the stands and see the same few familiar faces. Mr. and Mrs. Hayward, the older couple who attend every game, are here in their matching jerseys, and an exhausted mom is trying to wrangle her preschoolers out of the aisles and toward the playground. There is a family area of the ballpark that features a bounce house and face painting. Most days that area is more crowded than the metal bench seating in the rest of the stadium.

I know as the rookie I need to earn my spot and prove my worth. I get it. I do. Clark Davis is in his seventh season as the starting shortstop with this team, which is probably his last. If he doesn't get called up to the majors—and it's not likely when he keeps making errors like this one—he will probably retire after this season. He's going to hit thirty in a few months, and while he's a nice enough dude, I don't think his heart is in the game anymore. It's not personal. It's just that every play Davis makes lately is garbage, and that position should be mine because I'm objectively better at it.

"At least we have that crab feast tonight, hey Miller?" Rodriguez tries to lighten the mood.

"Yeah, I guess."

I have to hand it to the guy. Rodriguez never takes life too seriously. He is completely unfazed by the annihilation happening right in front of our eyes. This is the same dude who didn't let the fact that he doesn't know how to play the guitar stop him from performing absolutely horrendous versions of Ed Sheeran covers at open mic night this week. Lack of talent be damned, he still had almost the entire place on their feet, with the exception of two women in the corner who seemed lost in their own conversation.

I nod about the dinner, my fist still clenched from the bonehead mistake that cost us yet another run. I don't know what it is with this town and crabs, but it's a whole thing. I've never been anywhere else where you can walk in someone's front door and announce "I have crabs" and everyone would start to cheer instead of assuming you have pubic lice. Maybe I'll get used to them eventually, but if I'm being honest, the idea of eating crabs tonight seems nasty. They are scavengers who literally survive by collecting the dead, rotting stuff off the bottom of the bay. Then we're supposed to eat the thing that's been shoveling in all the decaying sea trash? Forgive me if I have reservations. It's weird.

We manage two more runs in the ninth, but in the end, we lose the game 14-4.

"Okay, Rookie," Jordan says as he jogs in from the field. "Let's get showered and go eat."

Chapter 3

Mike

Coach said attendance tonight was mandatory. He has the team doing one bonding activity per week during the season. Last week we drove out to Marnock, the next town over, to play laser tag. This week it's a team dinner at The Blue Crab restaurant in downtown North Bay. Calling it "downtown" is a big stretch, but that's how the locals refer to Main Street. Other than the Major Dollar over on Pinecrest, every store in the whole town can be found along this one street. Scattered among hundred-year-old homes, there's the tiny library, ice cream parlor, a coffee shop/karaoke/comedy club, one church, and an old Victorian-style house that serves as a yoga and dance studio upstairs and a hair salon on the bottom floor.

Main Street is a small peninsula jutting out into the Chesapeake Bay, and the properties on both sides are waterfront. The Blue Crab restaurant sits on the point at the end of the road, so the diners have a view of the boats passing by. There are wooden picnic tables inside and out, where people gather to eat various forms of seafood. Main Street might have a boring small-town vibe, but on the plus side, it's easier to keep myself out of trouble when almost everything is closed by eight o'clock.

I'd never heard of a crab feast before moving to the East Coast, but apparently you just sit at one of these picnic tables for hours and smash crabs with tiny wooden hammers until you can't eat any more. We didn't have blue crabs in Idaho. I still can't understand the appeal. I'd rather be spending this time at batting practice because my average lately is lower than I'd like it to be, but I guess I'd better get on board because, like I said, these grouchy little sea spiders are a *big* deal in North Bay.

I need to take a deep breath and readjust my attitude. It's time to shake off this loss. Well, these *five* losses. Nope. Not dwelling. Not me. Mindset is a huge part of the game, and negativity isn't going to get me anywhere. I didn't do anything to help on the field today, so I have no place blaming the rest of the team. If my high school coach were here, he'd tell me I can't erase what happened in the game, but I can control how I approach the next challenge in front of me. So, that's it. From this moment forward, I'm going all-in on these damn crabs. I'm determined to learn to love them, even if there's something ridiculous about sitting outside of a joint called The Blue Crab and demolishing actual blue crabs while also being a Blue Crab. It's crab cannibalism, is what it is. We are destroying ourselves, just like we did in the game. *No. Not doing that.*

I tap the scruff on my cheek harder than necessary to try to snap myself out of my funk. Jordan insists we shouldn't shave on game days, not that it seems to be making any difference.

The team and coaching staff take up all six outdoor tables at the only full-service restaurant in this tiny town. We are wearing matching white tee shirts and navy-blue hats printed with the Blue Crabs logo, so it's easy to identify who is here with the team.

"Can we get a round of beer and some water, please?" Coach Johnson asks the server. He grunts trying to fit his large frame in the limited space between the picnic table and the attached wooden bench.

"Yes, sir. I'll be right back with a few pitchers for each table. Can I get you anything else?" She's using a customer service voice that is an octave too high, and from this angle I can see that the skin at her neck is flushed. It must be intimidating to have an entire team of guys swarm in on you at once.

"Just your phone number, cutie." Smithy tries to shoot his shot with her and I roll my eyes. The nametag on her uniform says her name is Danielle.

"Sure thing. It's 555-in-your-dreams. You want my address, too? I live just over at the corner of You Wish and Never Going to Happen. So, would you like any appetizers for the table? Jackson's in the kitchen today, and he makes great crab fries."

Okay, maybe she's not intimidated then.

"Ha. Dang, Smithy. She didn't even need a second to think about it," Rodriguez says. A few of the guys rag on our teammate, and someone high-fives Danielle while the conversation turns to a debate about crab fries, which I gather from their discussion are french fries coated in crab seasoning and topped with crab dip. I still have no idea what crab dip is. The server heads back inside to get our drinks.

As we settle into our seats, I try to be intentional about using the strategies I've learned and look around to ground myself in appreciation of this moment. The whole town of North Bay really is picturesque, like it was spawned to life from an oil painting or a greeting card. The Blue Crab restaurant is no exception. It sits close to the water and has a pier where locals can dock their boats when they want to come in for a bite. Today there is a bit of a breeze that's causing the water to roll in tiny waves. The side lawn is set up with outdoor games like horseshoes and cornhole, which I'm sure the team will be hitting hard when we finish our meal, and there is a small sandy area near the water with gliding benches for people to sit and rock while they look out into the bay.

Each outdoor picnic table is covered with brown paper, and in the middle of each one sits a wooden bushel basket filled with cooked shellfish. None of my teammates seem to find this the least bit strange. They are all just rolling with it and digging in. A few of the guys are using crayons they snagged from a box inside next to the children's menus to draw inappropriate cartoons or play hangman on the paper tablecloths.

I take a crab out of the pile, but I have no idea how to even begin eating this thing. It's spikey and sharp. I already have a small cut on my finger from the shell, and it's coated in an inch of some sort of clumpy red pepper seasoning I've never seen anywhere else on Earth. Whatever it is, it sure stings like a mother when it touches that fresh paper cut-sized wound. The dead, yet somehow still aggressive, thing staring back at me also still has both claws and eyeballs. Who wants their food to gross out and attack them simultaneously? And why?

Shake it off. I can do this. It's just one little crab.

The guys who have offered some semblance of advice so far have thrown out such gems as "Make sure you scrape out the intestines," "Start at the apron," and "It's up to you if you want to eat its mustard." *Mustard* is apparently what they are calling the globs of yellow fat some of the crabs have inside of them. I would think this is some kind of joke or hazing ritual for the rookie, except the entire town is in on it. Everyone eats these little monsters constantly and seems to love them.

Our server returns carrying two pitchers of beer. I'm sitting on the end of the bench at the closest table to the restaurant, so she stops when she reaches me and sets one pitcher down. We aren't supposed to drink much during the season, and we certainly are not supposed to be getting drunk in public because we have a family-friendly image as well as muscle mass to maintain, but no one argued when Coach bought a round for everyone. It's probably his way to try to boost morale after the recent string of losses.

As the familiar sour smell hits my nose, I move it across to Jordan, who pours himself a glass and sets the pitcher on the other side of him, out of my reach. He knows I'm sticking with water. I should probably talk to Coach about my baggage, but I haven't found the courage for that conversation yet.

"Anybody need anything? We have enough paper towels over here?" our server asks cheerfully. The Blue Crab logo printed on her shirt looks similar to the one on my own. There's a small red apron tied around her waist, the kind that only consists of two pockets, to hold her notepad and a pencil.

I angle my face up to look at her. She's cute. Her brown hair is pulled back into a ponytail, and a few freckles are scattered across her nose. Her standard-issue polo shirt is tucked into a pair of tight jeans that are hugging her curvy hips in a way that is giving me ideas I probably shouldn't be having at a team dinner. I'm not going there.

While I'm not as serious about it as my roommate, I promised myself I wouldn't get distracted by any women this year. I have goals to achieve. Plus, I have already seen how the North Bay rumor mill works. The whole town blacklisted Lincoln for weeks after he went on a date with the mayor's daughter and didn't call her in the morning. Her friends came to our next three home games just to heckle him. I don't want to end up at the center of small-town gossip about my love life.

When no one answers her paper towel question beyond a few polite nods, I speak up.

"We're good, thanks."

Our eyes lock and she smiles at me. Then Danielle turns to the table next to us and sets their pitcher down before heading back toward the indoor dining section.

Jordan leans across the table to tell me, "You should definitely hit that."

"Shut up. Eat your crabs."

"I'm just saying, pickings are slim in this town, and we all saw the way your tongue was practically hanging out of your face just now while you were looking at her. You're an idiot if you don't make a play."

"Whatever, man. I haven't seen you bringing anyone around for months."

When I was signed to the team they told me our first baseman was looking for someone to share his two-bedroom apartment. His old roommate had just been called up to join the Orioles and was moving to Baltimore. Jordan's a good guy, and he never gives me any grief for leaving my breakfast dishes in the sink or playing my music too loudly, so it's worked out pretty well for us so far.

"You know that's because I took myself out of the game." As if he would let me forget.

"If you say so," I goad him, even though I know he won't react.

My roommate might be a superstitious, scatterbrained S.O.B., but he has the patience of a saint. It's a good thing, because he is going to need every ounce of that patience if he plans to make it through the vow of celibacy he insists on taking during the season. Apparently, three years ago he went two months without a date and his batting average coincidentally increased by a hundred points. He insists those two things are connected. He's taken the vow every season since, but he always caves before the playoffs. He swears that won't happen this year.

Unfortunately, that stupid vow means he has been bored and horny, which is a dangerous combination. Now he is invested in making sure the rest of us are getting some, and it's getting weird.

"I thought you had game, Rookie. Don't tell me you can't even talk to a good-looking waitress. Not up for the challenge after she put Smithy in his place? Where's the confidence you're going to need if you ever want Coach to let you onto the field?"

That's it. It's one thing to make insinuations about my lack of flirting skills, but it's another thing altogether to imply that not talking to this woman means I don't have what it takes to get in the game. This I cannot allow.

"You know what? Fine."

I lay my tiny, steamed archnemesis down on the paper-covered table and stand up. Jordan snickers from across the pile of crabs. "You make it way too easy to mess with you, man."

I ignore him and head over to the waitress. She is facing away from me, but I recognize the ponytail and those curvy hips. It only takes me a few strides to catch up to where she is standing next to an overgrown oak tree. I admire how she fills out her jeans from the back as I approach. She's shorter than she seemed a second ago when she was hovering over me and offering napkins. The top of her head only reaches my shoulders.

"Excuse me, Danielle?" I say from behind her, referencing the nametag on her uniform.

She startles a bit, probably because she never told me her name, but she recovers quickly.

"Yes, sir? Did you need something else?"

Now we are face-to-face and she cranes her neck to look up at me. My shadow falls over her, shielding her from the sun. Her deep brown eyes are staring straight into mine again, and something in the air between us changes, but I try to ignore the crackle of electricity and go for a friendly approach.

"Not sure I've earned the 'sir' just yet, I'm only twenty-two. We're probably the same age."

"Fair enough. Yeah, close. I'm twenty-one." She smiles, then looks down at the ground and shakes her head like she's scolding herself for sharing that personal detail about her life with me. She clears her throat and puts her professional persona back in place. "How can I help you?" Now she's using the same chipper customer service voice from earlier as she lifts her face back up to mine.

"This might be weird, but I think I need a crab tutor. And maybe a Band-Aid?" I hold up the finger where that little demon cut me. I know some guys think asking for help is emasculating or whatever, but I know my own skill set. I also know women can't resist a man who knows he needs them. If I can use that to my advantage and make a new friend in the process, so be it. Especially when that friend has curves like this woman. All three buttons at the collar of her polo shirt are undone, and I am working hard not to stare.

Danielle lets out an adorable little giggle, and leans closer to whisper, "You're not the only one who needs some guidance. I've seen some seriously terrible techniques at those tables. This happens every year. Even some of your friends over there aren't doing as well as they'd like you to think." Then she straightens up and speaks in her normal voice again, not the one she'd been using at the tables. I like that she is dropping the mask so quickly. I wish I could do the same.

"Let me just go grab the other pitchers. I'll be right back."

I follow behind as she walks inside the restaurant and take the opportunity to duck into the bathroom. When I come out, Danielle is carrying four more pitchers of beer, two in each hand. She spots me and nods to several more sitting on the wooden counter area.

"Grab a few of those, will you, Big Guy? Then let's get out there and teach you how to put those giant hands to use outside of the ball field."

Oh, if she only knew what I could do with these hands. After a deep breath, I oblige her and grab the pitchers. We walk together back to the outdoor tables.

"Not that I'd ever stop a pretty woman from referring to me as a 'big guy,' and I know I already told you not to call me 'sir,' but you can call me Mike. Michael Miller. I'm new around here. From Idaho, originally. I'm playing for the Blue Crabs this year." Like she hadn't already figured that out from the shirt, and the hat, and the fact that I'm sitting with the entire baseball team. She also *just* mentioned me on the ball field.

I need a quick recovery, so it's my turn to lean in and whisper, "Despite what you're about to see in regard to these crabs, I've been told I'm actually very good with my hands." I wink at her before I can stop myself.

What is wrong with me? Maybe Jordan got in my head. She probably thinks I have some of that crab seasoning in my eye. Who goes around winking at the restaurant server they just met and making innuendos about touching them? Creepy weirdos, that's who. And me, apparently. Get it together, Miller.

"Danielle Daniels." I can't tell if she's blushing or just flushed from the physical labor of her job and this heat, but she isn't rejecting me outright like she did with Smithy, so I'll take it. I think I can work with this and get her talking a little.

"Okay. Your parents must be fans of alliteration, too. All of my siblings also have names that start with the letter M, like mine. We're Michael, Michelle, Mandy, and Madison Miller. Me, three little sisters, and a whole lot of people mixing up our names."

"Yikes. At least I'm an only child, so the suffering starts and stops with me."

"It's not so bad for me either, being the only guy. Mandy and Maddy have it especially rough. People always think they are the same person until they see them standing next to each other. They hate that."

My sisters' names are a constant source of exasperation for them, so I'd be willing to wager Danielle Daniels isn't a big fan of hers either.

"I bet." She chuckles.

Tough break, being saddled with a name like that, although the *Danielle* part seems to suit her. It's pretty, but not flashy, and that matches the vibe she is giving off. Simple, approachable, but classy. I doubt she's the kind of girl to burp the alphabet in public, but from the way she was talking to Smithy earlier, she seems like the type who wouldn't bat an eye if she were at a party with people who did. Until this moment, I didn't know being unaffected by a belching contest was something I look for in a woman, but now that I think about it, it does seem like an important trait a partner should have. You know, if I were looking for a partner. Which I'm not.

We set the beer on the tables, and Danielle makes the rounds pouring it into red plastic cups for anyone who needs a refill while I return to my seat. Then she comes back to stand next to me at the end of the table, takes a Band-aid out of her apron pocket, and quietly sets it on the table next to my crab. Now she's the one winking at me. I guess that's a thing we do now.

"Gentlemen, if I could have your attention for a moment." She clears her throat dramatically, which brings my attention to her neck. It's a nice neck, and for a moment I picture getting close enough to run my nose from her shoulder to her chin and breathe her in. I wonder what she smells like.

"The Blue Crab restaurant would like to welcome the Blue Crabs baseball team for a dinner of, well, blue crabs." A few of my teammates whoop and clap. Coach Johnson nods his appreciation to

Danielle. Some people turn in their seats to get a better view as she speaks.

Meanwhile, my pants are tight because now my imagination is getting away from me. Jesus. This is embarrassing. I know it's been a minute since I've hooked up with anyone, but I can't sit here and fantasize about the waitress during a team dinner. I need to shake it off because I don't have time for those kinds of distractions. I also definitely don't need Jordan to notice and give me crap about it tonight at home, or worse, on the field. My teammates can't call me Rookie anymore after this season, so it's inevitable that I'll end up with a new nickname. The last thing I need is for something like Woody to stick. I keep my legs firmly planted under the table and just tilt my head to make it seem like I am engaged in what Danielle is saying.

I came to this town for a fresh start. I have to focus on my career and earn my spot in the majors. I need a clear head if I'm going to achieve that goal. I can't be going around thinking about necks or how much I want to let her hair out of that ponytail right now and run my fingers through it. Nope. No. Not going there either. There will be no thoughts of sniffing or roaming fingers. I take a deep breath and let it out slowly through my nose as she talks, then force myself to picture Cal Ripken's career highlights so I can cool down while Danielle continues her impromptu speech.

"I know we have some new faces this year, and steamed crabs are not a delicacy in all parts of this great country, so unfortunately not everyone is well-acquainted with them." She actually puts her hand over her heart and bows her head like it's a tragedy. Danielle is really making a meal out of this. A silent chuckle shakes my shoulders. Her voice gets louder and her smile widens as she goes on. It's a pretty great smile. The kind of smile that could make you forget your own goals for a second, which is exactly why this woman is dangerous.

"I'm willing to offer my personal crab-picking tutorial services for the low, low price of a good tip and the promise that you will return to The Blue Crab soon, which let's be real, you were going to do anyway. We're the only place in a twenty-mile radius, besides your ballpark, that serves both beer and food."

Some of the guys laugh, and even though I've only just met Danielle, it makes me proud to know she can hold her own with them. The whole team seems to like her. She continues in a more normal tone, "My shift is ending in a few minutes, but as soon as I wrap up my other tables, I'll be back for you all. I can stay on a while longer to help anyone who would like to learn how to properly and safely clean and eat a crab." There are a few more half-hearted claps, but most of my teammates just turn back to their food. I smile at Danielle.

Ten minutes later she returns and motions for me to scoot over so she can sit down beside me.

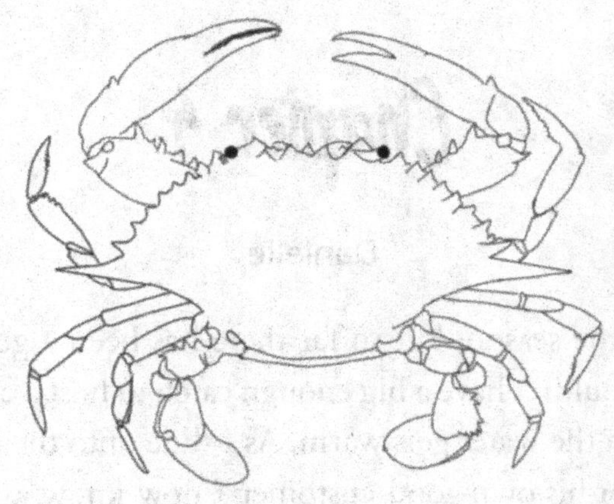

Chapter 4

Danielle

It's early in the season, but so far there has been a good yield. We normally wouldn't have a big enough catch to host a crab feast until summer, when the water gets warm. As I slide onto the bench next to the too-cute-for-his-own-good customer I now know as Mike Miller, the other baseball players at their table nod their hellos. They seem to be in a heated discussion about the way sports statistics are measured and if it's fair to compare college athletes and professionals using the same methods. The guy directly across from me waves with two fingers to acknowledge that I've joined them.

"Hey, I'm Jordan. First base," he says.

"Danielle. Waitress." He smiles and fists bumps me. His hands are already covered in crab guts and Jackson's signature steaming spices. After our brief introduction, he turns to rejoin his buddies in conversation. The short twists in his hair bob as he nods his head vigorously in agreement with someone. "That's exactly what I'm talking about," Jordan says to the player on his right. "You just can't compare them. It's apples to oranges."

I guess this will be a private tutorial for Mr. Miller then. Not that I'm complaining.

I try to make sure I am giving Mike enough personal space, but it's hard not to brush the person sitting next to you at a crowded picnic table, so my leg keeps making contact. I'm just going to ignore the fact that our thighs are touching and direct my attention to the task at hand.

"First, let's get you acquainted with this little guy, huh?" I point to the steamed crab resting on the table in front of us.

"Whatever you do, please don't give him a name. I'm not going to be able to handle it if you tell me I have to crack Santa Claws open and tear out his heart."

I want to laugh, but I don't know Mike well enough yet to be able to tell if he is kidding about not wanting to eat the crabs. It can be a weird experience for out-of-towners, so I try to reassure him, just in case. "First, solid crab pun, especially for your first time. Kudos. Personally, I probably would have gone with something more artistic, like Leonardo Da *Pinchi*. Second, never feel bad for eating a crab. He didn't have a heart. Not metaphorically, anyway. Blue crabs are straight-up sea murderers who eat their own babies. They're like the sociopathic kind of mean." I pause trying to think of a catchy name for a crustacean serial killer, but come up empty-handed.

"So, more like Jack the *Flipper* then." He chuckles. I'm a sucker for a cheesy one-liner and his dumb joke makes me snort.

"Ha. Nice, bro." Jordan must still be half-listening because he reaches across the table to high-five Mike for that one, not caring this time that their hands are filthy. I give an exaggerated roll of my eyes, but my smile gets wider.

When he sees my dopey grin, Jordan says, "If you're a fan of cheesy puns or dad jokes, Miller's your man." He points across the table to his friend, clearly trying to be Mike's wingman. I like these guys. I'm definitely going to have more fun staying here a bit longer with them than I will with the sociology paper I need to write when I get home.

Plus, sitting here gives me a chance to get off my feet for a minute. I'm not looking forward to the three-mile bike ride back to the house. My legs are dead after this shift, but Honey needed to use the car today to get to her spicy book club. Spread Those Pages meets twice a month to discuss the latest romance novels. I still can't believe Alice took Honey up on her invitation to join them and is off discussing the literary merit of *Stud in the Stable: A Cowboy Romance* with my grandma tonight. As much as I love books—and I love them a lot, which is why I'm slowly working toward a degree in library science— breaking down all of the erotic scenes in detail with my grandma while we share chips and onion dip sounds like absolute hell on earth.

"Okay, I am hearing that this can be a guilt-free experience." Mike's smirking. He was definitely kidding before, as evidenced by the continuation of terrible puns. He doesn't seem like the kind of guy who is going to leave the restaurant and write a scathing review on some internet message board for secret crab activists.

"Totally. We're basically avenging Nemo's mom right now. This is about justice. And vengeance." I nod solemnly and motion to the bandaged finger where the crab cut him. "We're like Batman."

"You must be big on movies, huh? I can honestly say that's the first time I've been compared to a super hero for sitting at a picnic table and butchering my dinner, but I'll take it. I can get on board with justice. Not sure about the vengeance part. I don't think Nemo's mom was taken out by crabs. I'm almost positive that was a barracuda. My sisters made me watch that movie like a thousand times."

"Yeah, I love pretty much all movies. Movies and party games are kind of my thing." I don't have the stamina to sit through a three-hour board game, but I've been known to rock a few rounds of Pictionary and I can hold my own in a DC versus Marvel discussion. "I concede that it was a barracuda in the cartoon version, but this is real life, and I promise these little crabby monsters have killed plenty of fish moms. They probably even took out their own wives and kids. They're vicious."

"Yes, I have heard they are very *shellfish*. But I had no idea they were so deadly." I probably hear that same joke at least five times a week from dads ordering crab cake sandwiches on their lunchbreak and I usually just smile and nod politely, but something about the way Mike says it makes me laugh for real.

He angles his body to face me and points to the cartoonish Blue Crabs logo on his baseball cap. "Glad to know this image will instill fear in the hearts of our opponents." Mike is what Honey would call "classically handsome." There's a tiny bit of light hair poking out from under his hat. His eyes are gray. They remind me of the misty fog that covers the bay on winter mornings. When he smiles widely enough to show his toothpaste-commercial-perfect teeth, there's a dimple in his left cheek. I drum my fingers on the table to avoid reaching out and touching it. Weird. I'm not usually tempted to touch people I just met.

Even if I didn't know Mike was on the baseball team, the tan he's already sporting in April gives away the fact that he spends a lot of time outside. His biceps and the veins protruding down his well-defined arms are showing the results of a lot of hours spent in the gym. Or the batting cages? I don't know, but they came from somewhere. His team shirt is stretched tight across his chest and shoulders. People have to put in a lot of work for that kind of muscle.

As he turns back to face the table, his shoulder nudges mine while he asks, "How can we be sure it's a him anyway? Seems a bit presumptuous to assume."

"He's definitely male, that's all we serve here. Our supplier is a big believer in throwing the females back to preserve the crab population."

"Show me how you can tell."

All the winking, smiling, and shoulder-nudging could make a girl think Mike Miller is flirting with her, and I just might be into that. Maybe. It has been getting a little bit lonely at night since Steve took the job in Richmond and decided I wasn't worth the effort of trying to make it work long-distance. If I'm being honest, I do miss having someone to sit with on the couch and watch Netflix with me. Although, to be fair, that's exactly what I did with Alice two days ago. I can imagine a night with Mike Miller would go much differently.

I turn the crab over so its white underbelly is facing up at us and point to it. There's a phallic shape right in the middle.

"See this part? This area is called the apron," I explain to Mike. "It's much wider and more oval on the females. The males are pointier." I keep talking while I pick up one of the discarded crayons on the table and draw pictures to illustrate my point. "My stepdad, Bob, used to say the female crabs wore big aprons and lipstick, because they also tend to have red marks on the end of their claws."

"Aprons and lipstick, huh? How progressive."

"My mom was a little more diplomatic and would tell me the boys had a ticket to the Washington Monument printed on their bellies, whereas the girls were destined for the White House because the shapes of their aprons matched those buildings."

I feel like I'm babbling, but he seems amused by the anecdotes and says the White House tip from my mom will definitely help him remember.

"So, here is the controversial part," I warn Mike. "I prefer to take the apron off and remove the shell first."

"Whoa, let me stop you right there." Jordan tears himself from the stats discussion to interrupt again. "Rookie, this is serious. We can no longer trust this woman. This tutorial is a sham. Demand your money back." He shakes his head with mock sincerity, looking at Mike first, then back to me. "Everybody knows you go for the legs first. This is common knowledge."

Mike's shoulders shake with another silent laugh. "Yeah? Well, I didn't see you stepping up to help me at any point over the past hour while I've been sitting here trying to crack into this thing," he tells Jordan. "So, let's give the lady the floor. Please continue, Miss Danielle." He gestures to the table with a sweeping hand motion.

"Like I said, controversial." I shrug. "But I prefer to take the legs off last. Once the legs are gone, it's harder to work with a smaller surface area. But *some* people prefer to take the legs off first." I purse my lips and tilt my head at Jordan. "That does help to pull out bigger chunks of meat. However, I think it also takes longer, and it makes the rest of the process a little bit harder. I'd rather jump straight to the main event."

"No foreplay?" Jordan teases from across the table and I can feel my cheeks heat with embarrassment.

"Behave," Mike admonishes him, then speaks to me. "You'll need to excuse my first baseman. Some of us actually do have manners and want to hear this," he promises.

"Teacher's pet," Jordan coughs into his hand.

After our lesson, Mike slowly picks his way through three more crabs. The guys offer a few to share with me, and I gladly take them up on it. We are still at our seats at the picnic table, but a few of the other players have dispersed to the grass to play cornhole. A boy who looks to be in about the third grade is going around and asking them all to autograph a napkin with one of his crayons. A player named Rodriguez gives up his turn at the game to let the little dude throw a beanbag for him. I recognize Rodriguez as the guy with the guitar from Brew-Ha-Ha. After being invited to play with them, the kid is positively beaming like this is the best day of his life. Hey, maybe it is. He's having dinner with an entire professional baseball team. Now he's on Rodriguez's shoulders and the players on the lawn are surrounding him, chanting "champ-i-on" with their fists in the air. Life probably doesn't get much better than that when you are eight.

As we finish eating, I offer everyone at the table a few wet naps from my apron pocket and point them in the direction of our outdoor sinks so we can all clean our hands. It's been a nice evening, but I have to get home to the sociology paper that isn't going to write itself. It will take me a while to ride home.

"It looks like you have mastered this art. I better get going. I want to get home before dark." I touch Mike's shoulder briefly with my goodbye and my fingertips tingle, so I pull them back quickly.

Must be static cling, like the kind that makes your hair stand up when you rub a balloon on it. That's the only explanation.

"Sure, no problem. I really appreciate your help. I think I'm going to be heading out too, actually. I need to stop at Major Dollar and pick up a few groceries before they close. Bye. Hope to see you around."

"Yeah, bye. Thanks for letting me steal your dinner."

I don't know if I should tell him he's headed my way. Mike seems sweet, but maybe it's not the best idea to tell a man I just met where I live. What if he turns out to be a psychopath?

I walk around the building while he heads to the parking lot. As soon as I pull my bike around from the side of the restaurant where it was leaning against the wall and move into the main parking area, I stop to buckle my helmet strap under my chin. I can see the whole parking lot from here and I watch as Mike climbs into an older hunter green pick-up truck that sits almost as low to the ground as a regular car. It only takes a second before he spots me and hops back out of the truck. He jogs over to where I'm standing.

"Nope." Mike shakes his head at me. "I'm sorry, but my mom would never forgive me if I let you take a bike home in the dark without offering to give you a ride."

I squint up at him, realizing the sun is setting and it's a bit later than I thought.

"I'm fine," I protest. "It's only a few miles, and I do it every time my grandma needs the car. I even have this fashionable night light, see?" Flicking the switch on the light attached to my handlebars doesn't seem to deter him, so I say, "No offense, but I'm not in the habit of getting into cars with men I just met."

"That's fair. Can you call someone? I'll wait with you."

"No, it's honestly okay. I need to get home and write a paper for school. Everyone I know is busy. My grandma and my best friend are together at their porno book club, and my parents are in Haiti doing relief work. It would be a pretty long commute from there." I don't know why I'm telling him any of this.

"Sorry, what kind of book cl—doesn't matter. I really don't mind giving you a ride. Friends don't let friends ride their bikes in the dark." He looks so sincere that I can't help but tease him a little.

"Oh, are we friends now? That was fast. Here I thought you were just using me for my advanced crab dismemberment skills."

"That too." Mike's eyes crinkle at the corners and I return his smile with one of my own. He continues, "I'd really feel much better if you'd let me take you home. We can throw your bike in the back of the truck. Besides," he grins and gestures to his tee shirt. "If I wanted to murder you, I wouldn't do it while wearing this. I'm too easy to identify right now." He winks again. What's with this guy and the winking? Normally it would feel sleazy, but when Mike does it, it's kind of charming.

"I live close to the Major Dollar. I guess I can accept a ride that far and make it the rest of the way from there?" So, I guess I'm doing this. No big deal. Just hopping into a car to be alone with a handsome guy I met only an hour ago. Nothing to see here. Totally a thing I do all the time. At least I haven't *really* told him where I live. It's not like I gave him my address. He nods and takes the bike from me and lifts it in the back of the truck. Then he opens the passenger side door and motions for me to get in.

That's how I find myself climbing into Mike Miller's truck.

"Choosing to keep the helmet on, huh?" he asks, still smiling.

I totally forgot I was wearing it.

"Yeah, well, I haven't seen you drive yet, have I?" I knock twice on the side of my head and hope to recover by making it look intentional. Because lots of people intentionally wear purple bike helmets when they are sitting next to cute guys in pick-up trucks. I make a show of pulling out my seatbelt as far as it will go and snapping it against my chest once it's buckled to really drive the point home.

Mike chuckles and puts his arm around the back of my seat while he reverses the truck.

"So, your parents are in Haiti?"

"Oh, um, yeah. My stepdad is a retired dental surgeon and he accepted a position with a charity that fixes cleft palates in areas of the world that don't have easy access to healthcare. My mom does the bookkeeping for them."

"That's really cool."

"I guess."

Mike looks at me from the driver's seat like he's waiting to hear more, but I don't elaborate. Now is not the time to sit with a stranger and talk about how it felt when my mom left me in North Bay with Honey so that she could run halfway around the world with her new husband to take care of other kids instead.

"I can't remember if you told me which position you play." I change the subject. Mike happily returns his eyes to the road and launches into a discussion about baseball, and specifically why he likes being a shortstop. Apparently, it's like being the leader of the infield.

I thank him for the ride as we pull into the parking lot of the Major Dollar.

"Sure thing. I just need to run in and grab a few dozen eggs," Mike says.

"Wow. Either you really like eggs or you are about to commit a crime straight out of a Bugs Bunny cartoon."

He laughs. "They aren't all for me. Jordan and I live over in the old Westwood apartment complex and we do a lot of quick, high-protein meals like omelets."

"Right." It makes sense that four crabs and a glass of water isn't enough to fuel a pro athlete. "Plus, it makes for a convenient alibi for all your drive-by egging activities."

"What can I say? You've caught me. I'm an egg-strodinary criminal."

"Hardly. You *cracked* way too easily, but *omeletting* it slide this time."

"That was a good one." He seems proud. "If you can wait a minute, I can take you the rest of the way home after I grab the groceries."

Since he's told me where he lives, I feel comfortable enough to tell him, "Thanks again, but it's okay. I live just down the road from here." I'm still being vague, but he doesn't push for any more information.

Now that it's time to say goodbye, I can't help the awkward babble that continues to fly out of my mouth. "Guess I didn't need the helmet after all, did I? Driving approved, good sir. I'll be off now." What am I even saying? He glances at me sideways and chuckles again, then he gets out of the car and motions for me to stay put while he circles around to open my door.

"We have another home game next Wednesday night. It's a scrimmage for charity. I'd love to see you there. You could bring some friends, you know, if you want. The team needs all the support we can get. Stands have been pretty sparse lately, and this one is for a good cause." The yellow fluorescent lights coming from inside the store give the parking lot an eerie glow and low hum as Mike hauls my bike off the bed of the truck. There are only a few other cars scattered around the lot. It's gotten dark and I can't quite see his face thanks to the shadows. Standing alone in a mostly-empty parking lot at night with a man I just met isn't smart. I know that, yet I'm not scared around Mike Miller. Something deep in my gut tells me it's okay to relax with him.

"Maybe. Thanks again for the ride."

I take the bike, swing my leg over it, and switch on the light before I pedal away.

I wonder if he's watching when I turn into the driveway right next door.

Chapter 5

Danielle

"You two are back early," I say, surprised to find Honey and Alice waiting for me in the kitchen when I open the door. Then it dawns on me that their book club didn't finish early. I'm the one who's late.

"We really aren't, but never mind that. Am I to infer from your mode of transportation that you've been asked out on two separate dates, with two different men, within the past twenty-four hours?" Alice asks, giddy excitement radiating off her as she bounces her pixie-sized self on the stool pulled up to the breakfast bar. "Shelia says you're going to a dance at Virginia Tech, and now we see you riding home with a handsome stranger. This is just like when Amelia had to choose between the ranch hand and the horse's veterinarian."

Honey nods her agreement.

"There's no way you could tell from here what he looks like or what we talked about," I argue. "Wait. Shelia Gibson? Are you telling me Jake's mom is going to Spread Those Pages meetings with the two of you now?"

It seems highly out of character for a woman who handed her son an anatomy textbook when he was nine because he asked what the word "erectile" meant after we saw an ad for E.D. medicine on TV. She told Jake to discuss any further questions with his doctor.

"She only comes for the appetizers and to socialize for a little while. She always leaves before the discussion heats up," Alice clarifies. That makes more sense.

"Shame because it would probably do the poor woman some good to read those books. She's more pent up than—"

"Nope. Not listening." I stick my fingers in my ears and cut Honey off before she can finish her thought, then I turn my attention back to my best friend.

It's no surprise to see Alice here. She loves the spicy book club as much as Honey does, and it's becoming a tradition for them to come back and share dessert with me afterward. She and Honey were expecting me to be riding my bike home, so they were watching for me through the living room window. Now I have some explaining to do.

"Sit and tell us everything," Alice insists. She pats the stool next to her as she takes bite of chocolate snowball from her bowl.

"Here you go, sugar." Honey hands me a dish of my own. It's a frozen chocolate milk concoction Honey started making when I was young, because before we got the Major Dollar in town we had to go all the way to Marnock for groceries. In the summer, any ice cream we bought would melt before we got back home. Honey's snowball tastes like chocolate Italian ice.

Alice chops at the frozen dessert with her spoon and I take a big bite of my own. It immediately gives me a brain freeze, so I rub my temples. Honey puts her own empty bowl in the dishwasher and picks up a tea towel from the counter. Then my grandma leans her back against the closed refrigerator and joins our conversation from the other side of the breakfast bar.

"Yeah. Tell us more about Mr. Green Truck." Honey wags her eyebrows at me and waves the towel like a tiny lasso.

"Yes. Details," Alice agrees. Her feet are swinging, nowhere close to touching the floor. She might be tiny, but she is still a force to be reckoned.

"Ugh. Fine." I throw them a bone. "His name is Mike Miller. He's on the baseball team. They were at the restaurant for the Blue Crabs team dinner, and he needed a lesson from Yours Truly on how to pick the crabs. He's from Idaho. I guess they don't eat a lot of seafood out there. Then afterward he was headed to Major Dollar anyway, so he invited me to tag along. He didn't like the idea of me riding home in the dark."

"Chivalrous," Honey muses.

"Ah, a protective romantic?" Alice practically squeals. "Did he ask you out? He did, I'm sure." She answers her own question. "I love it. Straight out of an Emily Henry book. I'm totally using this for inspiration in my own stories." She tucks a strand of pink hair behind her ear.

Alice always looks very punk rock, although I have my doubts about if she could name even one punk rock band if her life depended on it. Today she's wearing an oversized white tee printed with the words "the book was better." She cut off the neckline, so it's falling off one shoulder, and it's tied up at her waist in a tight little knot. She's wearing it over tight faux leather leggings with black Converse sneakers. She looks effortlessly hot, and it makes me self-consciously tug at my work uniform.

"Protective and romantic is a big leap from 'stranger with a car.' I don't know him well enough to call him either of those things. And I hardly think this one counts as a date," I object. "It was just one of the baseball players telling me there's a baseball game on Wednesday. It's his job. I doubt I would even get a chance to talk to him if I went. We didn't exchange numbers or anything." I ignore the sudden pang of disappointment that realization brings. "He was just being polite and dropping me off because he was stopping at the store and I live right here. I really don't think it's like that."

"Are you sure? Because I don't know many men in the habit of driving women home and inviting them out again in a few days if they aren't interested."

"I don't even think I want it to be like that. Not really. He's a baseball player. He already has one foot out the door. Why start something when we know it has an expiration date?" Sure, Mike Miller is nice and he has a mesmerizing dimple. And, fine, maybe I smiled a little when I was talking about him just now. Perhaps there are a few flutters in my belly because his car smelled like cedar and cinnamon. So our legs and our shoulders touched when we sat together on the picnic table, looking out over the water at sunset. So what? It wouldn't go anywhere.

It could be one season, or it could be a few years, but eventually Mike Miller's career will take him away from North Bay, and I already know I would not go with him. This is my home. I would never leave Honey, my job, and all of my friends for some guy. That's exactly why it didn't work out with Steve. I already know the same thing would happen with Mike.

"Maybe it's not officially a date *yet*, but we are totally going to that game together. Neither one of us has class on Wednesday afternoons. What else are we going to do?" Alice squeals and wiggles her fingers in the air, giving jazz hands. Under that tough exterior she's a hopeless romantic. I shrug because she has a point. Maybe I don't intend to marry the guy who invited us, but who says I can't go to a baseball game with a friend?

"Aaaaand, you're going to visit Jake. Because he asked you to go to a dance. Wearing a dress. That one is totally a date. Even if it is with Jacob Gibson." She shudders.

"As a friend," I add quickly. It does feel a bit different this time, though. My stomach does a little flop. I'm not sure why. I've known Jake forever, and over the years he's wiggled his way into a few naughty thoughts and a pretty intense crush on my end that lasted through all four years of high school (and possibly a little beyond). But he never felt the same way when we were teenagers and my crush has mostly faded over time. Now we are firmly rooted in the friend zone.

"I almost never look at him like that anymore, and I'm pretty sure he has never looked at me that way at all. And that, folks, is why I'm probably going to die alone surrounded by books and stray cats."

"Alone and snuggling cats actually sounds like a day you would enjoy."

"True. Is that so bad?"

I do like men. I like how they are funny and tend to take life a little bit less seriously, making everything into a game they believe they can win. I like being with someone who makes me feel safe and looks at the world through a different lens. Sure, I'd like to find a partner, but being surrounded by books and cats with as much alone time as I want also sounds pretty sweet.

"This is why you have me. I'll help you pick out what to wear. Trust me, that man will be thinking way more than friendly thoughts about you when I'm through. They both will, if I have anything to say about it." She wags her eyebrows the same way Honey did and giggles.

I shake my head and smile, following her when she hops off the stool and heads down the hall, but not before grabbing my snowball to take with me. We walk into the garage and up the stairs to my apartment. I can faintly hear Honey sorting the mail and grumbling at her bills in the distance.

"Project Redecorate is looking good. I love the paint color you chose." Alice points to the new seafoam green accent wall behind my couch.

"Thanks, I still need to figure out a few more storage solutions for my clothes and books. There is only so much space under the bed."

This place was originally built for my mom. She was young when she had me, and has always been kind of nomadic. We lived together in a camper van for five years when I was little, traveling the country. It was always just the two of us. When I was born, she didn't put my dad's name on my birth certificate. That's why my last name is Daniels, like my mom and Honey.

Honey wanted the apartment to be somewhere her girls could always come home. We would find our way back to North Bay whenever the weather got too cold. Then after my grandpa died, we moved here permanently. The garage apartment is one large room with a double bed and second-hand sofa, separated only by a waist-high book shelf. There's a tiny bathroom, a kitchenette, and one closet. It's not much, but it was ours.

I was only twelve when Mom married Bob and they decided they had to save the world, so I moved back into the main house with Honey until I graduated from high school. When I started college, Honey offered to let me have my own space and take over the apartment again. Lately, I've been feeling a bit guilty about it. I do try to contribute some of my earnings from the restaurant, but Honey insists I use most of them for school. She already feels bad about not being able to help more with my student loans. I keep telling her that's not her job, but she's a stubborn old broad. If I weren't staying here practically rent-free, maybe Honey could rent this space to someone to cover a few more of those bills. She hasn't said anything, but I know she's been feeling the pinch of the higher property taxes lately. The whole town has.

That's a discussion I'll need to have with Honey soon, but it can wait. For now, the question is… do I want Jake Gibson thinking more than friendly thoughts? That sounds terrifying, but also kind of fun.

I pull back the fabric curtain that serves as my closet door, revealing my entire wardrobe. Then I flop onto my bed, hanging my head off the side and looking up at Alice.

"Go ahead. Work your magic, my friend." I upside-down smile at her.

Work her magic she does. That sociology paper is going to have to wait one more day. After an hour, my bed is piled high with the discarded clothes I've tried on and tossed aside, and Alice is standing over me with tweezers, plucking away at my unruly eyebrows.

"I can't believe I'm wasting my talents helping you look this smoking hot for Jake freaking Gibson." She sighs dramatically. "Especially when there is a new baseball player in town with his eye on you."

"The feud between you and Jake is getting weird now that we are all adults. Don't you think it's time to kiss and make up?"

"Ew. Not likely. As if I would ever let him within ten feet of my mouth. We don't know where he's been. You had better keep that in mind this weekend." She scoffs. "If you're planning to touch him, you might want to think about getting a tetanus shot when you get home." She may not like Jake, but that doesn't stop her from taking two condoms out of her own purse and putting them in mine.

"I won't be needing those. No one will be touching anyone. It's just two friends going to a fundraiser." With dancing, which does imply touching, but we don't have to talk about that right now.

"If you say so. Maybe we should also pack some disinfectant spray in your bag, just in case. I'm sure his room is a biohazard."

Jake and Alice have been at each other's throats for years. We all played together constantly as kids, but they haven't gotten along since Jake joined the popular crowd in high school, leaving Alice and me behind. I still hung out with him a lot outside of school because we are neighbors. He didn't do it on purpose, but Alice started to get left out quite a bit. I think it hurt her, and she was too proud to admit it. She has been on Jake's case ever since, and he gives it right back to her.

"Again, I won't be needing that. Besides, it's weird to think about whether or not I want Jake to touch anything. He's like a brother to me." Except he's also *so not* like a brother. Jake is probably the hottest guy we know. At least he was until today. "Enough talking about him. What have you been up to?" I try to change the subject. I don't like spending too much time listening to Alice badmouth my other best friend.

"Really? I just spent the entire evening with your grandmother and several other of North Bay's finest seniors, so clearly nothing. You're not getting off that easy. Tell me more about Mr. Baseball and how you got him so invested in your well-being."

"His name is Mike," I remind her. "But I think it's a stretch to imply he's into me."

She waves the hand holding the tweezers through the air, dismissing my point. "It's not a stretch at all. Who wouldn't want to get with all of this?" she asks, motioning up and down my body. "I want it to be known that I support you and your choices, always. But in this scenario I'm Team Mike, all the way. Jacob Gibson does not deserve to be anyone's first choice."

"Noted. But I feel the need to point out you know almost nothing about Mike, and we also don't know what Jake's intentions are for this weekend. He might not even consider this a date. I'm looking at it as a favor for a friend."

"Either way, you have been too good for that boy for years. He bounced around everybody else's bedroom back in the day, even while he knew exactly how you felt about him. You deserve someone who knows how to sit still and give you his full attention. Now pass me that lip mask," Alice instructs.

I don't know much about Jake's recent dating life, but I do know I can trust him just as much as I can trust Alice or Honey, and she's not being fair to him. Dating people who were not me does not make Jake a bad guy. Especially because, while I think he knew, I never explicitly told him how I felt back then. I know better than to argue with Alice about Jake, though. Besides, she's right about one thing. Mike definitely knew how to sit still and give me plenty of attention this afternoon. My mind wanders to his thigh pressed against mine under the table while he told those silly dad jokes.

Chapter 6

Mike

I swore to myself that I would not let a woman be a distraction this year, but I can't stop thinking about a certain brunette. Even now, I'm scanning the stands for her as Jordan and I toss a ball between us before the game. I should have given Danielle my number. My sisters are always saying they prefer when a guy gives them his phone number rather than asking for theirs. That way they can decide if they want to contact him and not have to worry about some weirdo blowing up their phone with unsolicited messages, or worse, pictures. Gross. I gag. While I'm busy trying not to think about some dude sending my sisters unwanted pictures of his junk, I miss the easy throw Jordan sends me.

"You good, man?"

"Yep."

"Cool. I'm going to run a few warm-ups with Smithy before we get started." Jordan jogs away, leaving me with my thoughts.

I didn't give her my number. I considered it, but at the time I thought I should hold strong and keep it casual. Now I regret that all I did the last time I saw her was mention that the team has a game today, then watch her ride her bike away from Major Dollar in the dark. I hate regrets. Thankfully, she was telling the truth and didn't need to go far. I watched until she stopped next door, at the brick house with the crooked mailbox.

Now all I can do is wait to see if Danielle, the quirky waitress who kept her bike helmet on the entire time she was in my truck, is coming. She should be easy enough to spot if she does, the stands are practically empty. This is only a scrimmage game against the Navigators, another local team. It doesn't count toward our record. Even so, I have a job to do and I need to focus. This woman is already taking up a lot of my brain space. This is exactly the kind of distraction I shouldn't be messing with right now. I'm no stranger to how screwed up things can get when I let myself give in to temptation. I need to get my head on straight for this game. It doesn't really matter if Danielle Daniels shows up today or not.

So why am I still thinking about her? I bend down to stretch my hamstrings and shake off the memory of how my truck smelled like vanilla for two days after she rode with me.

"Get it together, Miller," I say to my feet. We're here for an important reason today.

There are a few scrimmages sprinkled throughout the season, and the ticket sales from these games go to the home team's selected charity. This year the Blue Crabs are partnered with Planting Hope, a cool organization that collects overstocks of fresh food from grocery stores and restaurants and redistributes them to people suffering from food insecurity. Unfortunately, unless our marketing team managed to bag a lot of corporate donations this week, all these empty seats today are going to equal a disappointingly small check for Planting Hope.

Because today's game is only a scrimmage, Coach is giving Davis a break and letting me start. This is my chance to show him I have what it takes. I finish stretching, then grab a bat and take a few practice swings on the sidelines.

It's not long before a voice shouting from behind me breaks my concentration and I turn to follow the sound. Danielle's here and she brought a friend. The short woman with a pink streak running through her hair is projecting her voice to get my attention.

"Hey, Mike Miller."

Danielle elbows her friend, then she hides her face behind her own hands. The ladies are standing at the metal railing separating the field from the stands, so I make my way over to say hi.

Danielle's wearing light wash jeans and a flannel shirt open over a tight white tank top, which I can't help noticing is doing an amazing job showcasing her chest. Her head is covered with a plain white baseball cap, which is adorable on her, and her long hair is braided and pulled through the hole in the back of her cap. She lowers her hands, smiles, and offers me a tiny wave in the process.

"You made it." I smile up at them. "I'm Mike," I say to her friend. "Although, it sounds like you already know that." We wave at each other because the fence is putting too much distance between us for me to be able to shake her hand.

"I think I prefer Batman, actually. That's what we've been calling you behind your back today. I heard something about seeking vengeance on our local crab population," the friend teases.

"Oh my god, shut up," Danielle mutters under her breath. I have to admit I'm really enjoying seeing her flustered about this.

"I'm Alice. The best friend. Always available for Dee's Wednesday afternoon adventures." Alice lightly nudges Danielle, and I can tell from that small gesture that, even though I haven't done much, I've already earned her approval.

"Nice to meet you."

"You, too."

"We brought some other people, too. That's our friend Regina and her daughter Emily," Danielle says. She points to a woman buying cotton candy from a vendor at the end of the row. There's a little girl next to her wearing a pink tutu and a Blue Crabs baseball hat that is so big that it's practically swallowing her head. I smile and wave at them as well, and the little girl gets shy and hides behind her mom's leg. "And just past them you can see Jackson in the blue polo shirt. He would be the one who prepared those crabs for you the other day."

"Ah. Okay. Please pass my compliments to the chef."

"You sure about that? You didn't seem like a huge crab fan."

"Shhh. That's blasphemy around here. Are you trying to ruin a man's career before it starts?" I joke with her, putting up one finger in front of my lips and using the other hand to point at the crabs displayed on both my hat and my jersey. She laughs.

"Miller, let's go," Coach Johnson calls to me from the dugout. That's my cue.

"Well, ladies, I'm glad you made it. Thanks for coming, and thanks for bringing your whole crew. It's nice to know we have some friendly faces in the stands. I need to get to work." I wave at them and turn around to jog over to join my team.

Danielle and Alice are whispering and giggling. I'm too far away to hear what they are saying, but I know they are talking about me. It seems to be in a good way, and a little bit of warmth spreads through my chest, making me stand a bit straighter. When I get to where Coach Johnson is standing, he lays a hand on my shoulder.

"All right, son, let's see what you can do."

I swallow and ignore the pang of homesickness those words bring. "I've got this, Coach."

"I like the confidence. Now go do your job."

When he returns his attention to his clipboard, I bounce on my toes a few times and move my head in a circle, feeling the stretch in my neck. I need to focus. I continue my stretches and pull my left arm across my body, wincing just a little bit at the familiar pinch in my shoulder. It isn't long before the announcer tells everyone to rise for the national anthem and the game begins.

I make the first catch and send it over to first base before the hitter can get there, giving us our first out. Everything is going well until the third inning, when a base runner collides with Jordan and he falls back into the dirt. The Navigator lands on top of him. They go down so hard I can hear the thud from my position, but it happened too fast for me to see much. From what I can tell, Jordan's outstretched arm seems to have taken the brunt of their fall. He might've hit his head, too.

"Shit. Come on, buddy," I mumble, watching helplessly.

The Navigator player walks away on his own, but Jordan is not getting up. All of the players freeze, and Coach jogs out with the medic to examine him. The longer he lies there answering their questions the more fans start to stand and put their hats over their hearts. Thankfully, after a few minutes Jordan is able to stand and walk off the field, but he's clutching his elbow, which can be the kiss of death when you throw for a living. He looks at me and I nod at him in solidarity as he is escorted down to the locker room.

We resume play and I'm reabsorbed in the game again. Even with Jordan's injury on my mind, by the ninth inning I've fielded every ball that came my way. I have base hits three out of the four times I'm at bat. The fourth time their pitcher throws too many wide of the plate, and they walk me. I have zero errors in this game, and we are ending with our first win in weeks. Hopefully, this will prove to the coaching staff I have what it takes to be a regular starter. Maybe it will even impress a certain flannel-wearing woman in the stands.

After the game, Jordan and Rodriguez find me in the locker room.

"Hey man, from what I saw, it looked like you played a great game," Jordan says, walking up to me. He's holding a pack of ice to his arm.

"Thanks." I point to his injury. "Do they think it is your UCL? How does it feel? What did they say?"

"Hurts, but I can move it, so it's not as bad as we first thought. They don't think anything broke or tore completely. Plan to see how it feels for the next day or two, then I'll get it checked further if I have to."

"Good. Just stay on top of it."

"Yeah, I know. Hey, was that the waitress from the other night we saw you talking to before the game? Rodriguez here says you left with her after the crab feast. Why didn't you tell me that when you got home, bro?"

"He absolutely did leave with her," Rodriguez confirms, a huge smile on his face. The two of them fist bump each other. I shake my head.

"Her name is Danielle. Nothing happened. I just gave her a ride and invited her to come out to the game today."

"Looks like she accepted the invitation. Nice. I can't lie. I didn't want to say anything, but I was getting worried that my roommate had no game," Jordan says.

I don't know what he's talking about. He did nothing but say exactly that the entire time we were at the restaurant. That was the whole reason I started talking to Danielle in the first place.

"Right. Sure. You're great at keeping your mouth shut about stuff like this," I say sarcastically.

"Worked, didn't it? She's here."

Coach Johnson walks in and congratulates us on the game. "Well-played, gentleman. You looked good out there. Let's use this energy to keep the momentum going." After a few more brief remarks, he asks a few of us to stick around. Everyone else is dismissed.

"Jordan, don't leave until we talk about that elbow. Miller and Rodriguez, I'm sending you both to Virginia Tech to represent the team at the charity gala on Saturday night. Wear a suit and you can present our check for Planting Hope."

"Um, yes, sir. Sure. But, can I ask why us?" It's a good cause and I'm happy to show my face for an hour at some stuffy charity fundraiser, but I have no clue why he would pick players he hasn't started in a single game until today.

"Don't overthink it, kid. Shockingly, there weren't many volunteers to drive for three hours to sit through a lecture about food insecurity in a hotel full of rich snobs who don't understand the irony of gorging themselves on a free buffet. But marketing says we need to show our faces, so a few years ago we starting sending the rookies. It's your turn. You and Rodriguez will share a room in the hotel for one night. Eat it up with the yuppies, and be back Sunday."

"Sweet," Rodriguez says.

"Fair enough, Coach. We'll be there."

I'm not about to complain about a free night away with my friend at an all-you-can-eat buffet, especially if the only thing we need to do is take a road trip and listen to some boring speech for a few minutes. Coach nods at us and leaves me standing with Jordan and Rodriguez again.

"Don't worry, Miller." Rodriguez says. "I'll handle all the ladies this weekend so you can save yourself for Danielle."

I roll my eyes and lightly punch him on the arm.

"It won't go anywhere with her," I tell them. "I need to keep my head in the game this season if I want to get a leg up on the competition. And I am including both of you idiots in that competition."

Jordan shrugs. "Who said it needs to get serious with her? You're allowed to just have fun sometimes, dude. And so is she."

"The lovin's even better when you're in it together." Rodriguez laughs at his own dumb joke and elbows me back. He's playing around, but the dude doesn't realize his own strength, and it still causes me to grunt. I retaliate and punch his arm again, this time harder than necessary, but he just laughs.

Maybe these guys are onto something. I can't spend my entire life on the field, and it never hurts to make a new friend, especially because I'm new here and she knows much more about this town than I do. It definitely doesn't hurt that she has a killer body, smells like vanilla, and fit right in with my teammates the last time we were together. I wonder if Danielle and her crew are still hanging around.

I have an idea.

Still in my uniform, I head out of the locker room and make a bee line for the snack bar. Hopefully she hasn't left. The line moves quickly and I make my purchase, grabbing a pen from the cup on the counter.

"Excuse me?" A little boy tugs on my pant leg. "Are you a baseball player?"

"I sure am."

"Can I have your autograph?"

It's the first time I've been asked to sign anything, and the moment feels so monumental I have to clear my throat before I answer him.

"Of course you can, buddy."

I grab a napkin, scribbling my name for him quickly.

"I'm going to play like you one day."

"Yeah? You play? That's awesome."

Looking up, I see a woman who must be his mom headed toward us. Her arms are full as she tries to balance a baby on her hip, carry a diaper bag, and push a stroller with a toddler sitting in it.

"Can I give you some advice?" I crouch down to get eye-to-eye with the kid. He looks back at me with wide eyes and an open mouth and nods. "Make sure to get your workout in today by helping to carry all of that stuff home. You look pretty strong, and it's important not to watch a lady like your mom struggle when you have two free hands. Your family is your most important team."

He listens immediately and runs to take the diaper bag from her, but it's almost as big as he is. It's hilarious to watch him try to balance as he walks with it next to the stroller. His mom laughs and only lets him wrestle with it for a second before she tells him they can hang it over the handlebars.

"Mom, look. I got an autograph."

"Thank you," the woman mouths to me, and I smile at her briefly before grabbing my snack bar purchase and jogging away. I need to go find Danielle before she leaves.

Hopefully, she'll think this is cute and not incredibly cheesy. Honestly, it could go either way.

It doesn't take me long to spot Alice and Danielle standing in the hall outside of the bathrooms, so I jog over to join them. Danielle's flannel shirt is now tied around her waist, which means her upper half is only covered by my new favorite piece of clothing: that very clingy tank top. It takes me a second longer than it should to redirect my eyes back up to her face. Her left cheek is covered in dark paint that I think is supposed to resemble the Batman logo. I wonder if she did that specifically for me and the thought makes me smile. Why does picturing Danielle visiting the family area for face painting make me so happy? I glance briefly at Alice and see that she is sporting a sunny yellow butterfly on one cheek and the Wonder Woman logo on the other.

"You're still here." I smile at them.

"Hi there, Big Guy. Good game." That's the second time Danielle's called me Big Guy and I don't hate it. Her compliment makes another pool of warmth spread through my chest and I can feel the tips of my ears going red. I rub the back of my neck and look down at my shoes.

"Yeah, nice job," Alice agrees.

"Thanks."

"How's Jordan? That looked pretty bad." Danielle's concern for my roommate is touching.

"He's doing okay, I just saw him. Just needs to take it easy for a few days. I'm glad I found you. I was hoping I would catch you before you left."

"You found two of us, but Regina had to head out early and put Emily down for a nap. Jackson took them home. Turns out a few hours in the sun after being stuffed full of popcorn and cotton candy can make a kid crash pretty hard."

"I can imagine. So, um, speaking of junk food, I got you a little something as a thank you for coming. No allergies, right?" I check, feeling awkward, but not as awkward as it would be to hand over a present that sends her straight to the hospital.

"No allergies," she confirms with a shy smile, so I hand her the pack of peanut M&M's I purchased. I wrote my phone number on the cardboard box and my initials underneath.

It may be corny, but hopefully she likes it. If there's one thing I've learned growing up with so many sisters, it's that if you want to impress a woman you can rarely go wrong with chocolate and a small, thoughtful gesture.

"Thanks. Now I have M&M's signed by M.M." She's definitely blushing this time. It's the cutest damn thing I've ever seen in my life.

"Nice." Alice gives me a solid nod of approval. I'll take it.

I tip the brim of my cap to them and thank them one more time for coming before heading back to the locker room.

Chapter 7

Danielle

Friday came faster than I expected. Between that sociology paper and the baseball game in the middle of the week, in addition to my regular classes and a few shifts at The Blue Crab, I have been busy. It's a long drive to Virginia Tech, which gives me a lot of time to think. I downloaded the audiobook of Great Expectations and it's playing now so I can get some of my reading done for British Lit on the way. I should be thinking about Jake and the weekend ahead of us, but my thoughts keep drifting to the baseball game.

I can't remember the last time a guy gave me his phone number, which very well might be because it was never. Honey already has the phone numbers for every family in North Bay, and it's not like I'm going to clubs and picking up men very often. Mike's M&M's move was smooth, not to mention sweet. I saved the candy for a road trip snack and I'm munching on them now.

Yesterday I contacted Mike for the first time. Texting with him was surprisingly easy and fun. The memory of our text chain brings a smile to my face.

Me: *This is Danielle. Thanks for the M&M's. Peanut is in my top three flavors.*

Mike: *Glad you liked them. What are your other favorites?*

Me: *If we are just talking M&M's, then my top three are the pretzel, peanut butter, and peanut, in that order. You?*

Mike: *Can't say I've given it much thought. Usually stick to original.*

Me: *Smart. Can't go wrong with a classic. Just keep the cold brew flavor away from me.*

Mike: *Why? Not a coffee lover?*

Me: *I love chocolate, and nothing against M&M's, they're fantastic, obviously. But coffee in general is the devil's bathwater. Blech.*

Mike: *Haha. I see. Well, I'm headed to practice. Talk soon.*

We left it there, and neither one of us has picked up the conversation yet, but I may have read over our exchange more than a few times since.

I shouldn't be thinking so much about Mike. I don't have time for a silly new crush. Jake needs me today. My attention should be on him and this charity event.

Jake lives a few minutes off campus in a townhouse with three other guys. Thankfully, parking is easy to find along the street, so I turn off the engine and send a text to let him know I've arrived. He replies right away.

BND: *Don't move. Be right there.*

While my phone is in my hand I can't help pulling up the messages from Mike one more time. I'm so absorbed rereading our texts that the soft knock on the window startles me. I sit up and turn to see a familiar face looking down and chuckling. Jake opens my door and wraps me in a bear hug as soon as I exit the car.

"There she is." He squeezes me tightly with his now fully-inked arms. Has he grown? My head is pressed against the center of his chest, and I swear he seems bigger. He must be working out more because I don't remember his pecs being this defined or his abs this hard. I pat his back and step back out of the hug. As he lets go I inspect his arms more closely. The left one has been covered in a full sleeve depicting a battle from *The Lord of the Rings* for two years, but now the other arm is completely tatted in what appears to be a scene from Harry Potter.

"Yep. Here I am. Love the new ink." I lean into the car to grab my bag off the passenger seat, ignoring a little pang of nerves when I realize my butt is in the air. I catch myself wondering if he's looking. Of course, I know he's watching, but is he *looking* looking? Ugh. This is so dumb. I don't know what this weekend is supposed to be for us, and I don't know how to act. Unfortunately, my default in unfamiliar social situations is awkward as hell.

"So..." I straighten up and rock on my heels, duffle bag now on my shoulder, as I turn to face him.

"So?" He pauses and waits. After a beat, when I don't say anything else, he fills the silence by offering to take my bag. I let him, and he motions for me to follow him back to his place.

I've been to his house before. Alice and I have driven together a couple of times to visit Jake on a Saturday and attend a football game. For all her grumbling about him, she has never turned down the chance to party on a big college campus. This is the first time I've decided to come alone. Just me, Jake, and no Alice. It feels weird not to have her here as a buffer to stop me from doing things I might regret. Boy-girl, friendship-altering things.

We enter the house straight into the living room, where all his roommates are sitting on the couch playing a video game. I recognize the one named Connor from my last visit. He looks up from the racing game they are playing, which causes his imaginary go-kart to smash into a wall. Accepting defeat, he hands the controller to the guy next to him and stands to greet me.

"Damn, is this Jake's friend Dan-Dan From Home that I see before me? Girl, you've had a glow-up since the last time you were here."

"Hi, Connor, right? It's Danielle." I point to myself.

"It sure is." He scans my body.

Alice really did work her magic. I felt a little ridiculous when she suggested this fuzzy cropped sweater and high-rise leggings combo, but once I put it on, I saw how much it works for me. It doesn't show much, but the sliver of skin between my top and my pants is more of my midriff than I'm used to exposing. Normally, when I wear leggings, I pair them with a shirt long enough to cover my butt. This time Alice insisted I needed to embrace my curves, so they are on full display. I slept with my hair in loose braids last night after the shower and took them out this morning, so now there are beachy waves falling around my shoulders. Alice also insisted on applying my makeup herself before I left. I have to admit, I do feel pretty. Connor's attention makes my cheeks heat up and I laugh, not sure what else to do.

Jake clears his throat and pulls on my elbow. "Well, I'm taking this one up to my room."

"Eager much?" Connor teases him. "She's barely in the door and you're literally dragging her to your bedroom."

Jake glances down at his hand on my arm and loosens his grip, but doesn't let go. He just glares at his friend. Connor laughs and holds up his hands in mock surrender as Jake guides me away, up the stairs. When we get to his room, he lets go of me and closes the door behind us. I kick off my shoes and sit on the bed, which is covered in the same plaid comforter he used for years at home. I arch an eyebrow and he knows I'm silently asking what gives.

"Sorry about that," Jake mutters. "I'll talk to him."

"About what? Nothing happened." I flop back onto his pillow and curl onto my side. I'm tired after the long drive. Maybe I can squeeze in a nap before the events start.

"The way he was looking at you was disrespectful."

"Ha. Was it, though? Felt pretty normal to me. You act like a guy has never hit on me before."

"Not in front of me they haven't." He crosses his arms over his chest. Why is he being weird?

"That can't possibly be true." I yawn and let myself sink further into the pillows.

"It is." He's serious.

"Don't be silly. You know Connor didn't mean anything. He knows I came here for you. He was joking. Besides, it was kind of flattering. It's not like I'm going to be hearing that kind of stuff from you, right? A girl needs to get her confidence boosted where she can." I put a lilt in my voice, trying to lighten his bizarre mood shift. He is still scowling, so I roll my eyes. "Fine. I promise not to run into the living room and boink your friend who I barely know and with whom

I have spent a grand total of forty minutes over the course of the last three years. Does that make you feel better?"

He grunts and an expression I can't read crosses his face.

"Just come here, dude." I pat the space on the bed next to me. "Show me this new tattoo. And then tell me what to expect tonight."

He takes a breath before joining me on the bed. He's sitting on the edge of the mattress. I'm curled up closer to the wall, facing him but not touching. I reach my leg out and poke him with one toe.

"Didn't realize I was going to be getting Grumpy Jake when I got here."

He shakes his head and morphs back into the guy I came to see. "You're not. Sorry. I have some school stuff on my mind, and Connor being a dumbass isn't helping. But it's nothing you need to worry about. I'll tell you whatever you want to know."

I jerk his arm closer and he shows me his new full-sleeve Harry Potter tattoo. It's done in the same style as the *The Lord of the Rings* battle he has detailed on the other side, but this one is the Battle of Hogwarts in shades of black and grey with a few patronuses floating through in white ink. Only Jacob Gibson can balance looking so badass with being a complete nerd.

"I want to know everything your fraternity has planned for the next few days so I can prepare myself."

He pulls up an itinerary on his phone.

"Tonight, there's a game of flashlight tag followed by s'mores around a bonfire. Tomorrow is hot dog eating."

Jake says we aren't required to be at every event, so we decide to skip tag and spend some more time catching up, then we'll join his fraternity brothers for s'mores later. I'm still not sure how any of this is raising money for charity, but if I can help someone in need by stuffing my own face with marshmallows, I'm here for it.

"Catching up" turns out to be watching two Adam Sandler movies on his laptop. Well, Jake watches. Big Daddy is normally one of our favorites. So many of our inside jokes are from this movie. I actually gave him thirty packets of ketchup for Christmas one year. No one else understood, but we both thought it was hilarious. Today it's not holding my attention. My eyes keep drifting to my phone and wishing I would see a new text in my thread with Mike appear.

A few hours later, I find myself sitting on the edge of a patio planter and sucking a smear of chocolate from my thumb. We are in the backyard of a four-story brick fraternity house. There are three small firepits in the yard, each surrounded by a few folding chairs. When we got here, Jake handed someone at a table twenty dollars for our cover charge, so I guess that answers how the money is being raised for Planting Hope. There must be at least two hundred people attending this bonfire. Jake slipped off to the bathroom at least half an hour ago, but now he's nowhere to be found.

We never ate dinner and it's eleven o'clock at night, so I am starving and shivering in the chilly evening air. My brain buzzes from the hit of sugar from the marshmallows, but my stomach still feels empty, so I stand and wander around the party trying to warm up and searching for something else to eat. Once I make my way past a group of what seems to be hockey players based on their towering height and the snippets of conversation I can overhear, I recognize Jake's familiar silhouette. He is bent down over a giggling red head, whispering something to her while he runs a hand through his own short black hair. When he straightens, I can see there's a flush on his cheeks. An unpleasant feeling burns deep in my belly. Either his face is heated because of the alcohol or because of something she said. I don't have any right to be upset with him just for talking to someone, but it is annoying that he invited me at all if he plans to ignore me all night.

I knew he planned to have a few drinks, but I didn't realize he'd be drinking quite this much. I saw him have two beers and two shots earlier, and there is another red plastic cup in his hand. Who knows what else he's had since he disappeared. I abandon my search for food and walk over to where they are standing, surrounded by other loud, giggling classmates.

"Hey." I reach up and put my hand on his shoulder in case he can't hear me over the noise.

"Dan-Dan, there you are." He grins. I roll my eyes. He knows I hate when he calls me that, and he also knew exactly where I was because until now I have not moved from the spot where he left me.

"Having fun?" he asks, raising his cup in a toast to nothing in particular. He's oblivious to my irritation.

"I think I'm ready to call it a night. Can I get the key to your place?" I lean in and raise my voice over the noise. Little Miss Red Curls doesn't even acknowledge my presence, she just turns and starts talking to one of her friends.

"Sure." Jake reaches into his pocket and pulls out his keys for me. Placing them into my palm he tells me, "I won't be too much longer. I'll see you back at my room." His words are coming out slowly with long pauses between them. One of the guys nearby whistles at the mention of Jake meeting me in his bedroom.

Okay then. I know it's what I asked for, but I wasn't actually expecting him to hand over his keys. I thought he would take the hint and come with me. Guess I'll be wandering around campus alone and finding my way back to his place in the dark. Cool.

My mom would never forgive me if I let you take a bike home in the dark. Mike's words from a few days ago echo back to me.

It might not be fair to compare my lifelong friend to a guy I hardly know, but I think I can be forgiven for not feeling especially generous toward Jake at the moment. I drove for three hours today because he said he wanted me to be here for these events, but he has hardly said a word to me since we arrived, other than to whine about his roommate giving me a tiny bit of attention. At least the guy I don't know cared enough to make sure I would get home safely, and Mike also didn't seem to have a problem talking to me in front of his friends or ignoring the pitchers of beer on the table at the crab feast. I can't say the same for Jacob Gibson tonight.

Turning on my heel, I walk away from the party without saying goodbye to anyone, not that any of them seem to notice. Shaking my head, I type Jake's address into my phone and pull up walking directions. About half a block into my journey, I hear a voice behind me.

"Dan-Dan, wait up." Thank God, maybe Jake came to his senses.

Nope. It's Connor, but at least his face is familiar. "I'm headed back too, I'll walk with you," he offers.

"Cool, thanks. Please call me Danielle. Dan-Dan is a weird thing Jake only does because he knows it gets to me."

"Sorry, he's being a downer lately. I promise I'll tell J to get his head out of his ass by tomorrow. He's not doing well in some of his classes, and I think it's really getting to him. But he probably wouldn't want me to tell you that, so just pretend I didn't say anything."

"The secret is safe with me." I'm zero percent worried about it. School has always been easy for Jake. Knowing him, "not doing well" most likely means he got a B-plus or forgot to do one homework assignment and turned it in a day late.

Connor is easy to be around and we make comfortable small talk on the way back to the house. He makes an effort to use my real name while we chat about the classes we are taking this semester, and he shows me a few funny memes on his phone. Before long, we are back at their place.

"My boy really likes you, you know." Connor's voice is sincere as he tucks his phone back into his pocket and lets us in the front door.

"Jake and I go back a long time," is all I know how to say in response.

"He's told me about it. You mean a lot to him, Danielle. I'm glad you're here. And I'm sorry if I made it weird earlier." At least someone is glad I'm here.

"You really didn't. That was all Jake. But thanks, Connor. I appreciate it. And thanks for walking me back. I think I'm going to turn in now. I'm pretty tired."

"Sure. Goodnight." Connor heads into the kitchen and leaves me to my nighttime routine. I drag my tired body up the stairs.

Alone in Jake's room, I set his keys down next to a box of protein bars on his dresser and help myself to one. I devour it in four bites before changing into pajama pants and a tank top. After going to the bathroom and brushing my teeth, I tuck myself into his bed.

I have no idea what time it is when Jake finally stumbles into the room. I wake up to him mumbling to himself and bumping into the furniture before he finally lays his body down with a thud in the bed next to me, the mattress sagging with his weight. He doesn't even bother to undress or get under the covers. It hardly takes any time at all before the dummy next to me is lightly snoring. I have half a mind to push him onto the floor, but instead I just turn to face the wall and fall back asleep.

In the morning, somehow Jake is already awake and dressed in a hoodie and dark gray sweatpants. He's standing across the room rifling through a few papers on his desk when I open my eyes.

"Good morning, Sleeping Beauty," he teases.

"What time is it?" I croak in my scratchy morning voice.

"Almost ten. Do you want to go to the diner and grab breakfast?" *Yes*, my stomach screams. *Finally, some actual food*. But my brain and my heart remember that I'm still irritated with him. Jake crosses the room and sits down on the bed where I'm still wrapped up under the covers. He ruffles my hair and smiles down at me, acting like nothing happened last night. Technically, I suppose nothing did.

"Um, I guess. Is anyone else coming?" I pretend to yawn and cover my mouth, trying to discreetly test my morning breath. Yikes.

Jake takes his hand off my head. "Do you want to invite anyone else?"

Should I suggest bringing Connor if he's home? He was nice to me yesterday, and since Alice isn't here, Connor could act like a buffer. Will mentioning him make Jake get all huffy again? Ugh. This is stupid and I don't have enough caffeine in me to deal with a cranky Jake again.

"No. Just give me a few minutes to get dressed and we can head out."

He nods and leaves the room, shutting the door behind him to give me some privacy. It doesn't take me long to throw on a pair of jeans and a sweater. I twist my hair into a quick side braid and duck into the bathroom to finish getting ready.

"Done," I announce as I head downstairs to find him. From the bottom of the steps Jake smiles and motions for me to follow him outside to his car.

Chapter 8

Danielle

The diner is actually a chain restaurant famous for being open 24-hours a day to serve their sub-par waffles, but they have food and caffeine, so bring it on. I order a stack of pancakes with bacon and home fries, hot tea for my caffeine fix, and orange juice because it's what I would rather drink. Jake orders a ham and cheese omelet with a cup of coffee.

He looks at me from across the booth. "Remember the first time you tried coffee? You spit it out all over the table and told Honey it tasted like there was burnt dish water in the mug she gave you."

I giggle. "Yeah. She threatened to smack me with her wooden spoon for trash talking her kitchen skills, but she couldn't stop laughing, so she just handed me a rag and told me to clean up the mess I made."

Jake smiles and his eyes soften. "You always stuck to tea or hot chocolate after that."

"Still do."

"Hey," he lowers his voice until it is almost a whisper and looks into my eyes as he changes the subject. "What's going on with us? Why does this feel weird?" He motions one hand back and forth between us. I puff out my cheeks and blow out a slow breath.

"Because it is weird, Jake. I don't exactly fit into your life here," I point out. "One minute you don't want Connor to talk to me because you want me all to yourself, and the next thing I know you're letting me sit alone on a huge potted plant all night so you can chat up some girl. What time did you get back? And did you even care if I was safe? I've hardly spent any time on this campus, I didn't know where I was."

"Damn. I'm sorry about that. I did know you were safe. Connor texted me to let me know he walked you home and you went to bed. That's why I stayed out later. But you're right. Connor also let me know what a dick I was being to you. I should have been more focused on spending time with you last night."

"That's the thing, though. You shouldn't have. You are supposed to be at those events to mingle with other people in the Greek scene or whatever. That's the whole point of this weekend, right? Networking and philanthropy. Not hanging out with your boring friend from home."

"Yeah, I guess," he says while his hands fidget with the salt shaker. "At least the networking and philanthropy parts. Still, D. I am sorry. That wasn't cool. And you're not boring."

"Right."

I am boring, and honestly, I'm okay with that. I like sitting here at a diner with one close friend, and I hate big parties with tons of strangers like last night. But Jake likes both, and he deserves to have both. I just don't want to make myself miserable trying to make him happy.

"You're definitely not boring. And to prove it, I dare you to try this one more time." He pushes his coffee mug toward me, knowing we never say no to each other's dares, no matter how dumb they are.

I sigh and try to choke down a sip of the coffee. At least he put three sugars in it.

"Ugh. No way. Still tastes like muddy feet sweat." I manage not to spit it across the table this time, but I give up pretending I will ever be able to stomach the bitter liquid and switch back to my orange juice. He just chuckles and drinks from the mug as if it's not the worst drink on the entire planet. After chugging half the glass of juice to cleanse the awful bitter taste from my mouth (which doesn't work because if there is anything worse than coffee, it's orange juice and coffee together), I decide last night isn't worth a fight. "It's okay. Let's just forget about it and start over. I've missed you."

"I missed you too," he says over the edge of the mug. "A lot. I do appreciate you coming this weekend, even if I haven't done a great job showing it." Jake sets the coffee down and folds his arms on the top of the table.

I see he means what he said, and my lips turn up at the corners. "All right. You can make it up to me today. Do you think we can lay low again? I like having you to myself." I place my hand over his arms and pat him gently. He nods his agreement.

"Yeah, sure. Since we were at the bonfire and we'll be making an appearance at the gala, I won't take too much heat if we skip the rest of today's events and stay in."

The introverted half of my brain is grateful for the chance to recharge.

"Although," I say, "I am bummed to miss my chance to become the hotdog eating champion of Virginia Tech."

"Somehow, I'm not buying that."

When our food finally arrives, I stuff my face full of fluffy, syrupy goodness like a champ. Jake laughs and helps himself to a small piece of my bacon. I retaliate by sticking my fork into his omelet and taking a bite.

"Maybe you had a chance at that contest after all."

"Told you."

It seems like things are back to normal, at least for now. For the rest of the day, things between us slide easily back into best friend territory as we hang out at his house. It's easy to be myself and laugh with Jake. I fill him in on the lives of everyone from home. He asks about Honey and, surprisingly, even Alice. I tell him about going to a Blue Crabs game with Alice and some friends from work, but omit the part about how I was personally invited by the new shortstop. He tells me that he only has a few exams to take at the beginning of next week, then he will be home for a few days.

"We should play a round of Truth or Dare for real," I say when I've reached the end of my stories about North Bay. We are both lying on Jake's bed, facing in opposite directions. His head is on the pillow, mine is at the foot of the bed.

He lets out a playful scoff. "You're such a girl."

I am a girl, but that's never kept him from playing this particular game with me. "Uh-huh. First of all, you started this with the coffee. You only have yourself to blame. Second, sounds to me like you're still afraid of my dares."

"Damn straight. You're the one who dared me to write a check for a thousand dollars made out to Captain Fartpants in my mom's checkbook. I was grounded for three weeks."

"I still don't believe that punishment fit the crime. It's not like Captain Fartpants was ever going to cash it. All she had to do was void it and the problem was solved. You would think she'd be impressed that her twelve-year-old son knew how to write a check in the first place."

He smiles and rolls his eyes. "Fine. Truth or Dare, Dan-Dan?"

"I dare you to stop calling me Dan-Dan."

"In your dreams. That's not how this works."

"It's not even your turn. You already gave me a dare."

"This is a new round. Do you want to play or not?"

"Ugh. Okay. Truth. I'm not taking my chances with more coffee."

"I take back what I said about you not being boring." He teases before asking, "How serious did things get with Steve?"

"I don't know what to say about that," I tell him. It's only been six months, but it feels like a lifetime since Steve and I were together. "I guess it was pretty serious? He tended to make everything about him, but he was nice enough and I was comfortable with him. I could have seen myself getting married, one day. But I probably wasn't as upset as I should have been when it ended." It was kind of a relief that it was over, if I'm being honest. I don't know if I ever really loved Steve, but it hurt to have yet another person in my life walk away from me.

"There are no rules about how to feel after a breakup. No one is saying you should have been shattered. I'm glad you weren't." He pats my leg. "But it's interesting that you just said you could have seen yourself getting married, and not necessarily that you were picturing marrying *him*."

"I think you're right." I never thought about it like that, but it's probably true. Whenever I think about the future, I picture things like buying a house, staying in North Bay, or having kids. None of it is specific to Steve. Or anyone, really. The guy in my fantasy future is just sort of a vague outline of a person, like a dream where you know what is happening but you can't make out the details of a person's face.

"Of course I'm right. I know you."

Something twists inside my chest and I swallow. Deep in the pit of my stomach I know it's because it has always been impossible to picture myself with anyone but Jake. Weirdly, though, it's also impossible to picture myself *with* Jake. It's not clear that he is the one in that dream, but a big part of me just always assumed it couldn't really be anyone else. At least not until recently.

"My turn. I also pick Truth. No way I'm taking heat for Captain Fartpants again." He sits up.

I laugh and shift toward him, which causes my shirt to lift just an inch. He takes one finger and boops the sliver of exposed skin, and I swat his hand away playfully. I should have thought about what to ask before suggesting this game. Now I am here without a plan. There are so many things I want to ask Jake. Like how many people he's brought back to this bed I'm lying on with him, if he ever thinks about me in that way, or if he is as scared to open that door as I am. I know it's none of my business how many other partners there have been, but there is still a growing weight on my chest as the questions on my mind get heavier. I decide to ditch that line of thinking entirely.

"What's your favorite memory?"

He scoots down and grabs the pillow from the top of the bed. He repositions it by my head, then lies back onto it, just a few inches away from me. "Are you sure you want to know?" Jake asks the ceiling.

"That sounds ominous, but now you for sure have to tell me."

"I think the honest answer is your grandpa's funeral." He glances sideways to see my reaction, but his response has made me more curious than sad. I nod to show him it's okay to continue.

"I remember that day. We were so young. I didn't really understand what was happening." My mom and I lived in our camper and traveled the country together. I never got to spend much time with her dad, other than when we would visit for holidays. I only remember him offering me mints from his pockets. I didn't like how hard they were to chew. But everyone in North Bay says Pop was a sweet, quiet man who was devoted to Honey and always did whatever he could to help his neighbors. Edna Plum has told me stories about how he would bring her all the vegetables from his garden when she first started the restaurant as a way of showing support. I was too young to realize how much I would miss my grandpa, or at least the idea of him being in my life.

"I was so excited to see someone else my age." I can hear the nostalgia in Jake's voice. "I don't know if you remember, but we got in trouble for playing hide and seek at the funeral parlor, so my dad offered to take us back to our house during the wake and give the adults a more peaceful place to mourn."

I pick up the story for him. "And then he took us out onto your pier and showed us the crabs hanging onto the pilings. He let me try to dip them with the net. I think it was the first time I went crabbing."

Jake laughs. "That net was bigger than you were, and you almost fell into the water in your church clothes."

"Your dad pulled me back in time."

"I wanted to catch you myself." His eyes lock with mine. "But I knew I wasn't strong enough."

Silence hangs between us, stretching a few seconds into an eternity. He's not just talking about that day anymore. Jake is talking about right now. He's admitting that he is curious what it would be like to make a move, but scared to go there with me. Well, same.

Although…is it?

Shouldn't there have been more of a spark when he touched my belly a minute ago? Should I be wriggling, and clenching, and feeling too warm lying this close to him?

Because I'm not.

I shouldn't feel guilty about that, but I do.

Briefly, my mind wonders how my body would react if Mike were the one next to me right now, and heat spreads through me, telling me I would feel very differently about it. A new wave of guilt hits me along with that knowledge. There is no romance handbook. If one did exist, I'm sure it would say not to think about another man while you are lying in bed with your close friend who seems to be moments away from confessing his feelings for you. I truly thought that if the day ever came I would jump at the chance to be with Jake, but maybe I was wrong. Or maybe we're just too late.

I can feel the words we don't know how to say to each other bubbling under the surface and threatening to erupt and destroy everything. Judging by the way he clears his throat and pops up from the bed so quickly, he can read my expression just as well as I can read his. It's a confession he doesn't want to make, and the truth is I don't think I want to hear it either.

"Okay. Enough heavy. Let's get ourselves dolled up for this shindig." I try to lighten the mood by using a retro radio announcer's voice. Because that isn't awkward at all.

He chuckles and says, "Remind me why I invited you again, you dork? I'll change in here so you can have the bathroom." Just like that, the tension is gone and my best friend is back.

Smiling my relief at him, I take my duffle bag and duck out of his room. Once I close the bathroom door behind me, I set my bag on the counter and get started. My curling iron is tangled in its cord, so I spend a minute untwisting it and plug it in to heat while I dig my dress out from the bottom of the bag. After searching the phrase *affordable fancy dress,* I found one online for twenty-three dollars and ordered it the day after Jake invited me. Alice told me to bring a garment bag for it, but the idea of carrying an extra bag as tall as I am into Jake's house for a dress that cost less than our breakfast at the diner felt embarrassing. Thankfully, the slinky black sequined material didn't wrinkle and it looks fine. I tear the tag off with my teeth, put it on, and give myself a once-over in the mirror. Not bad, if I do say so myself.

This dress was labeled "bodycon" and it is definitely hugging my curves in all the right ways. I love that it has long sleeves so I won't be freezing all night. I can wear a regular bra with it, and the sweetheart neckline is giving me some killer cleavage. Plus, it has pockets. Once my curling iron is hot, I use it to roll loose waves around the barrel and let them fall down my back and over my shoulders. A quick swipe of mascara, some smoky eyeshadow, and a touch of the red lipstick I swiped from Honey's dresser, and I'm done. This is as good as it's going to get. I unplug the curling iron and let it cool on the sink while I stuff the rest of my things back into my bag. The final touch is my trusty black heels, which I retrieve from the side pocket of my duffle.

I exit the bathroom and almost bump into Jake in the hall.

"Wow." His breath is heavy and his eyes are scanning my body in a way that tells me he is looking at *everything*. I just laugh awkwardly.

"Thanks. You clean up pretty well yourself." He's wearing a dark gray suit with a black button-up shirt and a thin silver tie. I reach out to straighten it for him. "Should we get going?"

"In a minute." He tugs me toward him gently until my body is pressed against his, our hands clasped at my hip. "Come here for a second. I really do appreciate that you came this weekend. You look beautiful." As I look up at his face he tucks my hair behind my ear. Jake looks at my mouth, then into my eyes. Neither of us blink. For a second, I think he wants to kiss me, but instead he lets go of my hand and wraps his arms behind me, pulling me closer into a hug. I can smell his cologne with my cheek pressed against his shoulder, and there is a faint hint of mint on his breath. I tilt my head up toward his face and our eyes lock together again. We are both still, frozen with the knowledge that if something is going to change between us then tonight will be the night. But in this moment neither one of us has the courage to make that leap. After a beat, I pat his chest and pull away.

When we arrive at the hotel hosting the gala, there are signs directing us toward Ballroom C. Jake leads the way and I follow slightly behind, a bit wobbly in my heels because I haven't had a reason to wear them for over a year. At the end of a long hallway an arched doorway opens to reveal a large space decorated with ornate wallpaper and oversized chandeliers. There is a buffet of food extending along the entire left wall and round tables adorned with pristine white cloths take up most of the space. The center of the room has been left empty for use as a dance floor, but no one is dancing yet. A small table in the corner is surrounded by speakers and Connor is standing behind it, plugging in his phone. Jake tilts his head in that direction and tells me Connor volunteered to DJ, which in this case just meant making a playlist and pressing pause when it's time for someone to speak to the crowd.

We find an empty table and I put my purse down to save our seats. A guy I don't recognize comes up to us and ignores my presence as he speaks to Jake. "There you are, man. Where have you been all day? Derrick is looking for you."

Jake turns to me. "I'm sorry, I need to go deal with this. I'll be right back."

"Sure thing. Can't keep Derrick waiting, whoever that is. I'm going to scope out the buffet."

"I'll be right behind you, I promise. I need to talk to a few of the guys first."

I smile at him, but inside my heart tightens. I hope this won't be a repeat of last night, but if it is, at least this time there is food. I refuse to spend another night hungry and alone in a crowd of strangers, so the first thing I'm going to do is make myself a plate.

The line for the buffet moves quickly. I'm balancing a dinner roll on top of my overflowing pile of roasted chicken, mashed potatoes, and green beans when I hear a low, familiar voice behind me.

"Save some room for dessert. There's a candy station over there. I heard a rumor they might have M&M's."

"Mike." My voice squeaks in surprise. My shoulder brushes against him as I turn, and I inhale sharply at the surge of electricity the contact sends through me. That seems to happen every time I touch him. I have to concentrate and make sure not to drop the plate in my hand. On their journey to his face, my eyes have no choice but to roam up his muscular body, which looks like it can barely be contained by the suit jacket he is wearing, and it makes my breath catch in my throat. Unlike most of the men in the room, he is not wearing a tie, just a dark tee shirt under his jacket. I can't explain why I think that is as hot as I do. "What are you doing here?"

"I was going to ask you the same thing. I'm here with my teammate, Rodriguez." I remember his friend from open mic night and the crab feast. The one with the little boy on his shoulders. "We're here to represent the team and present this year's donation to Planting Hope."

It's the name of the charity Jake's fraternity is supporting with their philanthropy events. I didn't realize there were other community organizations here for the cause, but it's nice that the Blue Crabs are helping to raise money, too.

"Oh. I'm here with my friend Jake." I hesitate before adding, "As his date."

Mike nods, but I can see a shift in his eyes. The playful heat that was there a second ago is replaced by something else. Resignation maybe? He reaches past me to grab a fork from the buffet table.

"Cool. Well, it was great running into you. Have fun tonight."

"You too." I smile and offer him an awkward side-hug while trying to avoid getting my mashed potatoes on his suit. Once Mike disappears into the crowd, I find my seat again. It isn't long until Jake sets his plate on the table and pulls up the chair next to mine.

"Who was that guy you were talking to?" His tone is casual, but in a way that feels forced.

"His name is Mike Miller. He's on the Blue Crabs baseball team. Rookie shortstop from Idaho. I met him when they had their team dinner at the restaurant a while ago, and I guess we're friends now. He's here as a team representative."

"Huh," is Jake's only response before turning his attention to the food. Maybe I should have told him about meeting Mike and the fact that he invited me to his game when I was sharing my other news from home. I'm still not sure Jake would have wanted to know, especially after seeing how he reacted to Connor checking me out. He probably wouldn't love knowing there was a professional athlete buying me candy or that I was also texting with Mike before I came to visit him. I follow his lead and pick up my fork, and we sit in awkward silence eating our dinner. Strangers come and go in the other empty seats at our table. I'm not sure what to say. Jake isn't doing anything specific, but I can tell he is feeling weirdly possessive, just like he did when Connor greeted me at their house. He's not my boyfriend, he has no right, yet I can't blame him because I felt the same low-key jealousy when he was talking to that red head last night.

Except it's not really the same, is it?

He invited me on what could reasonably be assumed to be a date, then went out of his way to ditch me and talk to another woman for almost an hour. All I did with both Connor and Mike this week was make polite conversation for a few minutes. Now I'm angry all over again at the double standard. I don't like what Jake and I are bringing out in each other this weekend. Folding my arms and leaning back in my chair, I take a deep breath and let it out slowly, suddenly hyper-aware of how uncomfortable I have become. It's hot and my dress is too tight, the music is loud, and my shoes are pinching my toes. I don't want to be in this stuffy ballroom anymore.

An older woman with sleek gray hair pulled into a tight up-do and wearing a conservative black dress approaches Connor's table, and the music fades. She taps the microphone and waits for the room to settle before she thanks everyone for coming and gives a short speech about Planting Hope's mission to reduce food waste and eliminate food insecurity. Then one-by-one, she calls several community organizations to the front of the room to present oversized novelty checks in a photo-op for publicity. Mike and Rodriguez are wearing their Blue Crabs baseball hats with their suits as they pose for the camera. He looks in my direction and our eyes connect in a way that sends a bolt of heat through my body and makes me squirm in my chair. Now I feel guilty again on top of everything else, but the moment is brief and he turns away to smile for the flashing cameras. Those of us in the audience clap politely as the music resumes.

"Let's dance." Jake's voice pulls me out of my brooding thoughts, and before I can think to protest, he is leading me to the section of carpeted floor where a few other couples have gathered. Maybe my moodiness isn't fair to him. He can't help the way he's feeling, if he even is being jealous. I suppose I could be projecting it onto him tonight. Unlike his little hissy fit about Connor, Jake hasn't really said anything other than asking who Mike was. It's a perfectly reasonable question.

When we are in the middle of the floor, flanked by other dancers, Jake puts his hand on my waist and leans closer to whisper into my ear. "I'm not sure why you're mad at me this time, but I'm sure I deserve it. Let's try to have fun. Truce?"

I exhale a laugh and a small smirk forms on my lips in response. I give him some strong side-eye, but relent and start moving my hips to the catchy beat of the Miley Cyrus song blasting from Connor's playlist. I like dancing with Jake. Always have. He's not one of those guys who just stands there swaying back and forth. Jake can actually dance. He has rhythm and he's not afraid to look silly. It reminds me of all the times we would dance on his parents' covered porch while his dad blasted an old Beach Boys record in the living room. To this day, I don't think I could find Kokomo on a map, but we sang our little hearts out about it. As we flail our bodies with the music blasting in this ballroom, the tension between us disappears. He's my Jake again.

We dance to two more songs before the music slows and the air between us changes to something thicker. I take one step closer and rest my head on his shoulder. His hands settle on my hips, and he bends to lay his cheek on the top of my head. We stay like that for a moment, before he uses one hand to lift my chin.

"Can we try this?" His face is just an inch from mine when he whispers the question, seeking my permission.

I know if I don't kiss him, I will always wonder what could have happened between us.

"Okay."

Jake moves his hand to the back of my head and I close my eyes while he kisses me softly, just once. His kiss is tender and chaste. It's nice, but nice is all it is. There is no spark. Then he puts his hands back on my waist and we continue to dance. We turn in slow circles, and I spot Mike, watching me from across the room while I dance in Jake's arms.

I take deep breaths, my heart still beating fast from the exertion of our previous dances. Breathing in Jake feels both new and old, like I've been doing it all my life, and now it carries a weight I don't know if I'm ready to accept. Or, more honestly, I do know and I'm disappointed that this is not what I always thought it would be if this moment ever came. It feels like I am letting both of us down.

Jake can tell I'm getting lost in my head.

"Truth?" he whispers. "What are you thinking right now?"

I swallow, because I don't know how to tell him. The truth is that his hand on my dress isn't lighting my skin on fire underneath the material, and there's another man in this room with us who doesn't even have to touch me to make me feel that way. A man who is still looking at me. At us.

"Jake." The tension hangs heavy in the air between us. We both know what I'm going to say, but neither one of us wants me to say it. I have to swallow and look away from him to make myself push out the words. "I think we are trying to force something that's not here. I love you, you know that. But romantically? This is not going to work. We each deserve someone who will be all-in, and we can't do that for each other right now."

Honestly, I'm as surprised as I am disappointed. I'm having a hard time believing the spark is not there. I do love him. I always will. But this doesn't feel right. It's like a puzzle piece found its way into the wrong box, but we are still trying to force it to fit in a space where it was never designed to be.

He inhales for a long time, shoulders rising until he finally says, "I know."

"You do?" A tear escapes my left eye and I sniffle. Jake reaches out and brushes it away with his thumb.

"Yeah. I do. Don't cry." He kisses the top of my head. "We shouldn't try to force this. You've been unhappy all weekend."

"That's not really because of you. I'm sorry. I think I need to leave. I'm going to head back home tonight." I give him a brief hug then pull away.

"You don't have to do that. I'll take you back to my place."

"No." I shake my head firmly. I need to do this without him. "I appreciate it, but I think I need the time alone, and you're supposed to be at this event. I've kept you away from enough of your responsibilities this weekend. I'll call you later."

"Are you sure?"

"Yes. Please. I just need a little time."

Jake is hesitant, but he reaches into his pocket. "Here, at least take my keys. You can leave them on my dresser. I'll go back later with Connor." Jake hugs me goodbye and kisses the top of my head one more time. He looks torn about whether it is the right thing to do, but respects my request. He puts his keys and valet ticket in my hand and watches me turn and walk out of the hotel. I manage to hold in my tears until I am in the privacy of the car.

Thirty minutes later, I'm back at his house gathering my things. It's getting late, but I do want to go home tonight. The idea of sharing a bed with Jake again is just too much, and I am not going to kick him out of his own room. He hasn't done anything wrong. My phone buzzes. Thinking it will be Jake trying to convince me to stay, I sigh and take it out of my purse, preparing myself for the conversation I don't want to have. But the silly Bat Signal graphic I uploaded as the contact photo stares up at me. It's not Jake. It's a text from Mike. Relief washes over me and the knot in my stomach loosens a bit, only to be replaced by some brand-new butterflies.

Mike: *Hey*

Me: *Hi*

Mike: *Your friend started hitting the bar pretty hard after you left. That have anything to do with me?*

The direct tone of his text catches me by surprise, but I think I like it. I don't want to play games, so I answer him honestly.

Me: *Maybe, but it's not your fault. It's been a weird weekend.*

Him: *How so? You okay? You left in a pretty big hurry. Did he do something? Want me to hold him down so you can kick his ass?*

That makes me laugh. I feel a pang of guilt about the way I left and the fact that I only came here for Jake, yet my chest is fluttering every time a new text pops up from Mike.

Me: *Not really. He's harmless. It's just odd being here. Doesn't feel like the right fit.*

Him: *I can definitely relate to that.*

Me: *Sorry. I'm sure you don't want to deal with my drama.*

Him: *You seemed upset when you bailed.*

He noticed the moment I left. What else did he see? He could have been watching me kiss Jake. Yet, it hasn't stopped him from texting.

Me: *I'll be fine. Thanks for checking on me. You're sweet.*

Him: *Can't say I hear that very often.*
Me: *Really? That's surprising.*

Of course Mike's sweet. He's also super easy to look at, but I'm going to keep that information to myself for now.

Chapter 9

Mike

She thinks I'm sweet? If anything, I've gotten used to hearing the opposite. Selfish, egocentric, arrogant, those are the kinds of words my dad would use to describe me. I used them as fuel because I knew I was betting on myself and I had to push hard to come out on top. But lately things have started to feel different, calmer, like it might finally be okay to take a breath and enjoy the climb on my way up. Maybe it's because I've been given a fresh start in North Bay. Or maybe it's just her.

I saw Danielle kiss her date. Then she left. It didn't even seem like a good kiss, but I hated seeing her with him and wanting it to be me. I'm usually not the kind of guy who lets women get to me like this. Watching her from the sidelines like a jealous, lovesick puppy felt pathetic. But I can't deny anymore that I want her. Something about Danielle makes me feel like she sees into a part of me that has been buried for a long time. Things feel lighter when she's around.

Which is ridiculous, because I barely know this woman.

Another text comes through as I lean against the wall in a dark corner of the ballroom.

Danielle: It's been a crazy night. Think I'm going to head home.
Me: To North Bay? Now? It's late.
Danielle: I know, but things got pretty awkward. Honestly, I need to get out of here. I don't want to sleep at his place tonight.

Jake, was it? Whatever is going on between them is none of my business, but I don't like this. I don't like this at all. But it's not my place to tell her to stay somewhere she is uncomfortable, so against my better judgment, I type again.

Me: Well, be safe.
Danielle: I will.

I may have only known Danielle for a few days, and I have no right to tell her what to do, but every part of me is fighting the urge to go get her. I clench my fist at my side, and start walking toward the ballroom doors. Jake is at a table sipping what looks to be bourbon with some of his frat buddies and they're getting rowdy. I can't stay in this space with him, I don't trust myself not to do something stupid and get myself thrown off the team. He just let her go? No one should drive that far in the middle of the night by themselves.

I wish I could tell her to come stay in my room, but I'm bunking with Rodriguez. Is she really planning on driving through the entire night alone? I don't know if she had anything to drink. Before I can think it through, I'm calling her.

As soon as she picks up, I ask, "Do you want some company?"

She doesn't respond right away, so I tell her, "Look, I don't want to make you feel weird. I know we haven't known each other long. But I really don't like the idea of you going all the way back to North Bay by yourself right now. It's dangerous. I was planning to go back in the morning anyway. You would be doing me a favor by giving me a ride."

That last part isn't one hundred percent true, I have my truck, but that is not the point. I make a big effort to be honest with the people in my life these days, but this tiny omission is for her own good. I hope my proposal doesn't creep her out. I can ask Rodriguez to drive back in my truck tomorrow, in the daylight after he's gotten a full night of rest. He won't mind.

"Really? Um, okay." Her voice is hesitant, but I can hear something else in her tone. Maybe it's only surprise, but I swear it almost sounds like she is excited. "It might be nice to have a road trip partner, if you're sure you don't mind. Promise not to murder me?"

I laugh. "Like I said the last time, if I wanted to murder you, I wouldn't do it while I'm on official Blue Crab business. And no, I don't mind. It will be fun."

"Honey would probably feel better knowing I had someone with me on the road."

"Who's Honey?" I hope that's not her pet name for this Jake dude. I try to keep my tone neutral so my curiosity doesn't cross the line over into desperate territory.

"Oh, Honey is my grandma. Everyone we know calls her that. She basically raised me. You could try calling her Mrs. Daniels when you meet her, but I can't promise she won't try to slap you for that. She's a bit of a wild card."

Seems like an unusual name for a grandmother, but what do I know? Most of my grandparents passed away before I was old enough to remember them.

"I see. Well, sure, I'm happy to ride back with you. Are you okay with picking me up outside the hotel? I'm staying in the same place as the dance."

"Yeah, I'll head over soon if that's all right, but can you meet me in the parking lot so I don't have to go back inside? I just want to get out of here and forget this weekend ever happened."

"Sounds like a plan. I'll see you in a few minutes."

It doesn't take long to throw my stuff back into the bag I brought. I'm still wearing my suit pants and black tee shirt, but I took off the jacket in an attempt to get more comfortable. As I expected, Rodriguez was fine with the idea of driving the truck home, although he did bust on me a bit for ditching him. He also made some very unsubtle hints about me getting it on with Danielle tonight that I had to shut down. Not that I wouldn't be open to it, because I very much would, but she was upset tonight, and she just left a date with another guy. This is not the right time to hit on her, and I'm trying this new thing where I show people the respect they deserve.

In less than fifteen minutes, Danielle texts to let me know she's here, so I head down to meet her.

Under the street lamps, I can see her sitting in the driver's seat of a Honda, tapping her fingers on the steering wheel. I wave and walk to the car, and she reaches down to press the button that opens the trunk so I can stow my stuff. Once my bag is dealt with, I slide into the passenger's seat and toss my suit jacket in the back.

"Hi." I offer a smile. She's no longer wearing that dress. Her hair is pulled back in a low ponytail and she has changed into a tank top with leggings and sneakers. She looks unsure of what to do or say. We've only been alone together on the short ride from the restaurant to Major Dollar and she's about to be stuck in the car with me for hours in the middle of the night. I can tell she's rattled from whatever happened with her friend, and now I'm probably making her nervous, too, which is the opposite of what I want to do.

"Good call switching shoes," is the next thing that comes out of my mouth. I point to her feet.

"Yeah." She chuckles. "Easier to drive this way. But that means the heels are up for grabs, if you want them."

"I do like them," I say because it's the truth. I swallow the lump that forms in my throat as I imagine her wrapping her legs around me while wearing those shoes. "But I doubt they'd fit me, and they look much better on you."

She ignores the compliment and asks if I'm ready. I give her a nod and she hits the gas. After a few minutes of silence, I ask, "Do you want to talk about what happened?"

She heaves a big sigh. "I'm not even sure I know what happened. Jake has been my friend since we were literal babies. He's always been a popular guy, and that's true here, too. He's doing awesome. Scholarship, fraternity, tons of new friends. I was excited to come up here and visit him this weekend."

"But?" I prompt.

"Things are fine whenever we're alone, but as soon as we are out of our bubble, everything is different. It makes me look at him and our whole friendship in a new way, and I don't think I like it. It's not his fault."

"Doesn't sound like your fault either. Sounds like childhood friends drifting apart. That's normal, but it does suck." I try to empathize.

"Did you have a friend like that growing up?"

"No, none that I kept in touch with." I clear my throat. "But my sister Maddy did. She was always close with this one girl, Kate. They did everything together until they went to high school, then there was a lot of drama. That's when I learned teenage girls can be really mean."

"True. They definitely can. Tell me about your sisters again."

"I have three younger sisters," I remind her. "Mandy, Maddy, and Michelle. Most people call her Shelley. They're all back in Idaho with my parents."

"Are you close with them?"

"With my sisters and my mom, yeah. Not so much with my dad."

"That sounds like a story."

"Maybe for another day." Or not. I like this new friendship I have going with Danielle. She doesn't need to hear why my own father hates me. Especially because that hatred is well-deserved.

It's quiet again. Too quiet.

"May I?" I reach toward the radio and she nods, so I turn it on in order to drown out my own thoughts. Her dial is set to a 90's station and I leave it there. Despite my nagging memories, it only takes me a few minutes to settle into the peaceful vibrations as we pass over the pavement. Riding with Danielle is comfortable. I don't want her to feel pushed to talk. Other than the low hum of the music, we sit together in the quiet, each of us lost in our own minds for another twenty minutes.

It's late, but a new text comes through on my phone.

Jordan: _This elbow is killing me. Can't sleep. Think I'm going to go ahead and schedule with the doc._

I'm looking down at the message when I'm jerked upright by Danielle's sudden swerving and a loud thump. She gasps. We've hit something, but I don't know what because I haven't seen another car for miles. The contact throws both of our bodies forward and I can feel my seatbelt dig into my collarbone before my head is forced back into the headrest. I throw my arm across her chest instinctively.

The brakes squeal as we come to an abrupt halt on the side of the road. There's another loud noise and a large, blurred figure rushes past the windshield. I think I saw white and brown. It must have been a deer. Shaking my head and taking inventory of my body, I realize quickly that I am fine, but I'm more concerned with the woman next to me.

"Are you okay?" I turn to Danielle. Her eyes are wide and she is holding the steering wheel so tightly that the knuckles on both of her hands are white. She doesn't look at me, but she nods once, then sucks in short, heavy breaths that make her chest rise and fall in rapid succession. We both look down and notice my arm is still stretched across her body. I pull my hand away quickly and get out of the car. "I'm going to go out and take a look."

From what I can see using my phone as a flashlight, the damage seems pretty minimal. There's a small dent in the hood and a busted headlight. Otherwise, her car seems drivable. I know from experience that it could have been much worse.

The driver's side door opens, and Danielle slowly makes her way to the front, tiptoeing over roadside debris in the dark.

"Careful," I tell her. "There's broken glass on the ground. But don't worry. We got lucky. No one was hurt, and I think the deer even got away." It probably didn't get far. I think I heard something fall in the trees, but she doesn't need to know that. Hopefully its injuries were minor and it will heal. That's the story I'm going with. There's not much I could do for a wounded animal right now. I need to focus on Danielle and getting us home.

She hasn't said anything, and she still has those wide eyes. Maybe she's in shock.

"Hey." I approach her slowly. "We're okay. The car is okay. Just a minor setback. We're still going to get home tonight." I reach out with both hands and rub up and down her arms. It's cold out here. She must be freezing. Ducking into the car, I grab my suit jacket and drape it over her shoulders. She pushes her arms through the sleeves, clearly distracted by the other thoughts running through her head.

"Honey is going to kill me for crashing the car," she murmurs. Then a little louder, "Oh no, what if I killed that deer? You weren't the murderer after all. I was."

"You didn't hurt the deer." I try to sound convincing. "Although, maybe it had a death wish. It jumped right into the only car on the road." Seriously, what are the odds? There isn't another vehicle around for miles.

She barks a loud, stressful sound that is half-laugh, half-tortured scream. "I can't believe I did that. I could have killed you. Or worse, what if I hurt you and ruined your baseball career?"

"That would have been a fate worse than death." I chuckle. "Again, this was not your fault. Accidents happen. That's why there are deer crossing signs all over Virginia. But you seem like you are pretty shaken up. Here, let me help you around to the other side. Watch the branches. I'll drive the rest of the way back."

She doesn't argue. She lets me guide her into the passenger seat and lean over her to buckle the seatbelt. As I'm reaching across Danielle's lap, her soft brown hair brushes my face. It smells just like the vanilla mist I remember and it tickles my skin. I have to fight the urge to kiss her forehead to comfort her, the way my mom used to do for me when I was upset. I don't know Danielle well enough to do that, so instead I press my lips together hard, walk around the busted-up car, and buckle myself into the driver's seat.

Before we leave, I use my phone to find our location and look up the non-emergency number for the local police.

"Hello, yes. I just want to report that we've hit a deer. There was only one vehicle involved and no injuries. Well, no human injuries. Deer ran away. There is some debris on the road." The operator asks for the location of the accident and after confirming again that Danielle and I are both okay and do not need medical attention, she wishes us a goodnight and tells us it's fine to go home. With that settled, I pull back onto the road and start driving.

It's quiet for a few minutes, then I realize Danielle is humming something softly. After a few bars I recognize the melody to *One Headlight* by The Wallflowers and I can't help but laugh.

"That song is a bit on the nose for our current situation, don't you think?"

"Seemed relevant." She finally gives me another tiny smile, then bites her lip and tucks her chin down to try to hide it. She pulls up her music app on her phone and the real version of the song starts to play. Once Jakob Dylan's voice is blaring through the speakers,

Danielle's shy smile transforms into a hysterical giggle that squeezes the muscle pumping in my chest. It's nice to know I am the one helping to take the stress of tonight away for her. The heightened emotions of the past few minutes are catching up to us. When she starts to sing along loudly I can't stop myself from joining in. Before I know it, the windows are down and both of us are screaming lyrics that are only half-correct into the night air.

The music fades and Danielle's chest heaves as she catches her breath. I squeeze the steering wheel and try to keep my eyes on the road.

"I really needed that." She pants, fanning her flushed face with her hands. Having her this close to me while she is breathless makes my body clench. She leans back into the seat and closes her eyes. I wonder briefly if she is praying. It is sort of a miracle we both walked away from that accident without a scratch.

I want to comfort her. I don't think Danielle's heart can handle any more stress tonight. Instead of responding, I reach over and place my hand on her leg, squeezing lightly but not saying anything. She looks down and lays her hand over mine, intertwining our fingers. My palm turns up to hold her hand. I want to keep my eyes on the road because one accident in the middle of the night is more than enough, but I can feel her looking at me.

"For the record, that was not how I envisioned you getting to second base," she says, making me laugh. So, she has envisioned it. Interesting. I'm glad her sense of humor is intact. "Seriously, though. Thank you, Mike. I'm really glad you were here tonight."

"Me too." I squeeze her hand.

I drive with one hand on the wheel and one headlight guiding our way for the next two hours until we pull into the parking lot of my apartment complex.

Danielle opens her car door and climbs out of her seat. She arches her back and reaches down to touch her toes, then walks over to me so she can get ready to drive herself the rest of the way to her house.

My jacket is still hanging loose around her body, practically swallowing her and making her stretches look silly. Letting out a long breath while she pulls one arm across her body, the same way I do before a game, she sounds resigned when she says, "Honey is truly going to kill me. I forgot to tell her I was coming home tonight in the first place, and now I'll be showing up in the middle of the night with a mangled car. I hope she won't have a heart attack when the door opens at three thirty in the morning."

"So, stay here," I offer without stopping to think how presumptuous that might sound. I quickly add, "Jordan isn't here. He's visiting a friend for the weekend. I can sleep in his room and you can take over my bed to get a few hours of sleep. You don't have to face Honey yet." She looks like she might actually be considering this. "Then just go home later like your grandma is expecting. And yes, once again, I promise not to murder you." I use my index finger to cross my heart, and I can't keep the smile off of my face.

Danielle hugs herself around the middle while she peers up at me. "Tempting. But I don't know if that's a good idea?"

I shrug in response, trying not to let on how much I want her to stay. "Why not? You already know I don't love the idea of you going home alone in the dark, and I have two beds right up there, in completely separate rooms." I point toward the window of my third-floor apartment. "But no pressure. If you need to go, I understand."

I'm not trying to be a creep. It's just that I know she's exhausted, and I can tell she really doesn't want to go home and deal with her grandmother right now. Yep. Those are the *only* reasons I would like her to walk up to my apartment and get into my bed.

She looks toward the building. "Are you sure you wouldn't mind?"

"Not at all. I'd rather know you're safe and getting some rest before you drive over there."

"Okay," she whispers. Before she has a chance to reconsider, I nod and retrieve both of our bags from the trunk, then lead her up the cement stairs to my front door.

"No judgment, deal? I didn't know we were having company." I try to hide my nerves under a chuckle as I turn the key and let us both inside. Relief washes over me as I scan the apartment. It's not as bad as it could have been. There are a few dishes sitting in the sink and an empty pizza box on the counter, but otherwise everything looks pretty decent. I show Danielle to my room and tell her I'm going to grab some clean sheets from the hall closet for her, but I also duck into the bathroom to make sure the seat is down and nothing too disgusting is happening in there. Seems like we are good, so I return to my room with the new sheets in hand.

"Oh, you don't have to go through the trouble. I'm fine. Honestly." She motions to the brand-new sheets I'm holding, still wrapped in their plastic packaging. Danielle is already sitting on my bed and removing her shoes. If I had a response, I've lost it. The air is stuck in my throat because, even though I've imagined it at least fifty times since we met, I wasn't prepared for the sight of her actually sitting on my bed, and I haven't had enough sleep to process it.

I should tell her how good she looked tonight. At a minimum, I should say goodnight or ask her if she needs anything. Some water? A clean t-shirt? Instead, I set the new sheets next to her on the bed and bow before I leave the room in silence. I *bowed*. It's time to admit Jordan was right. I have no game with this woman. None. Muttering to myself about what a dumbass I am, I walk across the hall and crash on my roommate's unmade bed.

Chapter 10

Danielle

Yesterday morning I was in Jake's bed, then last night I kissed him. Twelve hours later, here I am waking up in Mike's room, wrapped in the sheets that smell like his spicy body wash. Who does that? My mind is starting to spiral as I hastily try to make the bed and throw on a pair of sweatpants and a clean tank top from my bag. I toss my dirty clothes back into my duffle so I can get started on my walk of shame.

Is it even a walk of shame if all you did was sleep alone in a guy's bed until…um, what time is it? Eleven-thirty. Oh my god. A glance at my phone tells me the time, and the red battery signal alerts me to the fact that I forgot to charge it last night. At least Honey still thinks I'm traveling today and won't be wondering where I am for a while. Getting too close to a mental breakdown, I freeze in the middle of the room and call Alice from my dying phone. As soon as I hear her voice, I launch into all of the same questions I've been asking myself.

"Hi," she responds after I pause to catch my breath. "Listen, I need you to turn the drama dial down about five levels. You're an adult woman and free to do whatever and whomever you want. But are you telling me you slept with both of them?" There is no judgment in her tone, only curiosity.

I swear, if the writing thing doesn't work out, she would make a great therapist.

"I didn't sleep with either one of them. Well, technically, I guess I slept next to Jake for half a night, but it was just sleeping. Although, I did kiss him. Then I ran away. Last night I slept in Mike's bed, but he was in a different room."

"What?" I can picture her eyebrows scrunching together.

"This is going to have to be an in-person conversation. There's too much to tell you over the phone. Can you meet me at Brew-Ha-Ha in half an hour? My phone might die before I get there."

"Sure thing. See you soon."

There are pictures of Mike with friends and family thumbtacked to the back of his bedroom door. I'm tempted to cover their eyes as I open it so they can't see me tiptoe out of here. I don't see Mike when I walk out into the living room, and I'm not even sure if he is still home. Maybe he's still sleeping because last night truly was exhausting. Or maybe he has practice, or a game, or some other plans today.

Maybe he has plans with another girl. Sure, he held my hand last night, but anyone might do that for a friend after a traumatic event. It hits me that I haven't asked if he is seeing anyone, and he's never actually said he is interested in dating me. Now I'm too embarrassed to stick around to find out. In the past twelve hours, I made him drive with me all night and got us into a car accident, then I kicked him out of his own room. As quietly as I can, I slink through the front door of Mike's apartment, down to the parking lot, and into my car.

By the time I arrive at Brew-Ha-Ha, Alice is waiting for me with a chai latte and a blueberry muffin. Immediately, I sink into the chair across from her and take a huge, comforting bite of the muffin, talking to her through my food.

"Morning."

"This is a look." She points at my unbrushed hair and my face, still caked in last night's makeup.

"I left so fast I didn't even brush my teeth."

"I noticed," she deadpans, but I think she's teasing. At least, I hope she can't smell my breath from across the table. "Did Mike say anything to you this morning?"

"He slept in the other room. I haven't seen him since last night. I bailed before he could get a glimpse of this." I motion up and down the hot mess that is currently sitting in front of her, otherwise known as my body.

"Smart. How about Jake? Where are we with that situation?"

My shoulders slump and I pick off pieces of my muffin, popping them into my mouth as I relay the entire story and Alice nods along.

"Let me see if I've got this straight. In summary, Jake was kind of a butt, as per usual, but then he made up for it, and there was one lackluster kiss between the two of you. Mike played the role of the knight in shining armor in what could have otherwise developed into a Blair Witch Project situation, and you need to make a call to your car insurance agent as soon as your phone is charged. Would you say that is correct?" Alice asks.

"Yeah, that's pretty much it. Except Jake wasn't just a butt on Friday night. He was a very drunk butt. He did make up for it both before and during the dance, but it still got weird."

"Because he kissed you?"

"Yeah. The kiss was nice, I think, but also sad. It all felt so weird."

"Typical Gibson." She rolls her eyes. "For the record, I have never heard of a good kiss that could also be described as weird and sad." For my sake, she restrains herself and doesn't say anything worse about him. She makes a beckoning motion with her hand. "Keep going. Tell me more. What happened with Mike?"

"Nothing I haven't already said. He was so nice. He offered to keep me company on the ride. I hit a deer, which was terrifying, but he handled calling the police and driving the rest of the way home. Then he gave up his bed so I could get some sleep and not have to deal with Honey in the middle of the night."

"I see. And now you have it bad for Batman."

I can't look her in the eye. "Am I that obvious?"

"Yes. One hundred percent."

"Ugh. Fine. I like him, okay? But is it terrible to be thinking about dating Mike right now? What is Jake going to think when he finds out I left with another guy?"

"Who cares what he thinks? There is no such thing as an appropriate timeframe for meeting a new friend. Besides, Jake gets zero say here. He had his chance fair and square. For literal decades. He did not step up. He doesn't get to be mad if someone else does."

"I guess."

"Okay, sounds like we need a plan."

"For what?" I'm skeptical. Alice has a habit of looking at every situation like it's happening in one of her stories. Real life doesn't work that way, and I have a busted Honda in the parking lot to prove it, but when Alice Caulfield gets an idea in her head there's no point in fighting her, so I won't.

A wide smile spreads across her face and she points a well-manicured finger at me. "It's time to land you a baseball player."

Alice reaches into her purse and pulls out a portable charger so I can plug in my phone. As soon as I turn it on, my phone dings with an unread text notification.

Mike: *You disappeared. I was going to ask if you wanted to grab breakfast.*

I lay the phone on the table between us so Alice can see it, too.

"Is he saying he was planning to ask me out?" I don't know if that would have counted as a date. Probably not. Two friends who are awake at the same time both need to eat. I didn't really think of the diner as a date with Jake, and I definitely don't think he thought of it as a date with me, so Mike probably wouldn't count breakfast either. I didn't stick around long enough with either one of them to find out.

"Of course he is," Alice insists. "Time to enact Part One of the plan."

"What's Part One?"

"Stop avoiding Mike. You can't create something real with a person you are actively running away from."

Right. I can do this. I type my response.

Me: *Sorry. I had to go. Maybe we can do something later?*

I nod at my phone, patting myself on the back. Alice gives me a thumbs up. There. A perfectly non-committal response to a non-date, but still I'm leaving the door open if he *does* want a date.

I like Mike. A lot. But I'm not sure it would be smart to start something serious, even if after last night I *really* want to. I still don't love the idea of dating a baseball player. They are always traveling. We would hardly see each other. Plus, they leave. Every time. I've had enough people leave in my life. My biological dad didn't even stick around long enough to meet me. Grandpa died. Mom, Bob, and Steve all peaced out of this town. Even Jake chose to move hours away for school, not that I blame him. It's just, everyone leaves me eventually. Besides, even if Mike wanted to settle down here, that isn't necessarily up to him. No one sticks out their entire career as a pro athlete in North Bay. He could even get traded before the current season is over.

"I need you to level with me here, what is actually the problem?" Alice crosses her arms.

"I really like him," I admit. "But no matter what happens, I know Mike's not sticking around North Bay for good. We don't have a Major League Baseball team nearby, and I'm sure that's his goal, right? It can't work out with him long-term. He's only here temporarily. He *will* leave."

"I love you. I do. But I have to say, that's a load of crap. And it also sounds very similar to how you've always said it could never work out with Jake because you two are such good friends. Or how it couldn't work out with Steve because Richmond is too far away."

"What are you getting at? All of those things were true."

"Says who? And either way, you have a fresh start with Mike. You can't live your life avoiding people just because one day they might have a cool career opportunity."

"Except he'll definitely go if he gets the chance. That's not a maybe."

There aren't any Major League Baseball teams in the entire state of Virginia. There is no possible way Mike can achieve the level of success he wants in his career and stay close to North Bay.

"Excuse me." She shoots me a pointed look. "Before we grieve prematurely over hypotheticals again, I think we need to take a minute to review who left Jake at the gala and then snuck out of Mike's apartment this morning. Seems like you're doing all the leaving in real life lately, babe. Maybe you could consider not sabotaging your own happiness, just this once?"

"Did they put truth serum in the oat milk today or something? Ouch."

But I hear her. Only Alice can call me out so easily. She takes a long sip of her drink and looks at me over her cup. When she says it like that, my arguments sound lame, but I still don't want to let myself get too attached.

Yet, I can't help thinking about the way Mike worried about me going home by myself, or covered my shoulders with his jacket and tried to comfort me about the deer last night. He didn't blame me for the accident at all, even though I was the one driving and we could have been hurt. Oh God. My stomach drops when I think again about the fact that I could have ended his entire baseball career and taken away his chance at the majors if the accident had been any worse. My phone buzzes again and pulls me out of my spiral.

Mike: *Do you want to watch a movie tonight?*

"Yes. You do," Alice says, hovering over my shoulder to read his message. The way she's talking about all of this makes it sound like the answer is obvious.

"No, wait, I mean, you're right, I do. But not tonight. Gah. What do I say to him?" It feels like there's an entire butterfly garden in my belly.

"You know what I think you should say, but you need to make this choice for yourself." Alice gestures to my phone, encouraging me to respond.

I still don't know if I'm ready to jump into anything with him, but I know the thought of seeing Mike again makes me happy and the thought of not seeing him anymore makes me sad. If only the answers were really that simple. Regardless, watching a movie together seems harmless enough. I do that with all of my friends.

Me: *I think I might need a day to lay low and recover. Would tomorrow work?*

Mike: *Recover? Everything ok? Are you sore after the accident?*

Me: *It's fine. I'm not hurt. Just meant recover from the stress of the weekend. Happy to hang out in a few days, though.*

Mike: *I have practice until 6 on Tuesday. You free after that?*

Me: *Should be. I have class in the morning and work in the afternoon, but I think I'll be done by six. Not sure what my car situation will be. Can you come to my house?*

Mike: *Of course. Is it creepy if I tell you I think I already know where that is? Confession: I saw you ride your bike to the house next door to Major Dollar.*

Me: *Yeah, that's Honey's house. I give it a 2 out of 10 on the creep scale. I stay in the apartment over the garage. See you after you're done with practice.*

Alice smiles at me. "See? The plan is already in motion, and we didn't even have to lift a finger."

After I say goodbye to her, it's time to go home and face the music. I need to tell Honey what happened to the car. I lug my duffle bag full of dirty clothes back into the house, then I dig my phone charger out of the side pocket so I won't miss any more of Mike's messages. I want to throw everything else into the laundry and wash it away along with the awkward parts of this weekend. But I can't do that just yet because a message from Jake appears.

BND: *Hope you got home OK.*

I send a thumbs-up and leave him on read.

Chapter 11

Mike

Not to jinx it or anything, but things might finally be starting to look up for me. Practice went well. I think Coach might start putting me into the regular rotation. Rodriguez only ribbed me a little bit for ditching him last weekend. Jordan is back and gave his stamp of approval to the jeans and short-sleeved Henley I'm wearing tonight, and I'm on my way to see Danielle.

I'm not exactly sure if I should call this our first date because we're just hanging out at her place. Well, her grandmother's place. Still, I asked her to accompany me to a movie and she said yes, which means I am going to be prepared. There's a condom in my wallet and a gift bag stuffed with snacks on the front seat of my truck, along with two small bouquets that I picked up from the grocery store near the stadium. One bunch of flowers is white and the other is yellow. When I scanned them at self-checkout the receipt said they are carnations. The only options were these or roses, and the roses were twice as expensive, so carnations it is. I already spent enough on the bag, but what can I say? It made me laugh. I hope Danielle likes it, too.

After I pull to a stop in their driveway, I gather the flowers and the silly gift bag and head up to the house. Before I can knock, the door opens, revealing a tall, full-figured woman with bright pink flowers on her dress and equally bright lipstick.

"I heard there was a man coming for my granddaughter, that you?" She scowls, but it seems exaggerated. I think she's already teasing me. Or maybe testing me?

"Yes, ma'am," I answer, hoping my smile is as charming as I want it to be.

She barks out a laugh, and the scowl disappears just as quickly as it crossed her face.

"Well, come on in. I'm Honey. No need to tell me your name, I already know everything this town has to tell about Mike Miller. Heard you're our new shortstop, here all the way from Idaho. Met our DeeDee over at Edna's restaurant, did you? I saw you drive her home last week, you know. And I've since heard you might know a little something about my busted-up car." She raises her eyebrows and lowers her chin on that last point, but she doesn't seem angry, more amused.

"I can't deny any of that," I offer, holding out the yellow bouquet. "I'm sorry about what happened to the car, but it wasn't her fault. That deer came out of nowhere. Danielle handled herself well. These are for you, ma'am. Thank you for having me to your home."

Another voice floats toward us and Danielle appears, bouncing down the hall.

"Sucking up to my grandma is a solid strategy. I respect it. Don't worry about the car. Insurance is covering it, and Frank at the auto repair shop says it'll only take two days to fix, so it should be ready tomorrow morning," she says, then turns to address Honey. "Leave the poor man alone, you'll scare him away."

Honey waves one hand dismissively. "Eh. Any man who can be scared off that easy wasn't worth keeping in the first place. I like this one better than that old fuddy duddy you had coming around here last year. Philip never brought me flowers."

Danielle's eyes widen, but she is still smiling. "You know his name was Steve, and can you not? Poor Mike just came to watch a movie." It's fun to watch the rapport she has with Honey, but I like it even more when Danielle takes my arm and leads me into the living room. I thought we would be watching a movie in her apartment, but she seems to have changed the plan. I can roll with it, but if we are hanging out with her grandma today, I guess this means that condom will be staying in my wallet.

Honey's place is an eclectic mix of mismatched furniture and knickknacks that somehow manages to feel homey rather than cluttered. There are two patchwork quilts folded and thrown over the back of the sofa and about ten framed photographs lining the top of the credenza, which has glass doors showcasing the other knickknacks inside. Along the left wall, the doors of a wooden armoire are swung open, revealing the television.

"Is it okay if we watch in here? The TV is so much easier to see than trying to watch on my laptop. Plus, if I'm being honest, I didn't have time to clean up after work and there is laundry all over my bed."

"Of course." I chuckle and hand Danielle her own bouquet. "Your house, your rules."

"I'm glad you feel that way," Honey's booming voice interjects as she pushes past us and sets herself in the recliner in the corner, lifting the lever to raise her feet and propping a throw pillow under them. "Because this is actually my house." Danielle rolls her eyes, but Honey makes me laugh. She certainly has no problem making herself comfortable around me, which makes me more comfortable, too. Usually, I would be hesitant to meet a girl's family on the first date. But Honey's big, welcoming energy actually helps to take some of my own nerves away.

"Thank you. These flowers are beautiful. I'll go put them in some water and get the popcorn," Danielle offers.

"That reminds me," I say as I hand her the gift bag. "I also come bearing snacks." Then I turn to Honey and add, "No worries. There's enough for everyone."

Danielle lets out a loud laugh when she notices the ridiculous design on the outside of the bag. "Is this a Christmas tree with jack-o-lanterns, turkeys, dreidels, and Easter bunny ornaments on it?"

"Yep. The tag said 'for any special occasion.'" I'm glad she seems as amused by it as I was. Not everyone likes my cheesy sense of humor. In college, I went on two dates with a snobby girl who dumped me for, in her words, "thinking puns were a passable attempt at wit." Her loss. I still think puns—and ridiculous gift bags— are hilarious. At least Danielle seems to get me.

"Is that what this is? A special occasion?" Her voice softens as she looks up at me. I can feel something melt in my chest. That stupid gift bag cost eleven dollars, which seemed like way too much to spend on a paper bag at the time, but I hoped it would make her laugh. And it did. Now that I know it also made her look at me like this, I would have spent five times that much.

Nodding at the bag, I say, "Of course it is. It's the day I met the famous Honey Daniels. Plus, I have it on good authority the peanut butter and the pretzel flavors are the best ones." I hint at the contents of the gift.

As she looks inside, Danielle starts to laugh again. "What, did you buy out the store? This must be every flavor of M&M's ever made."

"All that the stores of North Bay and Marnock had to offer, except the coffee flavors. Well, there is one coffee flavor. I got the Caramel Cold Brew because I was intrigued, but I won't be offended if you abstain from that one. You mentioned a few I've never tried, and then I saw even more at the store, and I got curious. I may have gone overboard."

I definitely went overboard. There are twelve different kinds of M&M's in that bag. I've been collecting them from everywhere I've been for the past few days. At the vending machine in the locker room, the gas station, Major Dollar, the grocery store, every time I saw them they made me think of Danielle and I just had to grab a bag. Then it turned into sort of a scavenger hunt to find as many different flavors as I could. I had Jordan scouting the candy aisles for me, too. He added a few packs he picked up from rest stops on the way back from his weekend trip.

I smile at her. "I thought we could have a taste test. I never realized they made so many options. My sisters always put their candy in their popcorn at the movies. Maybe we could try that?" Pointing, I add, "There's also something else in there, under the mountain of chocolate."

She digs for a moment before pulling out two movies: *The Sandlot* and *A League of Their Own*. There was a bin of old DVDs being sold on clearance at Major Dollar. I took a gamble and grabbed a couple of them. I hope she still has a DVD player.

"Lady's choice," I tell her. Two baseball films, sure. I love my sport, so sue me. But they also both seemed like safe options Danielle would enjoy as well. Hopefully Honey, too, now that she's joining us.

"Maybe we'll have time for a double feature? I love both of these. Thank you." Danielle steps forward and kisses my cheek. It takes a surprising amount of strength to hold still. I force myself to look straight ahead and not to turn to meet her mouth with mine.

"Sounds like a plan to me," Honey says from her recliner. "Mike? What do you say you help me figure out this remote, and Dani can go pop us up the rest of our snack. There's a fresh pitcher of sweet tea in the fridge, too."

I take *The Sandlot* from Danielle before she heads to the kitchen and I set it up on the TV while she handles the food. It isn't long before she returns carrying a big tray containing three bowls filled to the brim with fresh popcorn, a pitcher of tea, and three stacked glasses. It takes an impressive amount of balance to carry all of that, but then again, she is a professional. She sets the tray down in the center of the painted turquoise coffee table. Settling on the sofa next to Danielle while we watch the movie, with Honey offering her colorful commentary from the corner chair in her even more colorful living room, I realize how much I've missed the feeling of family. I could get used to this.

I try my best to pay attention to the movie, but my eyes keep wandering over to Danielle. She's mouthing the words right along with the actors, like she remembers every line. When she catches me staring, she offers a shy smile then presses her lips together to make herself stop. Maybe she's embarrassed, but I think it's cute. And I can't say I'd mind staring at her mouth all night.

When the movie nears its end, Honey notices the M&M's are still on the table.

"We oughta play Pick My Poison with those," she tells Danielle.

"What's that?" I ask.

"Oh, I had almost forgotten about that. It's a game Honey and I made up when I was little. One of us would close our eyes or wear a blindfold, and the other would put some kind of food in the blindfolded person's mouth. You have to guess what you're eating."

"The only rule was it had to be edible," Honey interjects and Danielle nods and continues the story.

"Yep. We had some interesting combinations over the years. Remember that time I gave you a grape coated in peanut butter and hot sauce?"

"Sure do. That one was better than the ice cream mixed with vinegar."

"Oh, you got me right back with my own creation that time. The vinegar milkshake was the worst." Danielle twists her face and before long she is shaking with laughter. Honey is hooting and slapping her own thigh. Their joy is contagious and I can't help but join them.

"You two aren't selling this very well," I admit through a deep laugh.

"Oh, we wouldn't subject you to anything like that," Danielle promises. "At least not yet." Her own laughter has subsided, and she's out of breath. The way she's looking at me with her soft smile and her eyebrows raised in anticipation makes my stomach warm with promise, like the ascent up the first hill of a rollercoaster.

She touches my arm. "You were smart to bring all these flavors. We could do an all-M&M's edition and just try to guess which one we are eating."

"I could get on board with that."

That's how I find myself wearing Honey's polka dotted sleep mask while Danielle pops a brownie-flavored candy in my mouth.

"Want to try another one?"

"Sure." This time it's peanut butter.

Honey takes one turn, but it isn't long before she excuses herself from the next round.

"Well, this has been fun. Thank you for the flowers and the candy, Mike. You sure know how to make an old lady feel special. But I don't think I can make it through another movie, I'm headed off to bed." Honey exaggerates a yawn and stretches both arms dramatically. "I'm so tired I bet I could sleep through a tornado. Wouldn't even hear a sound." She winks at Danielle, who just rolls her eyes. "You younger folks should keep this party going a bit longer."

Honey is not subtle at all. She's totally giving me her blessing to hook up with her granddaughter in her house, which strangely makes me even more apprehensive about acting on my feelings for Danielle.

I want her to know she means more to me than just a casual hookup. Which, to be honest, is really inconvenient because I wasn't planning to catch real feelings for this girl. I don't know if I have the capacity for something serious right now, but the connection that is building between us feels too real to ignore.

We both say goodnight to Honey, and then Danielle and I are left alone on her overstuffed plaid couch. The TV goes silent as the credits roll to an end. Danielle scoots a little closer and turns her whole body to look at me.

"My turn." She pulls the sleep mask over her eyes and opens her mouth. Seeing her full lips form a perfect circle puts ideas in my head. Now is not the time to act on them, but when she's ready I know exactly what to do with that pretty mouth.

"You up for this?"

"For anything but the coffee flavor. Can I trust you?" I feel her question stir something inside me.

"You can." I pop a pretzel-flavored candy in her mouth, but after three guesses she still doesn't know what kind it is, so she takes the mask off to peek.

"Cheater," I tease.

We go back and forth, taking turns until there are four empty bags on the table, and several more laying open. I haven't laughed this much in a long time. Danielle leans back into the couch and sighs contentedly.

"Maybe we can get out of here one night soon. Sneak off somewhere by ourselves?" she says.

"Are you asking me out, Ms. Daniels?"

"What if I am?"

"Will Honey think I'm corrupting you? I'm scared of her."

I can see her try to hide a smile. "No, you aren't. But she wouldn't mind. Honey lives for gossip. It's more likely she'll throw us a parade if she thinks we're up to no good."

"Then sure. Let's make a plan to go get some ice cream or tea or something."

"As long as you pick me up, because I'm never driving you anywhere ever again. It's bad luck. Actually, maybe we skip the food and just make out in your truck instead? Then we don't have to drive at all."

I chuckle because I'm pretty sure she's teasing, but I definitely don't hate the idea.

"Does this mean we're planning our first official date?" I ask. "What will it be? Ice cream or tea?"

"I can't believe I'm saying this, but I can't even think about dessert. That was a lot of chocolate." Her giggle flits through the air like wind chimes and she rests one hand on her belly. "I'll take you up on a tea instead. I never turn down a good cup of chai. It's not going to be our first date, though."

"It's not? Please refresh my memory. That doesn't seem like the kind of thing I'd forget."

"Nah. We already had a waterfront seafood dinner with your friends, and you drove me home after. Very chivalrous, by the way. Then we took an impromptu road trip together, and tonight we saw a movie. Plus, you've met my grandmother, I've gone to visit you at work, and I've slept in your bed. I think we're past first date territory by now, don't you?" She inches even closer and her gaze lowers to my lips. "I hope so, anyway, because I don't kiss on the first date."

I lower my forehead until it's resting on hers, our noses almost touching. "Well, when you put it that way. I guess tonight is what? Our third or fourth date? Do you kiss on the fourth date?"

"Definitely," she breathes out the word and it floats from her mouth into mine, minty and laced with chocolate and anticipation. I watch, mesmerized as Danielle closes her eyes and tilts her head. Between all the M&M's and her toothpaste, she smells like Christmas has come in spring. I don't know if Danielle leans in first or I do, but our mouths are on each other now, and this night is perfect.

At least it was, until the doorbell rings and there's an aggressive pounding on the front door. Danielle startles and leans back, her eyes wide.

"Dan-Dan!" a deep voice yells. "Let me in."

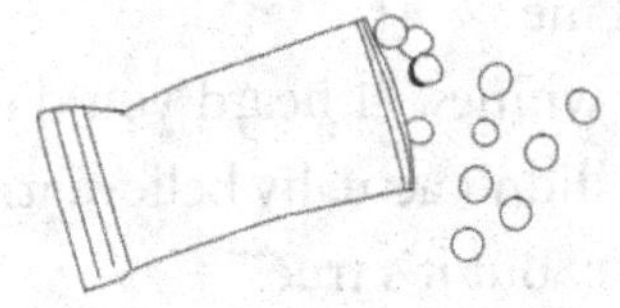

Chapter 12

Danielle

"What the hell, Jake?" I seethe as I open the door and he stumbles inside. "Seriously? What are you doing? Have you been drinking?" The last question is rhetorical. I can tell by the way he's struggling to keep his balance, and I can smell the liquor on him. Even in his current state, Jake immediately notices Mike standing in the hall a few feet behind me.

"He's here?" Jake whines. "I heard you ditched me for one of the baseball players, but I didn't actually believe it. I told everyone you would never do that to me. But it's true?"

"How are you even in North Bay right now?"

"I told you I'd be home this week. I drove back this afternoon, but when I got here there was a green truck in your driveway. I've been waiting for hours to talk to you. Letting you walk away after that kiss was a mistake." He squeezes his eyes shut like the overhead light in this room is too much. Mike clears his throat, claiming space in this conversation without saying a word.

This is ridiculous. I refuse to be the prize in some pissing contest between the two of them.

"I want both of you to hear this right now." I point my finger at Jake first, then at Mike. "Nobody 'lets' me do anything. Got it?" Mike smirks, seeming almost amused by my fiery side, while Jake huffs. "As for you, Jake, we both knew right away that kiss wasn't going to lead to anything more. We talked about it. Mike happened to be there that night, and yes, we drove home together. But my leaving the gala had nothing to do with him." The last part of my argument feels weak, even as I'm making it.

I appreciate how Mike is standing back, and so far he's letting me handle this. Although, he's a big dude, so just by standing at the edge of the foyer he is still making his presence known. Jake is glaring at him, and I can see how much Mike being here is getting to my intoxicated about-to-be-former best friend. Mike barely moves, except to cross his arms and take steady breaths through his nostrils. Jake is not small, but Mike is a professional athlete so he's even taller and more muscular. A drunken Jake stands no chance against him if this turns into a fight. I hope it doesn't get that far. Mike doesn't speak, even when Jake points at him and starts hurling accusations.

"You followed her."

Mike only nods at him once.

"Jake. It's none of your business who I spend my time with. For the last time, why are you here? What do you want?"

He scoffs. "Isn't that obvious? I want you, Dan-Dan. It's only been three days since you were in my bed." He's standing so close that little droplets of spittle hit my face as he talks. "We shouldn't have left it like that." Jake is speaking to me, but he is staring straight at the other man in my house. He's doing this on purpose. He wants Mike to think I slept with him. My eyes dart to Mike, too. He doesn't react. His body is still not moving, and the expression on his face is neutral.

I let out a heavy sigh, thankful that Mike doesn't respond. He knows that Jake and I were on a date at that gala, and even if he didn't see the kiss, he definitely knows about it now.

While there is a part of me that will always love Jake, I have never been more irritated with him than I am at this moment. It's becoming more and more obvious that I made the right decision when I walked away on Saturday night. Whatever small part of me that might have still been harboring a crush or any kind of hope that there could be something between us has been thoroughly squelched by this outburst.

"Let's talk about this in the morning. You need to leave. Go home and go to bed," I order Jake, then turn to Mike to explain. "This is Jake, the one who took me to the gala, although I'm sure you figured that out. His parents live right across the street. He can walk." I try to push Jake toward the door, but he is too big for me to move by myself.

"Mmm," Mike hums a non-committal noise.

"Can you just help me get him home? His dad is going to be so pissed."

Jake groans at that.

Mike sighs before he speaks.

"No."

I take a step back from him, surprised. Maybe Jake's words did upset him. "Okay. I'll handle him then, but that means our night is over."

"Sorry," he says quickly. "I wasn't blowing you off. I meant no, I don't think he should go home. Look, we can talk more about it later, but I've been there. Nothing good is going to come out of letting his parents see him like this. I'll take him home with me." Mike sounds resigned.

"What? Like, to murder him?" Because I kind of want to.

Mike lets out a loud laugh. "How many times do I need to promise you I'm not a murderer? And why do you always think that I would be so bad at it? If I planned to murder him, I wouldn't tell you I was taking him home with me. Have you never seen a single crime show? That's like rule number one. How about I just let him crash on my couch instead?" He shakes his head at me, but now he's smiling.

I'm still baffled by his suggestion. "You don't even know Jake. He just busted in and interrupted our first, or fourth, or whatever date. You want to do him a favor?"

Jake's my best friend and *I* don't even want to deal with him right now.

"Exactly. He's your friend. He's important to you, and you're important to me. Besides, I know him better than you think." Mike looks at the floor.

I'm important to him. We will so be circling back to that later. But about the second thing he said…

"What does that mean?" I can feel my forehead wrinkle in confusion. Balancing my relationships with these men is giving me a headache.

Jake slumps against the wall. His eyes are droopy. "I don't feel so great, you guys."

I ignore him and keep my attention on Mike. "How do you know Jake?" I don't think they've met before tonight, other than briefly seeing each other at the gala the other day.

Mike shakes his head again, more slowly this time. "I just meant we have a lot in common."

Jake wobbles and I move to prop him up with my body, pulling his arm around my shoulder while I continue the conversation. "How so?"

This seems important. Mike slides himself under Jake's other arm, taking the weight from me. He crouches down so he is at my level and we can guide Jake together. I try to ignore the fact that Mike smells like spices and fresh laundry, which is much more pleasant than the sour smell coming from my inebriated friend.

"It's really something we should talk about another time. If you want to help me get Jake in my truck, I'll take him back to my place tonight to sleep it off. Is this a regular thing for him? I saw how hard he hit the bar at the gala."

"I honestly don't know."

This was not at all how I expected the night to end. One minute I'm making out with Mike on the couch, and the next he's leaving for a sleepover with the guy who took me on a date last weekend? This feels so weird, but Mike's right. The Gibsons will be devastated to see Jake like this. Mr. Gibson gave us so many lectures growing up about the dangers of drugs and alcohol that he's still the voice in my head scolding me if I even think about over-indulging. If Mike is offering his couch, it might be a better idea than trying to sneak Jake back into his parents' house, but Jake is going to be so pissed when he sobers up and realizes what happened. He will not like the idea of me avoiding him and sending him off with my date, and he will like the idea of letting Mike play the hero even less.

But if Mike is offering to help, then Jake can go right ahead and be pissed off about it. Jake's the one going around interrupting other people's dates. He had his chance with me last weekend and he spent Friday night with a bottle in his hand and ignoring me.

Once Jake is in the truck, I slam the door shut and wipe my hand down my face, frustrated with the memories from last weekend. Mike approaches me slowly with both arms extended, like I'm a racoon he found in the garage and he's not sure if I'm going to attack.

"I'll take care of him, I promise," Mike tells me. He puts his hands on my shoulders.

"You shouldn't have to." I have half a mind to stomp my feet like a toddler. I don't like the whiny tone taking over my voice, but I can't control it. "This is ridiculous. Why is Jake doing this? This is the second time he's ruined an evening for me in less than a week. It's not like him. He's always been a good friend. I'm so sorry."

I sniffle as my eyes start to well up, which only makes me angrier. I hate that I cry when I'm mad. People have always treated me like either I'm too weak to deal with the situation or I am trying to manipulate them with my tears. Mike doesn't seem to think either of those things. He just continues the conversation as if my eyes are not leaking.

"Don't apologize. Only Jake can answer for his behavior. And he will. We all do." Mike's expression is solemn and he sounds lost in thought. "I'm sure he is not trying to hurt you, but you still have every right to feel upset. I haven't spent much time around Jake, and I know you say he is a good friend, but the way he's been treating you this week is shitty." His words make me feel seen and validated.

I sniff again and wipe my nose on my sleeve. Through the window of the truck, it looks like Jake has already fallen asleep. His head is back, eyes closed, and his mouth is gaping open. Mike closes the distance between us and wraps me in a tight hug. Welcoming the comfort, I reach my arms up and link my hands around the back of his neck.

"I had a lot of fun with you tonight. We'll get that tea soon," he tells me, pulling his torso back just a bit. His arms are still hooked around my waist and my legs are pressing against his.

I want to tug him back into me, but instead I bring my hands down and pat his chest. "I'm going to hold you to that."

"Good. I hope you do." He leans down to rub his nose back and forth on mine and whispers, "Can I give you a goodnight kiss?" As soon as I nod, he brushes his lips against mine so softly that I can barely feel it. It's over too soon. Resting my head on his chest, my eyes are still closed and I can feel the rumble of his deep voice resonate as he says, "I'm sorry I have to go, but I'll handle this. I'll text you an update later, but don't wait up. Try to get some rest. If you're here when I bring Jake back in the morning, maybe I can give you a ride to pick up your car from the shop. We can grab that latte then?"

"I'd like that."

"Me, too."

Goodnight."

"Night."

After a final squeeze, he gets into the truck and raises one hand to wave goodbye. I stand and shiver in the night air as my best friend is driven out of sight by the guy who came out of left field to steal my heart. I just met him a week ago, but I think I'm already falling hard for Mike Miller.

Chapter 13

Mike

In the morning, Jake is still asleep in my bed. I decided to put him in my room because I figured it would be easier to wash my sheets than to clean the sofa if he puked. I left some Advil and a water bottle on the nightstand next to a short note explaining where he was. I crashed on the couch last night. It was hard to sleep, and not just because I would need to have the skills of a contortionist to be six-three and lie comfortably on a two-seater couch. I tossed around most of the night remembering things I'd rather forget.

Around seven a.m. I gave up and snuck into my room to grab my computer. I was planning to watch a movie or check the scores from a few games, but seeing Jake snoring in my sheets knocked me right back to last night and the gut punch of seeing him so out of control. Maybe I should hate him for interrupting my night with Danielle and acting like such an ass, but I don't. I know what it's like to be that guy. That was me more often than I'd like to admit, and most of the time I was doing much worse than telling an old friend I liked her.

The problem with memories is that your body doesn't always realize they are in the past. My mouth is dry and when I look down I realize I've been scratching my forearm. A shiver runs through me.

"Dammit."

I feel like I'm crawling out of my skin. It would be so easy to drive to a clinic and tell a doctor I have an injury from practice, ask them to give me something for it. But I won't. I've been through this enough to recognize when I'm triggered and know that turning back to old habits is not actually going to help. Maybe I can find a morning meeting online?

North Bay has grown on me, but there are limitations to small-town life. For one thing, I haven't been able to find an in-person NA meeting within fifty miles. I've thought about calling the library or the church on Main Street to see if they'd be willing to host a group, but what do I know about starting something like that? Absolutely nothing is the answer. So, for the past few months, I've just been logging in online.

Virtual meetings aren't exactly the same as sitting down with people face-to-face. In some ways, that's good. In a town as small as this one, I doubt a North Bay chapter of Narcotics Anonymous would be very anonymous anyway. I'd be lucky if two other people showed up, and even if they did, they will probably have known each other for years and be able to spot me right away as a Blue Crab. There are no secrets in this town. Not that I'm ashamed, exactly, but I don't need to advertise it either. I don't know if I'm ready to sit with people I know in real life and discuss all the reasons I know I will never be good enough. Not for the team. Not for Danielle. Not for my dad. Not for any of this.

The online meetings also don't require the same time commitment or carry the heavy shame and embarrassment of having to walk into a new building and find the room with the NA sign on the door. There is a live meeting available, so I log in to the video chatroom and take a steadying breath.

Last night doesn't have to be a big deal, right? So, I brought my maybe-girlfriend's friend-who-wants-more-with-her home with me. So what? Beyond being Danielle's friend and neighbor, Jake is just a guy who I'm trying to help before he spirals any further out of control, the way I wish someone would have helped me sooner. I can do this. I can show up.

My heart is pounding so hard that it feels like it's going to jump out of my chest. I close my eyes to center myself for a second, then open them and blink into the camera on my laptop.

"My name is Mike, and I'm an addict. I'm in recovery. I've been sober for over three years." It's actually been 1,186 days. I'm counting every damn one of them. I might not deserve to be, but I'm here. I'm alive and I'm clean this morning, and I have to believe that counts for something. At least, I hope it does.

After I get the words out, I look up and see Jake leaning against the wall. I give him a nod letting him know it's okay to stay. Then to be candid with the other members in the meeting, I let them know, "I have someone joining me today."

"Hi, Mike and Mike's friend," a disembodied voice calls from the screen while my eyes are still on the mostly-stranger in my apartment. I motion for Jake to take a seat. He pulls out a chair from the dining table and sits a few feet away from me.

I don't actually share many of my own thoughts in the meeting, partly because Jake is watching, but also because I don't know how many times I can rehash the same story and maintain my sanity. Instead, I spend most of the time listening and empathizing with other addicts, throwing out occasional phrases like "I hear that" and "it's a fresh start from this moment forward." Hearing other people struggling with the same things I am and knowing I'm playing a small part in their recovery does help to calm the chaos in my brain.

Jake stays quiet and seems curious as the meeting continues. When we finish and I close the screen of my laptop he asks, "Do you do those meetings a lot?"

It's the first real conversation we've ever had, and this guy already knows more about my life than ninety percent of my teammates. He knows more about me than Danielle does. I squeeze my eyes tight, trying to push that thought out of my mind, but now it's lodged in my brain like a splinter. Last night with Danielle felt special. She makes me feel lighter than I have in a long time. But it isn't real. It can't be. She doesn't actually know me.

"Not as much as I used to." I deflate into the back of the couch. Then I redirect the conversation back to him. "There are meetings specifically for alcohol, if you're interested. We can find one. I could go with you."

"Nah, I'm good." His voice is small, forcing out the words we both know are a lie.

He doesn't need a lecture from me, so I only stand up and walk over to the table to lay a hand on his shoulder. "It's going to be okay, man."

"I wish I could believe that." His voice breaks while he twists out of my touch. This seems like something bigger than a crush on a girl, but I hardly know Jake. I don't want to pry. Well, any more than I already have. You could make a solid case that dragging him back to my place last night was pretty much the definition of prying.

"I know that feeling. Offer still stands if you change your mind." I try to leave the ball in his court.

"Why are you being nice to me?" He scoffs. To him, having someone be kind right now probably feels worse than if I'd punched him after what he pulled last night. Can't say I didn't want to, but I'm smart enough not to get myself kicked off the team over something stupid. Plus, that's not what he needs, even if it might be what he wants. Wouldn't be the first time I saw a guy come to me looking for a fight. When you're low and someone is beating on you, at least you feel like you're getting what you deserve. Grace is hard to understand and even harder to receive. I remember thinking the same thing about my mom. How could she just keep showing up and believing in me after everything I did to her?

"Like I said, I've been there, man." I shrug.

"Okay, whatever. Thanks for letting me crash here last night, I guess. I need to get home. My parents are probably freaking out. I'll call someone to pick me up."

"I'll drive you. I need to go back to Danielle's house today anyway. She told your parents you were going to stay with me last night. They think we're getting to know each other. Probably think we're fishing or something. I doubt they'll be suspicious of you wanting to check out the guy your best friend is dating." I notice him shift uncomfortably in the chair at the word "dating."

Maybe I shouldn't poke the wound so soon, but it's important to establish this boundary. I like Danielle and I'm not going anywhere. Jake's going to have to get used to it. I don't know him well enough yet to have a strong opinion about the man, but I'd like to think I do know something about Danielle, and I know he is important to her. I can respect a twenty-year history.

"My dad's going to be suspicious of just about anything involving me right now." Jake's voice cuts through my thoughts and makes me bristle. "I'm not exactly on his good side at the moment," he admits.

"Yeah, well, you're not the only one in this room with daddy issues." I pick up my mug from the side table next to the couch and take a long swig, then point to the kitchen counter and let Jake know he can help himself. "There's still some coffee in the pot. Cups are in the cabinet to the right of the sink, along with the sweeteners. I'm sure you can figure out where the milk is."

"Thanks." He nods before turning to pour himself a mug and shaking in a few sugar packets. At first glance the tats on his arms look pretty badass, even I have to admit, but now that I have seen them up close, I realize it's all fairytale shit like castles and wizards. Still, they are pretty sweet. I wonder if he drew the designs for them himself.

"Is this the part where we sit around and talk about why both of our dads hate us?" Jake asks, leaning against my kitchen counter and taking a long pull from the mug. He is clearly not fond of the idea. Well, bro, neither am I. There has been enough spilling of my guts in front of this guy today.

"No, I don't put out that easily. This is the part where we finish our coffee, then I put on my shoes and take your ass home."

As we bounce over the unpaved roads leading to Jake and Danielle's street, he leans his head back into the seat and closes his eyes. He's taking deep, controlled breaths, like he's holding everything back. I drum my knuckles against the steering wheel and try to keep my mouth shut, but that doesn't last long.

"There's clearly something else you want to say to me."

"On the contrary, I don't *want* to say anything to you."

I only grunt in response. He is quiet for a few seconds, but then it all spills out.

"This wasn't exactly my choice for how to spend the morning. I know you're coming out the hero in this scenario. Not that I don't appreciate you kidnapping me. I know it was a dick move to bust in on your date, and I clearly wasn't thinking last night. You did me a solid bringing me back to your place." At least he can admit that.

Jake closes his eyes and takes another deep breath through his nostrils as if the air will grant him the patience to overcome his irritation. "But damn, dude. I don't understand how I became the bad guy here. I was on a date with a woman I've known for twenty years, and I saw you chatting her up in the middle of it. Then she left with you in the middle of the night and ignored me for days." His voice cracks again. "It's been me and Dan for longer than I can remember, and suddenly a pro athlete shows up out of nowhere and she just takes off with him? No offense, but that story sucks."

I chuckle and he opens one eye to glare at me sideways. I'm sure he'd like to throw a punch my way, but he needs me to keep driving if he wants to get home, and he's got to be smart enough to know that throwing hands with me won't get him anywhere with Danielle. She was already pretty pissed off at him last night.

"When you put it that way, I guess I can see how it doesn't make a lot of sense from the outside. Look, man, I didn't plan this thing with Danielle. That's not how life works. Sometimes this stuff just happens. I met a woman, I like her, and she gets to decide if she likes me, too. No offense right back at you." I turn my head to face him directly and use his words from a moment ago. "But yeah, I didn't stop to think how her childhood neighbor friend might feel about it, because you don't get to decide how her story goes. She does. And I'm sticking around for as long as she wants me."

Jake rolls his eyes and groans before he throws his head back further. I can empathize with him. I know what it's like to be going through family drama and know your own part in it. Sure, it also sucks when you like someone and they don't feel the same way, but Danielle is the first woman I can see having a real relationship with. I'm not about to throw away my chance because some other dude had a boyhood crush on her and now he wants to whine about it. If Jake wants a fair shot with her, that's between the two of them, but it sounds like he already took a swing and he missed. He's going to need to step up his game if he plans to compete with me. I play to win. I might not deserve her, but if she wants me—and it seems like she does—I will gladly be here for that.

"That's the thing, isn't it?" His voice is flat. "You aren't sticking around. You're just passing through, and whether she has said so or not, she knows that." He angles his body toward me, seeming to gather a little more courage. "It doesn't matter if you're traded or called up, or if you strike out too many times and go back to Idaho with your tail between your legs. You'll be gone by this time next year. Dan has North Bay in her blood. She wants to be here. And I'll be right here with her. I'll be the one picking up the pieces when you break her. Which you will, the minute you leave."

There's a sinking feeling in my stomach. As much as I want Jake to be wrong about my time in North Bay, he's not. Failure is not an option I want to consider, but I could still get traded or called up, and if those opportunities come, I will have to take them. He is wrong about Danielle, though. She's stronger than he is giving her credit for being. Danielle's a free agent, and I'm going to do whatever it takes to keep her on Team Miller.

When we get to Pinecrest Avenue, I stop in front of Jake's parents' house. He climbs out of the truck and slips inside the front door without looking back.

"You're welcome," I mumble to myself. Then I swing the truck over into Danielle's driveway and shove the gearshift into park. It only takes a few long strides to reach the front door. I knock twice and she comes out to greet me. She has her hair braided in some kind of intricate knot that starts in the middle of her head on one side and falls down over the opposite shoulder. It makes the caveman part of my brain want to pull on it. I wonder if she would like that. I think it's time to show this woman that I do have game.

"Hey. How did last night go?" she asks. "Looks like you both survived."

"Morning, gorgeous. No worries, it was all good. Well, at least it wasn't all bad." I bend down and kiss her cheek. "Let's go get your car. Do you have to work today?"

"Yep." She smiles up at me. "But I get off at four. Can I come over after?"

Like she needs to ask.

Her question sends my mind to a dirty place. I'm not sure how she will react, but I decide that since the evening was disrupted just as things were heating up yesterday, it's worth the risk. I bend down to whisper in her ear with mischief in my voice. "You can come whenever you like."

"*Mike,*" Danielle squeals. She swats my arm and I laugh. "What got into your oatmeal this morning? Good Lord, it's not even noon and you're already standing out here on my grandma's porch trying to make me blush."

"If we hadn't been interrupted last night, I could have made you do a lot more than blush." I know I'm not the only one who feels the heat growing between us. Like I said, from this moment on, I'm pulling out all the stops. She may be shy about it, but I can tell by the way Danielle is wiggling now, shifting her weight from one foot to the other and smiling, that she likes hearing me talk this way.

She folds her arms and shakes her head, playfully scolding me. "That won't be necessary before breakfast. A ride to pick up my car will do just fine, thank you."

If that's the way she wants to play it, that's cool. I can be a patient man when I need to be.

"Then your chariot awaits." I make a sweeping gesture toward my truck and jog over to open the door for her. Danielle giggles as she climbs in. It's a complete 180 from where we left things last night, and I'm not complaining.

"Any fun plans for the rest of your day?" she asks once I'm in the truck and the seatbelt is buckled.

"I'm saving the fun stuff for later when you get back from work." I turn and wiggle my eyebrows at her. Her responding laugh is adorable. "I'm actually off today. It's a rest day for the team. Other than picking up your car, the only thing I have on my schedule is a trip to the post office." I ordered some vintage toys to send to Maddy for her birthday.

There's a joke about delivering my package on the tip of my tongue, but I hold it back. I just kissed her for the first time a few hours ago, and I have already made a few dirty jokes this morning. I don't need to come on *that* strong. Not that I haven't thought about delivering my package, I definitely have. But we have only been on one date. I don't want Danielle thinking I'm a total pig who didn't get what he wanted last night and came right back in the morning demanding more from her. There are plenty of other reasons she will discover eventually that prove I don't deserve her, but I won't let this be one of them. I'm fine with this going at her pace.

"The mechanic and the post office, both in one day?" Danielle teases. "Sounds like I have a real man-about-town on my hands."

This time I can't help myself and the joke slips out before I can even think about stopping it. "Always glad to be the man doing anything on your hands."

Oops.

Danielle's eyes go wide and her mouth hangs open for a solid two seconds before she throws her head back and lets out a full belly laugh.

"I'll keep that in mind." She dabs the corner of her eye with one finger where tears started to leak out from laughing so hard. "I can't believe you just said that."

"I know, me neither. I was trying really hard to behave. And I was doing so well holding back all the one-liners I had about my package." I shake my head with mock disgust.

She snorts. "Let's just go get my car before you get me in trouble. You are naughty, Mike Miller." She purses her lips and tries to pretend to look disappointed in me.

Oh, sweetheart. You have no idea. But if you're into it, maybe I can show you tonight.

Keeping the rest of my inappropriate thoughts to myself, I just smile and rest my elbow on the ledge of the open window while we drive the rest of the way to the body shop together.

Chapter 14

Danielle

Thankfully, the car is back and in great shape, but Honey decided she and Edna need to go watch tonight's improv show at the Community College. Alice offered to give me a ride after work in order to free up the Honda for their latest adventure. She pulls over on a secluded road along the way so I can change into leggings and the same cropped fuzzy sweater I wore to Virginia Tech. Mike hasn't seen this outfit yet, and Alice is right about the way it accentuates all of my curves. I use her rearview mirror to apply mascara and a new coat of lip gloss.

"You look hot. Whoever picked out that outfit definitely knew what they were doing." She smiles, then pulls a travel-sized body mist out of her purse. "Trust me. You need this, too. You just got off a shift at a seafood restaurant."

"True." I let her spritz me with the scent of raspberry blossom.

Fifteen minutes later, I knock on the door of Mike's apartment and hear footsteps on the other side. Jordan opens the door with a friendly smile and gestures for me to come inside. I'm a few minutes early, but I wanted to get here as soon as I could. A hint of heat creeps into my cheeks as I think about Mike's jokes from this morning. He may have been kidding, but some of the things he said sounded like a lot of fun. That might also be a big part of the reason I hurried over here as soon as my shift ended.

"Hi." Jordan greets me, then calls to Mike. "Our favorite crab tutor is here, Roomie. You better hide all of those My Little Pony magazines, man. She's going to think you're into some kinky shit."

He winks so I know he is teasing, and I smile back at Jordan, then turn and direct my own yell down the hall toward Mike. "Oh, please don't hide anything. I went through a serious Twilight Sparkle phase myself."

Jordan chuckles. "Dude honestly does have a bunch of My Little Pony paraphernalia back there. Fair warning. No judgment if that's your thing, but in this case, it is not usually in his room. He's been trying to find a gift for his sister's birthday. I can't remember which sister, but he said something about putting together a collection of retro toys from their childhood to send her."

"Seriously? That's really sweet."

"I guess. I mean, it would be cool if someone thought about giving me some Ninja Turtles once in a while." He pretends to pout.

"Exactly." I laugh and nudge him in his good arm. His other elbow is wrapped with some kind of beige bandage. "How is your arm?"

"Eh. Not the best, but it will heal eventually. Thanks for asking."

I make a mental note to look for a little Ninja Turtle for Jordan the next time I'm at Major Dollar as a get-well gift for him.

It doesn't take long for Mike to join us. His hair is damp. He must have been in the shower recently. I swallow and try to clear that image from my head before he can catch me in the middle of some very dirty thoughts about his freshly-cleaned body. Mike smiles and quickens his pace until he is standing directly in front of me.

"You're early. Not that I'm complaining." He bends down and kisses me in front of Jordan and I can feel my cheeks turning even more pink than they already were. It's not the first time he's kissed me, but it is the first time anyone else was watching, and we still haven't talked about whatever is going on between us. I didn't expect him to be so open about staking a claim to me in front of his roommate, but I like that he has no problem being affectionate.

"Hi," I say after he pulls away.

"Hi back."

"Well, as much fun as it would be to sit here and look at old, used rainbow unicorn toys while the two of you suck each other's faces, I'm going to pass. I'm headed out to poker night with a few of the guys. Rodriguez just texted that he's waiting for me outside. I might crash at his place tonight, so you two can have some privacy," Jordan tells us.

"Have fun. I'm sure we will find a way to entertain ourselves without you." Mike is talking to Jordan, but his eyes never leave mine. My stomach does a mini somersault. Those eyes seem to be making a lot of promises, and I am here for all of them.

"I doubt I'll be having quite as much fun as you will," Jordan says right before he grabs his keys from a hook next to the door. Then Mike's roommate is gone and we are alone in his apartment for the second time.

I stand there for a moment, awkwardly staring at Mike and waiting for him to make the first move. He seems content to just stand in his kitchen and trace my curves with his eyes. Sweater and leggings for the win.

Finally, he says, "Oh, I almost forgot. I believe I promised you a chai latte. Sorry, it's probably cold by now." He picks up a Brew-Ha-Ha to-go cup I hadn't noticed on the counter and hands it to me. It's still warm, but just barely.

"Better latte than never." I raise cup and toast the air before taking a sip and wince at my own bad joke, but he laughs because Mike has never met a pun he didn't appreciate. "Thank you. That was thoughtful," I tell him.

"You're welcome. Is the car doing okay?"

"Yeah. Honda Sykes is fine. Back to her old self." He chuckles, and I love that I knew it would make him laugh again when he heard I nicknamed the car after the actress Wanda Sykes.

"Good. How was work?"

"Um, work was fine." I've been in and out of the kitchen all afternoon. I probably still smell like sweat and seafood under Alice's body mist, but he doesn't seem to care.

"Cool. Can I show you something?" Mike asks. When I nod he takes my hand and leads me down the short hallway and into his bedroom. Jordan wasn't kidding. I'm glad he warned me because otherwise the gigantic pile of Barbies and ponies thrown all over his bed might have taken me by surprise.

"Oh my god, is that a Polly Pocket?" I pick the toy up from its resting spot on top of the grey-striped comforter and sit down on the bed. "I loved these."

I run one finger over it gently, remembering how precious the small plastic bin of toys I had in our camper was to me. We didn't have much space for extras, but I had a vintage set that Mom had purchased at the thrift store, from back when Polly's whole house really was small enough to fit in your pocket.

"Yeah. I'm just trying to figure out the best way to get all of these things into this box to send to my youngest sister, Maddy." He motions to a shoebox sitting on the dresser. "Like, should I bubble wrap them all together or just put some tissues in there and call it good?"

"It might be fun to giftwrap each one individually, so when Maddy opens the box it's like you sent her twenty gifts instead of one."

"That's a great idea. I can wrap them in the comic section of the newspaper like our mom used to do. Wait, do they still put comics in newspapers? I'm not sure I've ever bought a newspaper before."

I hope my stupid cheeks aren't turning as red as they feel when he smiles at me. I listen while Mike tells me a little more about his sisters. I know there are three of them, and they are still in Idaho with his parents, but he shares more about how Michelle is planning to go to law school, and Mandy is really involved in community theater. We chat for a bit longer about our families before Mike clears his throat and changes the subject.

"So, how's Jake doing?" He is trying to be casual, but there's a hint of something else in his voice. Worry, maybe? Is he jealous? I hope not.

Weirdly, though, I don't get the impression Mike is a jealous guy. I guess I assumed that because he plays sports for a living he would be more competitive, but he hasn't shown me that side of himself. He seems to want to like Jake, which is really endearing because, even if he's been making some dumb mistakes lately, Jake is always going to be important to me.

"I think he's fine. We haven't talked since you took him home," I admit.

Mike nods and makes a small humming sound. Then he makes one of the My Little Ponies dance for me. He is trying to lighten the mood, but I think we do need to have this talk if we are going to continue hanging out so much.

"Would it bother you if I did talk to him?"

"I'm not the kind of guy who tells my girlfriend who she can or can't talk to, but from what I saw yesterday it doesn't seem like he's in a very good place right now. Just be careful. Please. I know what it's like to be having a rough time, and it can be easy to hurt the people you care about the most."

"Excuse me? Your girlfriend?"

We are definitely finished talking about Jake now.

"You caught that, huh?" He looks sheepish as he runs a hand through his hair. "Is that okay?"

"Mike Miller, are you asking me to go steady?" I tease, hopping off the bed to close the space between us. He sets the toy down and turns to face me with a bashful shrug. "You like me," I pretend to taunt like a kid on the playground.

"I do," he admits while I throw my arms around his neck.

"Well, that's good, because I like you, too. A lot." I plant a brief, chaste kiss on his lips.

"Is that a yes on the girlfriend thing?" He chuckles.

"Definitely." There's a giddy smile plastered on my face, but I manage to keep my cool and hold in the squeal that wants to escape.

"Good. Then I think it's finally time we had that make-out session you mentioned, but we can skip the truck. I think you should stay right here and get used to kissing your boyfriend."

"I could get used to the sound of that."

There are flames dancing behind his eyes, and his Adam's apple bobs when he swallows. My fingers itch with the need to feel his hair, and I want to jump up and let him catch me while I kiss his neck. It takes a good bit of effort to keep my feet on the ground. It sounds silly, but I'm not used to having these kinds of intense thoughts about the guys I date. Here I am alone with this slender, six-foot-three wall of muscle, and he's officially my boyfriend. This is the kind of occasion that needs to be sealed with a kiss. Or several.

So, that's exactly what we do, leaning against his closet door. I breathe in the soft cotton of his tee shirt. It smells spicy and clean, just like him. I'm all tingly when he pulls back.

His face twists in an uncomfortable way. Something's wrong.

"What is it?" I ask.

"We need to have a conversation before we take this any further. I want to be honest with you, but I'm afraid it's not going to be easy for you to hear." Mike rubs the palm of his hand along the scruff on his jaw and my stomach drops. I hope he's not changing his mind because of what happened with Jake.

"What did I do?" Is my breath horrendous? Maybe I'm a really bad kisser and have never known.

"Absolutely nothing."

Tentatively, I ask, "I thought things were going well?"

"They are," he agrees. "Really well. I like you so much." Mike assures me with a kiss on the forehead. The tension in my shoulders eases a bit.

"I like you, too." It's so true that it almost hurts to say. "But I thought we already established that."

This is not the time to tell him that I already know it's more for me. For the first time, the guy in my imaginary future is starting to have a face, and that face looks an awful lot like the baseball player in front of me.

Mike's voice is softer, careful. He glides a finger down my arm as he starts to speak. "That's why I have something important to tell you. I told Jake a little bit about myself today, and there was something specific we discussed. I know you're close, and he will probably think he needs to tell you. I just want to make sure you hear this from me first."

He leads me to the bed and waits for me to take a seat before leaning himself on the edge of the dresser so he can face me. This really must be serious.

"Are you being traded? Are you leaving?" I voice my fear, although he wouldn't really have any reason to talk to Jake about that. "Is everything okay? Oh god, are you in some kind of trouble?"

I can hear the panic rising in my voice. I realize we haven't known each other very long. Maybe this is going to be something much worse.

He shakes his head.

Mike moves forward and squats down in front of me so we are eye-to-eye, then he reaches through the space between us to put a hand on my knee. He looks down at his hand while his thumb draws small circles on my leggings. He's hardly touching me, but the tiny movement is comforting and the warmth of his touch burns straight through the fabric to heat my skin.

"I'm really screwing this up." Mike takes a deep breath before launching into his explanation. "It was a long time ago, and I don't talk about it much. There aren't many people here who know because I wanted a fresh start in North Bay. Jordan is the only one on the team I've told. But things feel like they could be getting serious with us and I need to share this with you."

He swallows. "I haven't had to have this conversation this quickly with anyone I was dating before, and I wasn't really prepared to have it tonight. I'm not going to say everything right the first time. Let me get it all out first, okay? Then you can ask me your questions."

I bite the inside of my cheeks to stay quiet and nod for him to continue. He closes his eyes and takes a deep breath before he speaks. What could be so bad that he is this afraid to tell me?

"You need to know I'm a drug addict." The words rush out of him in a single breath.

I don't know what I was expecting to hear, but it wasn't that.

"What?" I blink.

Right. I promised to be quiet. It's just that his confession makes no sense. I haven't seen a single red flag from Mike. My chest is getting tighter, but I try to focus on the story he is telling and reserve judgment. I pick up Polly Pocket and run my fingers over her dress while I listen.

"My sophomore year of college, I busted my shoulder while I was playing pick-up basketball with some guys from the gym. Thankfully, it was my left side, so not my throwing arm. Since it was in the off-season, it didn't mess with baseball too badly. But I did need to have a minor surgery. Afterward, the doctor prescribed some pills to help me deal with the pain. Shoulder injuries are a real bitch, it can hurt for months afterward."

I lean in to show him I'm listening, but he asked me to let him speak, so I am going to try to sit here and take it all in before I respond.

"I was only supposed to take the meds for a few weeks and then taper off, but I couldn't do it. When my prescription ran out, I felt like I needed more. It was a craving so intense I don't really know how to describe it to you." He pauses to take a deep breath. "It wasn't like getting a craving for tacos or chocolate. It was more like once they were gone, I thought I was going to die if I didn't get them back. The closest feeling I know is when you are swimming and you stay underwater for too long. You know how your body can start panicking?" I nod to encourage him to keep going, although I can't say I've had that exact feeling before.

Mike's eyes are closed while he speaks.

"My grandmother was in hospice at a nursing facility not far from campus. I started visiting more often and stealing her medication. That's the biggest regret of my life. I sold some of her pills at school to get the money to buy stronger ones. When my dad found out I was turning into a junkie who was willing to hurt his mom while she was dying, he was so angry and disappointed that he cut me off completely. He stopped paying my tuition and left me to figure out my shit on my own. We haven't really spoken much since. My mom and sisters never gave up on me, though. Michelle knew what was going on, but my younger sisters were so little back then, they couldn't understand why

I was being mean to them. I hate that I put them through that. And then there was the accident."

"A car accident?"

He nods and pinches the bridge of his nose. That must be why he is so overprotective about me traveling in the dark. Now it's my turn to reach out to him. This is all so hard for him to talk about, I can't imagine how much it hurt to live through. It's breaking my heart just watching him tell the story.

"I don't think I need to hear anything else." I take his hand softly and pull it away from his face so I can look into his eyes. I only see sincerity in them. I have never seen him act strangely or even touch the alcohol at the crab feast or the gala. I have definitely never seen him take any pills. "It doesn't seem like you are using right now," I tell him.

"I'm not. My mom and my coach worked together and got me into a rehab program in Boise. Thankfully, I was able to turn it around and my coach really stepped up for me. I guess he was also like my sponsor. He had struggled with addiction, too, and it cost him his marriage. He never gave up on me. The program didn't take the first time. Or the second, but after the third time in treatment, I really did get clean. I missed a lot of time on the field to attend those programs, which might have hurt my chances at the majors, but I've been sober for three years."

I smile, the air lightening a bit. "Mike, that's amazing. I get that it was a rocky start, and I appreciate you sharing, but everyone makes stupid decisions when they are young. Look at everything you have accomplished since then. You finished college, where you played a Division One sport, and you are playing professional baseball now. It sounds like the rough patch is behind you."

He lets out a long breath. "Thank you. I did work really damn hard for all of that. I'm not afraid to work for what I want." His eyes burn right into me. I know he's talking about us now. "But if we are going to be together, you need to know this is always going to be a big part of who I am. You need to think about if that's going to be a problem for you."

"Of course not," I tell him immediately. Despite my best intentions to reserve judgment, I can feel more questions forming in the pit of my stomach. Intrusive ones that I don't know if I have the right to ask. So, I stick with the obvious.

"This is why you took Jake home with you? Because you were an addict and you thought he needed the same kind of help?"

"Not were. Am. Present tense. I am and will always be an addict. It's still something I struggle with every day. Yes, it's why I brought Jake here. I'm not sure how much good it really did, though. We aren't going to be planning a buddy camping trip anytime soon. But when I saw him like that I couldn't let him go home to his dad. It's just…I know how it feels to self-destruct and ruin everything."

There's a heaviness in his tone and I want to take it away, so I do the only thing I can think of: try to kiss it and make it better. He leans into me and kisses me back, hard, like he needs me more than air. It's heady and intoxicating, but also terrifying. Not because of anything he is doing, but because of my own growing need for him. Things with Mike are getting so intense, so quickly.

After a few minutes of mind-bending, life-altering kissing, Mike lowers his head and brushes his nose against my neck, sending shivers through me. There are goosebumps on my arm now, as I raise it to run my fingers through his hair. His mouth finds mine again, and this time his kiss is light and sweet at first, but soon I find myself pulling him toward me and we press further into each other. He's putting all of himself into this kiss. It's the kind of kiss that can only happen when people have no secrets between them, and the intensity is overwhelming. I have no control over the whimper that leaves my mouth when he pulls away again to suck on my neck. His hands are on my hips, toying with my waistband, and he brings his forehead to mine so he can look into my eyes. Our chests are both heaving. I want him. His eyes and his hands are begging for permission to take this further.

"You okay?"

I nod and bite my swollen lower lip.

"This okay?" He looks down toward his hand.

"Yes."

Please. I want him. Now. My body is begging, too, and I push my hips forward, urging him on. He slips his hand under the waistband, down the front of my pants, and strokes the top of my thigh. This is torture in the best possible way. Mike gently plays with the elastic on my panties, sliding his fingers over the fabric, then cupping his hand so that the heel of his palm is pressing into my most sensitive spot. I have no control of the way my hips are grinding into his hand.

"Talk to me, tell me what you want." His voice is low, a gravelly whisper next to my ear.

"Just…more…please." I can't even think. I don't know how he expects me to give directions.

"Like this?" He slides one finger inside my panties and touches me with long, slow strokes. I'm panting.

"You're so ready for me." There's a sense of awe in his voice.

Between everything he has done for me this week and the vulnerability of what he shared tonight, I'm gone for him. As his fingers continue their steady rhythm, my vision narrows and my body contracts and pulses around him. He kisses me through my orgasm. When he pulls his finger away I want to protest and ask for more, but he brings it up to his mouth. Oh God, he's going to su…

That's blood.

I come crashing down from the high I was riding a moment ago. Did he hurt himself somehow? No. It must be coming from me. Oh, dear God, it has been about a month, hasn't it? Mike's only noticeable reaction is that his brow furrows when he realizes at the same time I do that the liquid on his finger is dark red. I can feel my cheeks heat and I know my face must be a similar shade of crimson. I shake my head and pull away, not wanting to believe what I am seeing. He takes a step back.

"Are you a virgin?" he asks, confused but not judging.

"No," I squeak. That's all I can manage in terms of an explanation. How exactly do you say, *"Thanks for baring your soul and sharing your deepest secret as well as providing me with a life-altering orgasm. In return, how about I cover you in my menstrual blood?"*

Understanding dawns on him.

It's official. This is the most embarrassing thing that's ever going to happen to me. It's worse than that time in seventh grade when I sat on a candy bar wrapper and walked around with brown smears on the back of my shorts for half the day.

I got my period all over his unsuspecting hand in the middle of our first intimate moment as a couple. I'm never going to live this down. The only option now is to be a mature adult about this. So, obviously, I turn and run down the hall and lock myself in the bathroom. Then the tears come. This whole evening has been full of emotional turbulence, and all of it hits me at once.

"Danielle." His knock is soft and his voice is kind.

"Sorry, there's no one here by that name," I call out, sitting on the toilet and burying my face in my hands, resting my elbows on my knees. I can't catch my breath. I think I might be hyperventilating.

"Look under the sink," he says. "Take whatever you need. I'll be in my room when you're ready." I hear his footsteps carry him away.

Look under the sink? Reluctantly, I wipe my eyes and bend to open the cabinet door. Sure enough, there's a small plastic bucket containing some pads, tampons, and even a few brand-new pairs of women's underwear, with the tags still attached. Wait, is that a Diva cup still in the packaging?

I take a new pair of underwear and a tampon, clean myself up, and wrap the soiled panties in toilet paper before tossing them in the bathroom trashcan. The new ones are a little big for me, but given the circumstances, they'll do. After three deep breaths, I dig my phone out of the pocket of the leggings I'm wearing and text Alice.

Me: *S.O.S. Hypothetically, what would you do if you were going to third base with your boyfriend for the first time, but during the act you accidentally got menstrual blood all over him?*

Alice: *Yikes. But obviously, the answer is you text your best friend and ask her to bring you some new clothes and a ride home. I can be there* *in fifteen minutes with supplies. Also? Boyfriend??? It's official? That was quick. Told you that outfit is fire.*

Me: *Actually, he already had supplies. And yes, it's official. He asked me before the floodgates to the Red Sea opened.*

I snap a photo of the little period bucket under the sink and send it to her.

Alice: *Oh, I see. So, we love him. You have what you need. He understands periods. He admitted his feelings. This does not seem like a problem. I assume he knows how to wash his…I'm going to say hands and hope it wasn't his mouth.*

Why can't she freak out with me like I need her to, just this once? She always has to be so level-headed and logical.

Me: *Yes, it was his hand. But not a problem? Only the single most embarrassing moment of my life. What if he's pissed? We haven't talked about it. I ran and hid in the bathroom.*

Alice: *If he's pissed, he's a jerk. But that doesn't seem likely. It's not like you did it on purpose. Babe, bodies do all sorts of embarrassing stuff. Remember when I accidentally drank cow's milk in my latte and we had to pull over for three emergency potty breaks in the grass on the side of the road?*

Me: *That was different.*

Alice: *It wasn't. Besides, he's a professional athlete. Probably not the first time he's gotten a little bit of blood on him. I don't think this is going to scare him off.*

Is she right? Maybe I am overreacting. The evidence is on her side. My shame spiral, on the other hand, is not going to let up anytime soon. Unfortunately, I can't stay locked in this bathroom forever, even if it is tempting.

There is only a small stain on the inside of my leggings. I'll probably be able to get it out if I wash them at home. After a few more shaky breaths, I force myself to open the bathroom door and walk down the hall, back to his bedroom. He's standing at the dresser, occupying himself by putting away some laundry.

"So, um, the bathroom's free if you want to, you know, get cleaned up." I wince.

"Already took care of it." He shrugs. Right. The kitchen. There is another sink in the apartment. He also probably wouldn't be smearing my blood on his clean laundry, which I seem to have just implied. His voice sounds normal, unbothered. My stomach is still gurgling from nerves. I wonder if he can hear it. This might turn into an Alice's latte situation after all. As if it can get any worse. Am I sick? I feel sick. I'm dying. Literally dying. The answer is yes, you can die of embarrassment, in case anyone was wondering.

"I'm so sorry. This is humiliating." I can't look at him, so I stare at the carpet.

He turns and walks to me, cupping my face with both of his hands and raising my head to look into his eyes, but I can't do that yet, so I squeeze my own eyes shut while he talks.

"Are you kidding? Do you know how ashamed I felt to share all that stuff with you earlier? This tiny blip? It's fine. We are fine. You have nothing to apologize for. You didn't do anything wrong," he tries to assure me.

Not on purpose, maybe, but my body betrayed me. He bends down and kisses the tip of my nose. He's being really sweet, actually.

"You good? Did you find what you needed in there? I wish I could say I'm thoughtful enough to stock up for occasions such as this, but the truth is Michelle got her period the last time she visited. She sent me out to buy her supplies, and I didn't know what to get, so I just bought all the stuff the store had on the shelf." He takes my hand and leads me back to the bed, which has been cleared of toys. I sit, fidgeting with my hands while he stands in front of me. Alice was right, he doesn't seem weirded out at all, but that doesn't mean I'm comfortable yet. I still can't quite bring myself to look at him.

"I need to wash my pants," I blurt and sneak a quick glance up at him.

He chuckles and nods. "Okay. Do you want to borrow some sweatpants? I'm sure they'd look better on you anyway."

Although I doubt that anyone could look better than he does in gray sweatpants, the hint of a smile plays with the corners of my mouth. I'm not ready to let it out.

"Thanks for being nice about it." I swallow and whisper at the ground. He's never been anything but sweet to me, but after his confession, now I feel like I am walking on eggshells not wanting to upset him.

He stills.

"How did you expect me to react?"

"I don't know. Grossed out? Disappointed? I thought maybe you would make fun of me for it or get angry. Just generally act like someone who doesn't appreciate getting people's blood on them, not that anyone could blame you. Or a guy who thought he was going to get some action, but then…didn't." *And might need something to take the edge off.* I don't tell him that last part. It feels unfair to jump to that conclusion, but I mean, I feel like I could use something to take the edge off after what just happened, so why wouldn't he? If he does, are we supposed to talk about it? Are we not? I don't know the protocol for being an addict's girlfriend.

"Wow. Okay. Well, I don't know who that guy you're talking about is, but he sounds like a dick, and that's not me." He sits down next to me on the edge of the bed, causing the mattress to sink a bit under his weight. "Come here." He pulls me into his lap and wraps his arms around my waist. I rest my head on his shoulder, and we sit still until I'm ready to talk.

I sniff and finally look at him. "You're not mad?"

"I'm concerned that you assumed I would be, but no, I'm not. At all." Mike is being so gentle. But can I trust this? He just told me he's a drug addict. Present tense. What if I do something that makes him snap? How will I ever be able to know what might trigger him?

"Okay." I hate the doubts that are creeping in now that he's shared his deepest secret with me. I want to believe him. "Thank you. I appreciate it. But it's probably best if I go." There is no way the mood from earlier is coming back any time soon. I am mortified about the way things ended tonight. This is not the kind of thing I get over easily, but there is more to it than that. I also need to think about what his past means for us moving forward.

"You sure? I'm not going to push you to stay if you're uncomfortable, but please don't feel like you have to leave just because of this."

Sighing, I tell him, "I think I'm ready to call it a night. But thank you. If that had to happen, I guess I'm glad it was with you."

He breathes a small laugh through his nose and pats my knee. "That's not much, but I'll take it. I had a lot of fun before that little interruption."

"Me, too." I really did. "But let's never talk about this again."

"Talk about what?" He winks. "Do you want to grab your stuff? I'll drive you home."

I gather my things and follow him to his truck, where he opens my door and puts his hand on the small of my back as I climb inside. He must not be too disgusted if he's still touching me.

We drive in silence for a few minutes before Mike speaks.

"When I was in the third grade I threw up in the middle of a spelling test. Not that I had any control over it, but at the time it was really embarrassing. All the kids started yelling about how gross it was, and the teacher had to call the janitor down to clean it up. Remember that orange-smelling sawdust stuff they would sprinkle over it?"

I wrinkle my nose. As adorable as it is that he's telling me this story to try to make me feel better, it's still gross. "Yeah, I can still smell it. I used to live in fear of being the one to puke in class. I'm sorry that happened to you."

He shrugs. "I got over it pretty quickly."

"How?" I don't think I would have. I kind of want to cry right now for poor little Mike who wasn't feeling well and had to deal with his classmates teasing him on top of it. And I definitely want to cry for Danielle of fifteen minutes ago.

He reaches over the center console and squeezes my leg. "Eventually I realized those things happen to everyone. Just part of life. Can I tell you a secret?"

Another one? Intrigued, I nod. He's making a real effort to let down his guard tonight, and I appreciate it. I feel like a coward, but after what just happened, I'm still not ready to do the same for him.

"When I screw up during a game, sometimes I go home and watch videos of other players making epic mistakes. I probably shouldn't be laughing at them. Bad karma or whatever. But it helps to know I'm not the only one. There are guys in the majors who still trip over their own feet and faceplant on occasion."

I'm glad he doesn't seem to need me to participate in the conversation. I'm starting to feel better, but I don't want to talk about The Incident from tonight yet. I think he can sense me retreating into my shell, because he continues. "That's why there are so many online forums for people to share their own embarrassing moments. People bond over them. They're humanizing."

"That's true, I guess. I used to read the ones in the back of teen magazines, even though I'm sure at least half of them were made up by the editors." There. I can do this. I'm still talking to him and I survived my humiliation.

"Exactly," he nods. "I'm sure we are not the first couple this has happened to." Okay. He just called us a couple. Now I'm all tingly. "I know you're embarrassed, but you don't need to be. This moment stays between us."

"And Alice," I clarify. "I already told her."

He laughs. "I thought we were never supposed to talk about it. But, sure. Between us and Alice. And hey." He puts his hand on my knee again. "If you need to talk to her about anything I told you tonight, it's okay. I understand."

I've only officially been Mike Miller's girlfriend for a little over an hour, but so far dating a professional athlete with a secret past has been a heck of a ride. I hope I have it in me to hang on.

Chapter 15

Mike

After dropping her off at home, I need to blow off some steam. I text Jordan to let him know I will be free for the rest of the night and he invites me to meet him at the poker game. By the time I get to Rodriguez's place, the guys are a few hands in. The air is thick with the smoke from the cigars Jordan and Smithy have sticking out of their mouths. Lincoln is sitting at the table, too, nursing an IPA with one hand and holding his cards close to his chest with the other. My eyes start to water from the smoke, and I clear my throat to cover the cough that wants to escape. There are a few empty bottles on the table and Rodriguez stands with outstretched arms and rakes the chips toward himself.

"That's what I'm talking about. This pot is mine."

As he sorts and stacks the chips into towers, he glances up, noticing me. "Oh, hey, Miller. Grab a beer. Smithy said he has to bounce in a few minutes, you can take his chair when he leaves." He tips his head toward Smithy and deals the next hand.

I nod my thanks and make my way to the kitchen, but take a water bottle from the fridge instead.

Confession is the fifth step in recovery. I'm no stranger to it, but telling Danielle as much as I did tonight was rough for me. It's easier to talk about the things I've done in meetings. It's always much harder when you are looking into the face of someone you care about. She needed to know, I don't regret it. It went better than I expected, but I could do without all the old guilt about things I can't change that's now festering under my skin. There have been a lot of ups and downs today. I'm not used to feeling this many highs and lows off the field.

"The Rookie is my D.D." Jordan says, giving me a knowing look when I walk back to the table without the beer I've been offered, but the others only respond with grunts. They are too focused on the cards in front of them to care what I'm drinking. One nice thing about getting older and no longer being in the college party scene is that people rarely notice my efforts to stay sober, and even if they do, often they assume it's a choice I'm making to stay in shape or focus on my game during the season. Which, in a way, I guess it is.

I lean against the wall and watch the next hand.

Hearing Jordan say "D.D." reminds me of Danielle. The designated driver abbreviation is the same as her initials, and the fact that I realize this means I'm already thinking about her more than I should. She is constantly in my head, and it's only going to get worse now that I know what it feels like to touch her. I hadn't planned on asking her to be my girlfriend tonight, the words just popped out of my mouth like I had no control. My feelings for her are getting intense too quickly. Keeping myself in check is how I survived the past three years, and I know it's what I need to continue to do in order to make it in the pros.

But that's a problem for tomorrow. Danielle is safe at her house, and the rest of tonight is for having some much-needed fun with these guys.

My roommate folds his cards after the second round and turns his attention to me. "Wasn't expecting to see you until the morning. What happened? Your girl get spooked by all the tiny purple horses?" he ribs me.

"Nah. Women love that shit. Three sisters, remember?" I point to my chest, not taking the bait. "Danielle just had a long day so we decided to call it early."

"Fair enough."

Everything else that happened tonight can stay private. All of that is between me and her.

"Dude. You're still seeing that waitress from the crab feast?" Smithy asks, pushing a few more chips into the pot. "She was hot."

"Yeah, she is," Lincoln agrees with a smirk, rearranging the cards in his hand.

Smithy uses his hands to mime cupping half-circles in the air.

"Watch it," I warn.

"Oh, someone's feeling protective. This must be getting serious." Jordan talks around his cigar. My truck is going to smell like smoke for days after I drive his dumb ass home. It makes me miss Danielle and the way I could still smell vanilla in the cab of the truck after I drove her home that first night. The vanilla is definitely preferable.

"Actually, we just made it official tonight."

"No shit?" Smithy raises his bottle in the air for a toast. "Then to Miller and the waitress."

"Danielle." I correct him.

"That's what I said. To Miller and *Danielle* the waitress."

"I am taking full credit for this. You never would have even started talking to her if it hadn't been for me," Jordan says.

The guys raise their bottles and clink them together before they each take a swig. I roll my eyes and do the same with the plastic bottle in my hand.

A few minutes later, Smithy stands up and looks at his phone. "My ride is here. Miller, take over for me. Try to do my chair the justice she deserves."

When he heads toward the door, I put my hand on my heart and answer with mock earnestness, "I will do my very best."

"Hold up." Rodriguez takes out his phone. "Don't leave yet. Let's take a picture real quick."

Smithy comes back to the table and everyone stands and crowds together while Rodriguez extends his arm for a selfie.

"Got it."

"Okay, I'm leaving for real now."

"Later, Smithy."

I take a twenty from my wallet and hand it to Rodriguez to buy in to the game, and he counts out some new chips for me in return.

Three hands later, I'm up five bucks. Jordan glances at the clock on the wall and I follow his gaze to have a look for myself.

"Is it really only eight-fifteen?" It feels like it should be later. I managed to cram a lot into the afternoon. "I think I'm done for tonight."

"Yeah," Jordan says. "I'll come with you. Do you think we could run out to the pharmacy first? They don't close until nine and I got a notification that my prescription is ready. I was hoping to grab it tonight."

The elbow seems to be healing little by little, but I can tell from the way Jordan has been favoring it for the past few days that he's still in a lot of pain.

"Um, yeah, I guess. It's not too far out of the way." I can stay in the car, away from the triggers.

"Cool. Then this will be our last hand," Jordan tells the rest of the guys around the table.

My cards are trash and I fold immediately, but at least I ended on a high note, which is more than Jordan can say. He lost his buy-in and then some.

"Rough luck, man," I tell him as we head out the door. He doesn't seem to care. Jordan is always in a good mood, even on nights like this when he loses a hundred and fifty bucks to the other rookie.

When we pull up to the pharmacy, I wait while Jordan runs inside. No reason to put myself in the path of temptation. Instead, I pull out my phone and send Danielle a gif of two cartoon crabs dancing and I write *Look, it could have been us at the gala last weekend.* It only takes a few seconds before she replies with *next time* and a smiley face. I'm still grinning when Jordan comes out of the store and jogs back to my truck. As he slides into the seat next to me, he puts the small white paper bag between us.

"Dude. Are you starving? Because I am. And do you know what I just remembered? We're already halfway to Marnock. You know what is open late and is only like fifteen more minutes from here?"

"Of course I'm starving. Rodriguez had no food at his place, unless you count a stale bag of tortilla chips." I know what Jordan's thinking, and the rumbling in my stomach agrees with him, so I answer at exactly the same time that he says, "Taco Terrace."

When we get there, I'm out of the truck before Jordan is even finished unbuckling his seatbelt. I walk in first and order a party pack that includes a dozen tacos, and Jordan takes forever to join me.

"You get lost between here and the parking lot?" I ask when he finally comes inside.

"Aw. You missed me." He makes kissy faces in the air.

I roll my eyes. He was probably stalling so I would pay for our food. It worked, but I don't even care because I'm hungry. We sit down at a booth and crush the entire party pack before we head home to crash. We need to be up for an early practice in the morning.

Chapter 16

Danielle

Maybe I shouldn't be here after everything that has gone down with Jake recently, but the last few days have been intense, and the Gibsons' pier has always been my happy place. This is the same pier from the memory Jake shared with me. It's also where he, Alice, and I met to swim in the summers. We held hands and jumped off the end of the dock, tucking our knees as we perfected our three-person cannon ball technique. We caught lightning bugs in the yard closer to the house. When we were five, somehow Jake managed to tie one of the glowing little insects to a blade of grass, and then he twisted his creation into a circle to make me a ring. I wore it for a few minutes, feeling like a princess as I watched my finger glow, before we untied the knot and let the bug fly free.

Now my bare feet are in the water as I sit on the edge of that same pier, holding the end of a thick line of string. The insulated, lunchbox-sized cooler next to me holds a retractable knife alongside the recycled ice cream container that is now the home for all of the raw chicken necks and gizzards Honey saves each time she buys a whole chicken to roast for dinner. I tie a small piece of bait on to the string and throw it out as far as I can.

One of Bob's faded old baseball hats keeps my hair in place, pulled into a ponytail through the hole in the back, but even with my face shaded by the bill of the cap, the warmth of the sun burns my nose and I can almost feel new freckles forming. I will probably have a sunburn tomorrow, but for now I want to bask in the warmth of this spring afternoon. I don't even care that my allergies are acting up and I've been sneezing all afternoon. This pier has always felt like a hug for my soul. I close my eyes and breathe deeply. No matter what else was happening in our lives, Jake and I found peace here. As much as I like Mike, the knowledge that what I have with Jake could be ending over this is heavy on my heart, and the worry I'm carrying since Mike told me about his addiction is weighing on me even more. I need this place. I need home.

The fishy smell that permeates the air isn't exactly pleasant, but there is a calmness to it that makes me feel like I belong. Jake and I have shared this place for so long it is a part of us now, and we are a part of it. Even if we aren't going to be together, I don't think I can separate myself from him. But that doesn't mean Mike can't belong in my world, too. I just wish I could get rid of the doubts that have been clouding my thoughts ever since he told me about his past.

This morning I got a friend request from Mike's teammate, Rodriguez. When I accepted, the first picture on his profile was a group shot from last night. In the photo Mike and Rodriguez are with Jordan and a few other guys, and several of them are holding beer bottles. It didn't look like Mike had one, but there's no way to know that from one picture. Regardless, he was still surrounded by alcohol, and he didn't tell me he was going out last night. Maybe it's naïve, but I assumed he was going back to his place after he took me home. Not that he needs my permission to hang out with his friends, he's a grown man and he can do what he wants, but it doesn't sit well with me that he would omit that information. I didn't know he liked to party. Actually, I'm realizing I don't know much about my new boyfriend at all.

He said he's been sober for three years, but that is from pills. Maybe he wasn't talking about alcohol? I shake my head. I doubt he was drinking, but seeing him in that photo made my stomach drop. Now I'm thinking about the crab feast, and the gala, and every time the team goes out to a bar after an away game. Mike's always going to be in situations that could compromise his sobriety, and as long as we are together, I know it will be a constant worry for me. Even if he is physically present, I could still lose him to the pills. As much as I like him, I don't know if I'm ready to take on the weight of being in a serious relationship with an addict. I said yes to him before I had a chance to think about what it would mean. There are so many things I need him to clarify.

I feel a tug on my string and then there's a tautness on the line, pulling it straight out into the water. I grab the metal net and balance it in my hand while I start to pull in my handline. I dip it quickly, just like Mr. Gibson taught us when we were young, but the baby crab clinging to the frozen chicken neck is too small, and it easily slips through the holes in the net.

"Give him a few months to grow and you'll get him before the summer is over." Jake's voice comes from behind me and takes me by surprise. I turn to see him standing with both hands in his pockets and his shoulders slightly hunched.

"I didn't hear you walk out. Sorry. I should have asked before I came down here."

"You know you never need to ask." He removes his hands from his pockets and uses them to help him balance as he sits down next to me, keeping his feet on the pier and crossing his arms over his bent knees. My eyes are drawn to the intricate artwork on his forearms.

"Jake," I start, but the word hangs in the air, because for the first time I can remember, I'm not sure what to say to him.

He starts talking before I can form the rest of my thoughts. "I'm so sorry. I acted like such an asshole. I don't have an excuse. Just tell me we're okay, Dan. I get that you're with Mike now, and as much as it kills me to say this, he's a decent guy. I think I'm even happy for you. Or I will be. It might take a minute. It's just…" He blows out a long breath and shifts his body toward the water. There's a vulnerability in his voice, slipping past his usual easygoing exterior. "This is going to sound so stupid, but…"

"It was supposed to be us in the end." I finish his thought. "I know. I always felt the same way. It's weird the way things work out sometimes. Getting together with Mike just sort of happened. I wasn't trying to hurt you." Tears threaten to fall, but I blink them back.

"I know. I shouldn't have thrown it back at you like that. He's a good guy. He tried to get me to go to an AA meeting, did he tell you that?"

"No, he didn't." It warms my heart to know Mike would do that for my friend and that he kept Jake's business private. I wonder exactly how much of his own past Mike shared with Jake. "Are you going to the meeting?"

"No. I don't think I really need to. It was cool that he tried to help, but it felt like he was projecting a bit." Jake gives me a look, but doesn't say more about Mike's addiction. I can tell he is weighing how much I might already know.

Instead of airing Mike's business, he continues, "He's wrong about me, but it was a wake-up call. I haven't had anything to drink since I walked in on your date, and thanks to the massive headache I had all day yesterday, I don't have a desire to do it again anytime soon. Plus, I have no problem realizing I was a jerk to you and apologizing. I am sorry, D. You have every right to date whoever you want, and you were right. Now is not our time. We'll be okay."

"Thank you. I appreciate it. Although, it's not like Mike and I are getting married. It's still new."

A small scoff slips out of Jake. "We'll see. You're different with him."

"How so?"

"More yourself, I guess. Like somebody turned up the volume. He lights up something in you, I can see it. And I think you do the same thing for him. You deserve to be happy. I wouldn't stand in the way of that."

Strangely, I know what he means. I do feel like a more complete version of myself when Mike is around. But even if I do marry Mike, one day, a *very* long time from now, Jake is also always going to be a part of my life. I know it's corny, but I think he is the first person who taught me what it means to love someone besides my mom and Honey. I can't throw that away.

"You would know. You know me better than anyone." I sniff and wipe a tear that managed to escape.

"I'm not sure that's true anymore."

"You knew you'd find me here," I offer.

"That didn't take any advanced detective skills. I can see the pier from my bedroom window."

I smile, although the tears are coming faster now. It feels silly to cry. I'm not exactly sad, but it does feel like we are mourning the end of an era and marking the beginning of a new chapter in our grown-up lives. I'm not sure I'm ready, but I'm learning that life tends to come at you whether you are ready or not.

He pauses, as if he's not sure he wants to share what he is about to say. "God, you have no idea how many times I've watched you on this pier."

"Really?" I rub a ribbon of snot on the back of my hand, then wipe it on my cut-off jean shorts.

"Yeah, well. Don't let it go to your head. You know my parents wouldn't let me have a TV in my room." He playfully punches my shoulder. It makes me smile again, and a little bit more of the tension we have both been carrying melts away. Even if nothing romantic ever happens between us, he is always going to be my Jake. I pull up the neckline of my tee shirt to wipe the tears and sweat from my face.

"We good?" he asks.

"Always." It's a truth I know in my bones. It would take a lot more than two nights of overindulging to make me turn my back on twenty years of friendship. He's not getting away that easily. "Now make yourself useful."

I nod at the cooler, and Jake takes out the knife to cut a new line from the coil of string. While he baits his handline with a fresh chicken neck, I pull my line in, then toss it further out again.

Time stands still on the water, so I can't say how long we sit together, not catching much. It's long enough for twilight to come and the mosquitos to nip at our feet. When footsteps creak along the pier, Jake and I both turn to see Mike walking toward us.

"Honey told me I might find you here," he says. My heart catches in my throat, and for a second I'm worried he will be angry, finding me in the dark with another man who hasn't been shy about his feelings for me. But Mike is smiling when he reaches the end of the dock. Instead of taking me away from Jake or putting himself between us, he sits down on my other side and kisses the top of my head to say hello.

"You guys will need to show me how to do this one day when the sun is out and we can see what we're doing." It's a peace offering, Mike talking about making plans that include Jake. I reach over and squeeze his leg in a silent gesture of thanks.

"Sure, man," Jake says.

"I thought you didn't even like crabs," I tease.

"I'm a North Bay man now, I'm sure they'll grow on me."

Smiling and sandwiched between the two most important men in my life, I ask, "Anybody want to go back to Honey's house and have a sandwich? I'm starving."

"You two go ahead," Jake answers first. "I should put in some face time with the folks tonight." He doesn't sound excited about it.

"Okay, drive safe when you head back to school." I tell him, but he only nods once in response. Something still feels just a little bit off. I want to get up and give him a hug, but the idea of touching Jake in front of Mike still feels awkward.

"Yeah, take care," Mike tells him as Jake stands and salutes us with two fingers before heading back toward the house.

"You haven't eaten dinner yet?" Mike asks, turning his attention back to me. "I think I can do better than a sandwich."

"Oh, yeah? Mike Miller cooks? I'm learning new things about you every day."

"For sure. Omelets, pasta, grilled cheese. Sometimes I even microwave a frozen burrito." He smiles. "Stick with me, baby, there's a lot to learn." He's teasing, but it doesn't stop my stomach from doing a tiny flip when he calls me baby. "Come on, I'll make you dinner. Unless you want to go out to Marnock and get something else?" Mike stands and pulls me to my feet. I throw my supplies hastily into the cooler and place one hand in his as we walk together off the pier.

"I think I would rather have the Miller Special, please."

"That can definitely be arranged."

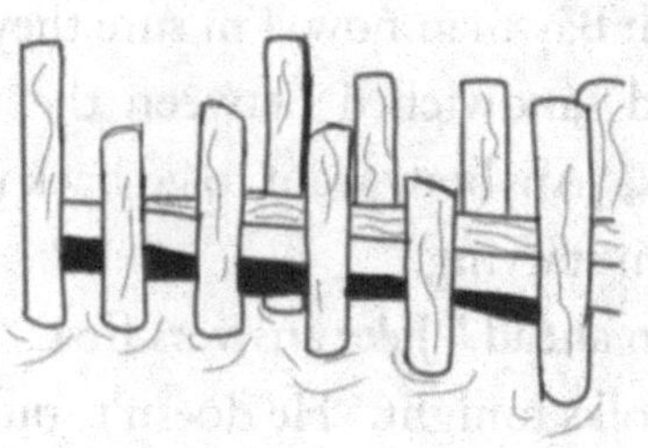

186

Chapter 17

Mike

Once we are in the truck, I turn on the radio and adjust the air vents while Danielle fiddles with her seatbelt. "So, what exactly is the Miller Special?" she asks.

"In this context it means I'll make you my spaghetti carbonara." I might not be the best cook in the world, but that is one dish I'm confident I can knock out of the park.

"Sounds amazing. Who doesn't love pasta, bacon, and cheese?"

"Exactly. Plus, it only takes fifteen minutes, and then we can move on to more important things."

"Oh? Do you have something specific in mind?"

"I was thinking we could continue where we left off last night, as long as you're into it. I can show you what else is included when you order the Miller Special."

"I might be able to be persuaded." She laughs and we fall into a comfortable silence.

When I sneak a peek at her, Danielle is rubbing her eyes. Come to think of it, they are looking a little red. I hope she wasn't crying with

Jake, but the two of them seemed to be in a good place when I walked in on the conversation.

She is quick to offer, "Oh my gosh, I was outside for hours. The pollen is worse this year than I remember. I've been stuffy all day. Do you have any tissues in here?" I know she was sitting outside for a while, so maybe it really is just allergies, but I get the sense it's more likely that there are also some memories making her emotional. It's okay if she doesn't feel ready to share those with me yet.

I nod at the glove box and she opens the latch. Danielle glares at me as she pulls something out.

"What is this?"

I see it too late, the pill bottle in her hand.

"Wait. They aren't mine." The words fly out of my mouth.

She closes her eyes. Her lips stretch into a thin, hard line, and my stomach drops.

"This bottle has Jordan's name on it. Why are Jordan's pills in your truck?"

Dammit, Jordan.

"I guess he forgot them." I know how it sounds, but she has to believe me, right? I'm telling her the truth.

"Mike, you have to know how this looks. This morning I saw a photo of you at a party surrounded by alcohol, and now you're telling me Jordan forgot that his…*acetaminophen with codeine* was in your truck?" She emphasizes the words as she reads them. After the discussion we had last night, I understand why Danielle is upset about the pills. I'm not sure how she came across that photo from last night, but I haven't done anything wrong.

"You said you were sober, but this is an opioid. It's a narcotic," Danielle says, her eyes glued to the little orange bottle in her lap. "I don't know what I'm supposed to believe."

As if I didn't know that. I bet I could list every opioid on the market in under a minute if someone asked. "Look, you have every right to be skeptical. I don't know how Jordan could have forgotten. But I didn't know they were there." It sounds like a lame excuse, the kind I used to give my mom when she would ask why the money was missing from her wallet.

Danielle dumps the contents of the bottle into her hand.

"What are you doing?"

"Isn't it obvious? I'm worried about you. First that picture, and now there are narcotics in your car." She picks through the medication in her hand. "The bottle says they issued thirty pills, Mike. The date on this prescription is yesterday. Why are more than half of them missing already?"

"Are you serious?"

"There are only twelve pills here. Where are the other eighteen?"

"What?" I can't believe this is happening. "Do you think I'd be thinking straight enough to have this conversation if I took eighteen pills?"

"How should I know what you did with them? Maybe you stashed them somewhere? Maybe you sold them? Just tell me the truth."

I blink at her. "I am. I don't know where the other pills are."

She doesn't answer, she just draws a shaky breath and shakes her head. This is bad.

"I can tell you this much, if I had known those pills were there I might have been tempted. But I didn't." All I can do is be honest with her. "I know how it sounds, but…"

She doesn't let me finish the thought before cutting me off. "Stop the truck."

"Seriously? You're being ridiculous. Just talk to Jordan, he'll tell you." I should know better than to call a woman ridiculous or say that she is acting crazy. That's like one step away from blaming the fact that she is mad on her period. But what am I supposed to say if she *is* being ridiculous and she *does* have her period? "Those pills are not mine. It's that simple. Ask him."

Except I know it's not.

"Jordan? Your roommate who was drinking with you last night, and then had his pills around you? Never mind the photo and the bottle I saw with my own eyes, that's the guy you want me to believe?"

"No, actually, I'm the guy I want you to believe."

"Stop the truck, Mike. I'd like to get out now."

"Danielle, come on. I haven't used for three years. I'm telling you those aren't mine." I've said that last sentence plenty of times before, but the difference is this time it's true.

"Clearly, they are not yours. That's why they have another person's name on them. But that doesn't really mean much, does it? You said so yourself. Things belonging to someone else never stopped you from taking them before. You told me that."

Her words steal the breath right out of my lungs. It's only been one day since I told her about my addiction. She's already throwing things in my face that happened years ago. Things she knows nothing about. Not really.

I once took a fastball in the sternum. I swear that hurt less than this. But what sucks the most, as much as I hate it, is that I understand. After what I've told her about taking meds from my grandmother and what happened with my dad, why would she take my word for it when some pretty damning evidence just fell into her lap? Logically, she shouldn't. I guess I just hoped she really saw me. I need her to believe I am a better man now than I used to be. Clearly, she does not.

I hit the steering wheel in frustration and she jumps. *Shit.* I need to rein it in.

"I'm sorry. I didn't mean to scare you." I squeeze the wheel until my knuckles are white and try to keep my voice calm.

All of the softness in Danielle is gone, and she is all business when she speaks again. "Michael, I asked you to pull over. I'm not comfortable with you driving right now."

I'm Michael now? I don't think I have ever heard her use my full name that way. The only time I have seen her anywhere close to this angry is when Jake interrupted our date. Her contempt has never been directed at me. This is different. She isn't just mad, she's legitimately frightened. I hate it.

"You honestly think I would get behind the wheel with you if I were high?"

"Pull. Over." Her voice is firm, but her body language is killing me. I can tell by the way she is leaning away from me with one hand on the door handle that I'm scaring her. Just by sitting here. She's uncomfortable because of me. Or at least what she thinks of me.

My chest cracks in half as I fight against every instinct I have to pull her toward me, and I roll the truck to a stop on the side of the gravel road. But then a new wave of righteous anger hits.

"I have been sober the entire time we have known each other, not to mention years before that. I work damn hard every day to stay that way."

Yet, obviously Danielle still doesn't trust me, and that is bullshit because I have never lied to her. Not once. Not about anything important. The only thing even close was asking to ride back to North Bay with her after the gala, and I have no regrets about that.

I didn't have to tell her about my past, but I did because I'm invested in making a real go of this thing between us. Apparently, she can't see that. This blows. How long am I going to have to pay for the choices I made when I was nineteen?

As soon as we are stopped, she opens her door and hops down into the grass.

"Danielle. Please. Get back in the car," I say through gritted teeth.

"I can't do that. I need a minute to think." She puts her hands on her hips and tilts her head toward the sky, like she's searching for answers in the clouds. After a deep inhale, she sneezes twice. Maybe she wasn't totally lying about the allergies. I lean over and get the tissues out of the glove compartment. When I toss them to her gently, she catches them and sighs a reluctant "Thank you." I just grunt. Even if she can't stand me right now, and I'm pretty pissed right back at her if we're being honest, I can't seem to stop wanting to take care of her.

I get out and slam the door then sit on the tailgate while Danielle paces back and forth. She alternates between chewing on her thumbnail and wrapping her arms around her stomach. She isn't talking to me, but I want her to know I am right here in this with her and I'm not going anywhere. So while she mutters to herself and pokes angrily at her phone, I sit still, frozen on the back of my truck until Alice pulls up in her Volkswagen and parks behind me. I'm still sitting and watching helplessly when Danielle gets into her friend's car and they drive away. I have no choice but to get back into my truck alone. Now it's just me and the bottle of pills she left on the front seat.

Chapter 18

Mike

Opening the door to Jordan's bedroom in the dark, all I can make out is an oversized lump on the bed, so that's where I aim when I throw the bottle. The pills land with a soft, unsatisfying thud on the mound of blankets covering my roommate.

"Thanks a lot, asshole," I say, loudly enough to wake him.

"What the hell, man?" He opens his eyes and rubs his face with both hands. "What's going on?" He switches on the lamp next to his bed and looks around the room, then his eyes land on me, and finally, down at the medicine resting on his comforter.

"I told Danielle everything. Then she found your pills in my truck."

"Oh, shit. You told her? That's a big step, right?" He takes the small bottle into his hand. "I was wondering where these were. I'm sorry. For real. I didn't realize I left them in your car."

"Why didn't you tell me they were gone?"

"The over-the-counter stuff was working out okay, and I felt stupid for losing the pills two seconds after asking you for a ride to pick them up." He rubs his eyes. "I remember now that I pulled them out to take one at Taco Terrace, but I dropped the bottle and spilled half of them in the parking lot. Then I forgot I stashed the rest of them in your glove box. Honestly, I didn't remember doing it until you came in here. Between the beer and cigars and the meds, I was pretty toasted. I just knew they were gone, and I didn't want to ask you to go back out looking for my missing drugs with me. Guess I thought that could be triggering for you or something."

Jordan knew his meds were gone and didn't remember why, but he didn't blame me? I shake my head because I almost can't compute that thought. He trusted me. No one has given me the benefit of the doubt for years. It's still his fault that I am in this mess, but now I want to hug him almost as much as I want to pound him, although the anger is still winning.

"Yeah, well, Danielle thought I stole them. Blamed me the second she laid eyes on that bottle, and didn't even give me a chance to explain."

"That's harsh. Obviously, you didn't take any. I dropped them. They are probably pulverized all over Taco Terrace's pavement if she wants to go check."

"There are twelve left. You can count them."

"I don't need to count them, dude."

As much as I appreciate the sentiment, I think I actually want him to count the pills. I need someone else to confirm I didn't do what Danielle is accusing me of doing. If there are still twelve pills in that bottle, it proves I could be trusted to overcome the temptation on my way here.

"Please."

Jordan rolls his eyes but sits up straighter and dumps the contents of the bottle into the palm of his hand. He counts one-by-one as he places each pill back into the container. Of course, there are a dozen pills, just like Danielle said. Not a single one has gone missing since we found the bottle. Even though I knew that's what was going to happen, I blow out a long, slow sigh of relief.

As much as it hurts to know that Danielle doesn't trust me yet, it's good to see that Jordan does, and it also feels damn good to realize that I could trust myself today. I didn't say anything to Danielle that I regret. We were fighting, but I kept my head on and didn't let anything get out of hand. I had opioids in my grasp after a heated argument, I was under a lot of stress, but I didn't even think about taking any of the pills. I didn't stash them for myself or try to trade them up for something stronger. Instead, my instinct was to drive here and hand them over to Jordan. That's progress.

I'm still pissed at the situation, but I'm almost proud of myself for being able to handle it. Almost. Even though my own dad and the woman I've fallen for both think I'm still a loser. I suck in another shaky breath and run my hand through my hair.

"Thanks for trusting me, I guess."

"Yeah, man. Of course. We need to hug now or something?"

"Shut up."

Jordan puts the bottle in the top drawer of his nightstand to signal that we are finished talking about this and he changes the subject.

"Are you going to tell your folks about Family Night at the ballpark? It's coming up pretty soon. They might need time to make a plan if they want to come."

I shrug. "I was thinking about texting my sisters, but I doubt they can make it."

"I didn't ask about your sisters."

"I know." The door closes behind me as I leave his room.

Family Night has been the last thing on my mind. It's a long way from Idaho to Virginia. I don't expect them to make the trip, but Coach says we need more butts in seats or we will be in danger of facing more budget cuts. He worked with the marketing team to get this event on the schedule, and he wants us to invite as many friends and family members as possible. He's convinced that if we can pack the stadium the newly generated interest in the team would appease the higher-ups and get them off his back about the money, at least for a little while. I was planning to ask Danielle to bring her crew, but who knows if that has any chance of happening now? I hate the way we left things.

I head to the kitchen because I need to eat something, but there's no way I can stomach that carbonara now without thinking of Danielle. Instead, I pop a plate of leftover chicken breast and broccoli into the microwave and think about her anyway. Sitting down in front of the TV with my dinner in my lap, I can't taste anything because I'm numb inside. I allow myself to shoot off one text to the woman I hope is still my girlfriend.

Hope you made it home safe. I promise I had nothing to do with those pills. If you want to talk more, I'll be here.

There. The ball is in her court. I'm not going to chase her. She's the one who needs to figure out what she wants. Either she trusts me or she doesn't. It's that simple. But if she does want to be with me, she's going to have to meet me where I am. I can't go backwards to a place where the most important people in my life are always walking a tightrope around me, waiting for me to screw up. At the first sign of trouble, she jumped to the worst possible conclusion. That's not fair to either one of us. For now, all I can do is hope that she will realize I'm not that guy anymore, and I never have been that guy around her.

I turn the channel to ESPN in time to catch the last ten minutes of *SportsCenter*. Jordan comes in and flops down next to me with a bag of shelled sunflower seeds in his hand. He holds them out to offer me some, but I shake my head.

"They show the highlights from the Phillies game yet?"

"I don't know." I shrug. "I'm not really paying attention."

"She hasn't called?" He nods toward the phone in my hand, which I've been checking every two seconds.

"She was probably too good for me anyway." I try to sound indifferent, but it just comes out bitter. "I'm not boyfriend material."

"Oh, come on. Enough with the whole 'I don't deserve anything good in my life because I made some mistakes when I was nineteen' sobfest. Don't sell yourself short, man. You're a different person now. No one worth being with is going to fault you for having a story. We all have them. We move past our shit and grow up. Growth is a good thing." Jordan leans back and crosses his arms. I get the impression that mine is not the only story he's referencing, but he can tell me about his baggage later. Tonight, it's my turn to sulk.

If only it were true that no one blames us for our pasts, but it's not. I lost my relationship with my dad and now things with Danielle seem to be over before they really started just because of who I used to be.

"I can't grow if people keep cutting me down," I argue.

"What are you talking about? I told you I'm sorry about the pills, man. But you're in rare form tonight. This has to be about more than just Danielle finding the prescription."

"It is about that. But yeah, there's other stuff, sure. My own dad won't speak to me. I can't earn a starting spot even though I'm working my ass off. Oh, and our entire team thinks I'm someone I'm not. They have no idea I'm an addict, and I can't tell them because look what happens as soon as people find out." I throw up my hands, then immediately bring them down and cross them across my chest, bouncing my knees.

"Yeah, all of that sucks. But you know what? Just own it," Jordan says, seeming annoyed. "Move forward. Stop letting this control you." I don't know if the "this" he is talking about is Danielle or my addiction, but either way, this impromptu speech of his is rubbing me the wrong way. She is not just some girl I saw a few times. I've never felt this way about anyone. I don't want to move forward from her. But I don't know how to move past all the things I've done. If I did, I would have done that a long time ago. I've been holding in too much for too long, and his lame advice is the spark that makes me explode.

"I'll own my shit as soon as you do. At least I make an attempt to own mine. I went after what I wanted with Danielle. I told her the truth. What the hell are you doing about your own life? All I see is a guy criticizing me for not doing things exactly the way he wants."

"I'm not criticizing you, dude. I'm just trying to help. You're not really owning it though, are you? If you were, you would be out there fighting to save what you have with the first person who has made you happy since I met your grumpy ass. Instead you're sitting here, sulking on this couch."

"Well, let me just get a notebook so I can jot down this sage wisdom from the king of functional relationships. Oh, wait. That's right. You're also sitting here alone, except you're pretending you can blame that insane vow when we both know your real problem is you."

It's a low blow that he doesn't deserve. He is just trying to help me. My words hit their mark, just like I intended, but instead of fighting back Jordan decides to take the high road. It's too bad, because it would have felt good to punch something tonight. He pushes himself off the couch, then walks down the hall and shuts himself back in his bedroom. The guilt hits me immediately, and I come crashing down just as fast as I went off.

"Come on, don't be like that," I call after him. It's not an apology, but it's all I've got right now.

Own it? Easy for him to say. What does that even mean? I already put in the work. I went to treatment. I go to the meetings. Why can't that ever be enough? I don't want to be forced to announce my flaws to the world. I don't want my addiction to be the thing that defines me for the rest of my life, the thing that makes people suspicious every time I walk past a prescription sitting out on their counter, or the reason they aren't sure if they can trust me around their kids.

But it is, and I don't know if I will ever be able to change that.

Chapter 19

Mike

When I still haven't heard from Danielle four days later, it is not looking good. At least we have a stretch of away games to serve as a distraction. Our hotel has a wall of windows overlooking the Pocono Mountains. There are trees and rolling green hills for miles. The ski slopes are covered in thick grass during their off-season, which is peak playing time for us. It must be incredible up here when it snows. Maybe I can come back with some of the guys over the winter, not that we are actually allowed to ski. Our contracts specifically forbid it, but this place has a cool vibe, and we could hit up the pool tables and hot tubs.

For now, I'm sitting with my teammates and drinking a seltzer water at the hotel bar while they nurse their beers after a tough loss to the Pocono Avalanche. They think I'm pouting because our team didn't win. As much as I hate to lose, that's not the reason for this funk I'm in. I wish I could call Danielle and talk to her about how much all of this sucks, but right now she is the biggest part of my problem. The other part, that small and unrelenting voice of constant regret, is all me. It's eating at me that, other than Jordan, none of these guys even know why Danielle left. They think what I had with her was just a casual hook-up with a local that ran its course, and I'm sitting here acting like that's the case when it couldn't be further from the truth. I haven't known her long, but somehow this woman has become an important part of my life. Which is exactly what I wanted to avoid.

"Hey, Rookie," Lincoln calls from a few stools down. "You look like you could use something stronger."

"Nah." I shake my head. I might have a laundry list of problems, but there's only one thing on it I can control, and I'm taking the reins back on this one. I slap the palm of my hand flat against the bar top then tap it down twice more to get everyone's attention. I'm tired of the shame and drama attached to dragging my addiction along quietly everywhere I go. I don't want to keep this secret from the team anymore.

"Hey, um." I clear my throat and a couple of heads turn my way. "Just so you guys know, I'm sober." I make my impromptu announcement.

"Well, that can be rectified pretty fast. Somebody get the rookie over there a drink."

"No, I mean on purpose. Been that way for three years. Just thought I should tell you."

It feels awkward to say the words out loud, but it was easier to get that out than I thought it would be. Jordan steps up behind me and rests a hand on my shoulder while a few of the other guys offer small gestures of support. A nod from Davis. A thumbs-up from Lincoln.

"Oh. Okay."

"Cool."

"Yeah, I noticed you never drink. Is it a health or a religious thing, or something else?" Smithy asks, no filter as always.

"I had a problem with pills a few years back. Now I just try to stay off of everything."

"Gotcha."

There are a few more murmurs and nods, and I feel Jordan's grip tighten to squeeze my shoulder, but overall, my reveal is not nearly as big of a deal as I made it out to be in my head. Most of the guys jump right back into their previous conversations.

"We cool?" I turn to ask Jordan.

"Yeah, man. No hard feelings. Way to own it." He pats my back.

"Can you pass those pretzels over here?" Rodriguez calls from down the bar. "And for the record, you're not the only one not drinking."

"That's just because you're still too young to order alcohol, kid. We had to bring our own beer to your apartment. Should I get you an apple juice? Or maybe a Shirley Temple?" Smithy stands to put Rodriguez in a headlock and gives him a noogie like a big brother would, and Jordan goes over to join in. Over the past few months, these guys really have started to feel more like family. North Bay is starting to seem like a place I could actually make a home. Now if only Danielle would call me back.

Davis slides onto the stool next to mine and helps himself to a handful of the pretzels from the basket on the bar. He takes a sip of his drink and nods at me.

"Hey, Rookie. You looked good out there today."

Coach has been playing me more since the charity scrimmage. It's obvious that he is phasing Davis out, but the guy doesn't seem to have any hard feelings about it. I think he's ready to hang up his glove and move on to the next step, whatever that is for him.

"Thanks, but we still lost."

"Yeah, it happens." He shrugs and takes another sip.

"What are your plans for next year? Do you know what you'll be doing yet?" I realize how awkward the question is after I ask it. Either he has to find a way to sound humble about an offer the rest of us would kill for, or he has to admit no one wants him. As far as I know, he hasn't received any offers and his contract is ending.

"I dunno, man. I can't believe I'm almost done playing ball. I'm ready, but I'm not sure what to do without it. That diamond's been there for every part of my life, you know?"

"I do."

It's the same for me. I can't remember a time when I wasn't on the field.

"Been thinking of sticking around North Bay, maybe picking up some odd jobs. I took an old mattress to the dump for Edna Plum last week, and ever since she has been telling all of her friends that I can haul their junk. I have twelve more appointments lined up next month. It's actually turning into kind of a lucrative side gig. These older folks need someone to help them downsize all their stuff when they retire or move into assisted living."

"Huh." I don't know what else to say, because what do you say to the man you're replacing on a pro team when he tells you he will be leaving your dream job in order to drag trash to the dump for elderly widows?

"Let me know if you ever need a hand with something. I have the truck." Let's go with that. Probably better than *thanks for giving up on your dream so I can take over your spot*.

"Thanks, Miller."

"Yep."

After that, we sit quietly and nurse our drinks before everyone starts to peel off and head up to the rooms to get some sleep.

Before I go to bed, I check my phone one more time, but just like every day since our fight, there aren't any notifications from Danielle. The turmoil from the past few days is making me exhausted, so I set my alarm to sleep in as much as I can before I need to get down to the bus.

In the morning, before the alarm goes off, my phone wakes me up anyway. For a millisecond, I allow myself to hope it's her, but of course it's not. It's my mother.

"Hi, Mom." I answer on the third ring, my voice still rough with sleep.

"Mikey," she greets me with her patented mom energy and the same nickname she has used since I was a kid. "You'll never guess what's happening soon." She stretches out the words with a sing-song lilt in her voice.

"Can I have a hint?" I play along, groggily.

She doesn't bother giving one, but launches straight to her reason for calling. "The Coffin Conference is in Virginia Beach this year, so we're going to be on your side of the country. Maddy and Mandy are going to visit Aunt Jeanie in Quebec, so they can't make it this time. But Shelley is tagging along with us. She wants to scope out those east coast law schools. We figured we could stay a few extra days and make it a beach getaway. Maybe we can even swing by one of your games while we are close by."

The event is not actually called the Coffin Conference. That is just the nickname Maddy gave the business convention my dad attends every year, and my parents thought it was so hilarious they have called it that ever since. Conveniently, this year it's being held in the same state where I am living, and my mom sounds way more thrilled about this news than I am.

Virginia Beach is two hours south of North Bay, but it's an easy day trip. Definitely closer than Idaho. East Coast beaches are still pretty cold in May, but I'm sure the Miller women will find a way to make it fun. My mom and sisters always do.

"Oh yeah? That sounds nice. It would be great to see you at a game, Mom." It doesn't go unnoticed that the conference will give my dad a perfectly reasonable excuse not to see me. I consider mentioning Family Night, but I've learned by now that having expectations only leads to disappointment. If they're going to come to a game, I want it to be because they want to be there. I'm not going to guilt them into attending a specific event.

"Oh, I would love that. You're welcome to join us for a beach day, too, if you can get away. Although, I'm sure you will have a packed schedule of games and practices while we're there. I can't believe my son is a *professional athlete* now." She whispers the second half of her sentence with a reverence that somehow adds even more emphasis than if she had screamed the words. Then she lets out a little squeal of excitement she must have been holding inside. That's my mom. Beverly Miller was Miss Corncob 1996 and is still an avid cheerleader for each of her kids. Even the screwup of the bunch.

"Your father is so proud."

Her words land in my gut, and I grunt into the phone. I know she is just trying to make me feel good. She hates the rift between my dad and me probably as much as I do. But if it were true, if he were actually proud, then he would come to the phone and tell me himself. He wouldn't hide behind the Coffin Conference and his business trip. He would come out for my games or send me emails about the latest trades. We could compare Wordle scores in the morning or Facetime while I'm shaving, like that one commercial with the father and son. We would talk about old times the same way Honey and Danielle reminisce about their games of Pick My Poison. Those things are not happening, so it's a waste of time to even think about them.

I swallow a lump of emotion and clear my throat. I don't acknowledge what she said about Dad any further. Instead, I redirect the conversation so my mom can do what she does best: talk about my sisters.

"How's Shelley doing? I heard she broke it off with that guy, right?" I say, even though I've heard nothing at all. I'm not in the habit of keeping up with my sisters' dating lives, but Shelley never stays with anyone for long, and I know this will get my mom to talk about something else.

"Ugh. Yes. George. Nice enough boy, but he was never right for her. Too myopic. Shelley is going to have a big life. She needs someone who won't be threatened by her ambition, who can handle her big dreams."

"Well, good luck to whatever poor fool thinks he can handle Michelle Miller." I laugh because there is no one who can handle Shelley. She practically has a PhD in ballbusting.

"He'll come along," Mom says as if it's a fact, just as Jordan knocks on my door.

"Got anything to eat?" When he sees I'm on the phone, he apologizes. "Sorry. Didn't realize you were talking to someone. Wait. Is that Danielle?"

I shake my head. "It's my mom."

"Hi, Jordan," my mom yells into the phone so my roommate will be able to hear her. I wince and rub my ear, then turn it on speaker for the last part of our conversation. She greets him again.

"How are you doing, Mrs. Miller?" Jordan asks.

"Certainly can't complain. I'm headed your way to visit the beach, and now I find myself talking to two handsome baseball players at once. You've made my day."

"Mom." I roll my eyes, but Jordan chuckles at the compliment.

I scrounge up two granola bars from my bag, hand one to him, and tear into the other one.

"Well, good luck with your next game against the Dolphins, gentlemen," she tells us in that way moms have of slipping little details into the conversation to prove they are paying attention to your life. I would not be surprised to learn that she still has my schedule up on the refrigerator, under the purple turtle magnet, just like she did from the time I was in Little League, all the way through college.

"Thanks, Mom. Love you."

"I love you too, Mikey. Always," she says. "And buh-bye, Jordan."

"Bye," we both say at once.

Jordan houses the granola bar and steals a sports drink and an apple from my minifridge.

"Did you tell her about Family Night?" My annoying friend asks the same question he did the other day.

"What do you think?"

Jordan narrows his eyes and shakes his head, letting me feel his disapproval, but thankfully, he lets it drop. I don't know why he cares so much.

Chapter 20

Danielle

As I'm stacking plates from the empty tables at the end of my shift, I notice Jordan enter The Blue Crab with a woman who looks vaguely familiar. They take a step apart when they see me looking. Interesting. I don't think I know her, but I swear with her dark blonde hair and crazy long legs she almost looks like Mike. Oh, that's it. I think I recognize her from the pictures tacked up on his door.

"Danielle," Jordan greets me. "This is Mike's oldest sister, Michelle, but pretty much everyone calls her Shelley."

"It's a way to help keep all of the 'M' names straight around my house," Shelley says.

Then he tells her, "This is Danielle Daniels. If you need someone to teach you how to pick a crab, she has been known to provide her services." He doesn't offer another title for me because who knows what Mike and I are to each other right now. I suppose Jordan would have no reason to introduce me as his own friend either, although it stings a little to know he doesn't think of me as one.

"Hi, Jordan. Nice to meet you, Shelley. Do you need a table?" I act professional and treat them like all of my other customers.

Shelley smiles warmly at me. "No, we're actually here to pick up the takeout order my parents called in. I was told you serve an amazing seafood club sandwich."

Mike's parents are in town? Both of them? Is he speaking with his dad now? How much have I missed since we had our fight? I stumble through my thoughts before finally answering her.

"Um, yeah. We do. That's my favorite thing on the menu, actually."

"Oh, you don't say." She elbows Jordan softly in the ribcage before she excuses herself to go pick up their order. It's waiting in foam boxes in front of the kitchen window. Jordan stays behind and rocks on his heels.

"Hey, look, whatever is going on between you and Miller is none of my business, but you should know one thing. I put the pills in his truck. He really didn't know they were there."

Looks like the time for small talk is over and we are doing this now. I sigh, balancing the tray of discarded dishes on my hip.

"That's what he told me. Said he had no idea how eighteen pills were suddenly missing one day after the date on the bottle. I suppose you have an answer for that?" I don't mean for the question to come out sharp and accusatory, but it does. This whole mess hurts, and I'm not good at hiding my feelings.

"I get that it looked bad, but I swear he didn't know. We had just picked up my prescription at the pharmacy. When we stopped for dinner I took a pill, but I dropped the bottle and spilled about half of it in the parking lot. He was already inside and didn't see it happen. I wasn't thinking, and I shoved the rest of them in the glove box and went in to meet up with him. Then I forgot to bring the bottle inside when we got home. That's on me. Anyway, I'm sorry."

I search Jordan's eyes for any signs that he might be making up a story to cover for Mike, but he seems sincere. I can tell by the way his face twists while he looks at the ground that he truly regrets leaving the pills in the truck. He doesn't strike me as the kind of guy who would lie about something like this. We both know that not only did it cause Mike to have a fight with me, but it could have derailed his friend's sobriety, which is so much worse. Then it hits me that I did the exact same thing. I also left the pills with Mike when I walked away.

Suddenly it's harder to breathe. The weight of my own role in this situation hits me like a freight train. Mike was telling the truth the whole time. I didn't even give him a chance before I threw a bunch of blame onto him that he didn't deserve, and then I left. I was so worried that he wouldn't stick around or that he couldn't handle a relationship, but I ended up being the one to bail at the first sign of trouble. Not only did I leave, I left him alone with narcotics.

"Oh, shit."

"That's the same thing I said."

Edna Plum walks by and takes the tray from me. "Better watch that mouth around the customers, Dee, or Honey might come by and wash your mouth out with my dish soap." She smiles to let me know she is teasing. Our customers have heard her and Honey both say much worse. "Your shift is over, darlin'. Go ahead and get home." She tilts her chin toward the door, encouraging me to hurry up.

"You're off now? Perfect," Shelley says, coming back with two plastic bags full of takeout in each hand. "Join us at the Marnock Hotel for dinner?"

"Oh. Um, thanks for the offer, but I can't," I lie. Actually, it's only a half-lie. I do have the time to join them for dinner, but I'm too ashamed. I don't know if I can face Mike yet, and I certainly don't think I am ready to meet his entire family. Besides, I still have a lot of thinking to do.

Shelley nods and looks at Jordan.

"If you talk to Mike, don't tell him about his family being in town yet, okay? We're planning to surprise him and bring them all out for Family Night at the stadium tomorrow."

"Sure. I hope it goes well. I know it will mean a lot to him. Oh, and Jordan? I have something for you." I hold up a finger and motion for him to wait while I grab my purse. Unzipping the front pocket, I pull out the miniature Ninja Turtle figurine I picked up for him. "I saw this in Major Dollar the other day and thought it needed a good home. I've been carrying it around in case I ran into you."

Jordan blinks a few times and swallows hard. "Thank you," he whispers.

Shelley touches his elbow lightly and looks at him with understanding. Something passes between them silently, and I can tell this is an important moment, although I have no idea why. She turns to me and says, "Mike really likes you, Danielle. I hope you know that." She waves as they walk away.

The truth bomb Jordan has dropped seems like it should fix everything, and yet it doesn't. I still don't know the first thing about dating an addict, and my overreaction to finding those pills just proves that. I'm still scared, but I know I need to reach out.

Me: *I saw Jordan today. He told me everything. I believe you. I'm sorry. I still might need some time. This has all been a lot.*

It isn't long before the dots appear to let me know Mike saw my message and he is typing. They disappear and reappear several times. Finally, just two words come back in response: *I understand.*

Chapter 21

Mike

The stadium lights are casting a white glow over the field for our evening game. There is always something magic about playing under the lights. The hum of the electric charge they put in the air and the way the crowd cheers just a little bit louder when they let down their guard after dark adds another layer of enthusiasm. The stands are more crowded than usual, I guess Coach was onto something about Family Night. Stepping up to the plate, I tap the bat against each of my cleats before hoisting it over my shoulder. I check my stance and raise my elbow a bit higher. Ever since the shoulder injury, it tends to drop a bit, and I need to be careful to keep it in place. The opposing team's pitcher nods and pulls back for the throw. I can't see their catcher behind me, but I'd be willing to bet he called for a splitter because we've been struggling to hit them all night.

Sure enough, the pitch makes a sharp drop at the end, but I'm ready for it. I make contact and the crack of the bat is the most beautiful sound in the world. The ball flies into the outfield and I take off for first base, then second, and third. I've already sent Rodriguez home when the throw overshoots their third baseman, so I chance it and run for home. It's going to be a close one, but I have to go for it.

"Safe!" the ump calls, as I slide across the plate ahead of the throw.

"Nice, Miller."

"Way to bring it home."

"We might actually have a shot at this one."

My teammates congratulate me in the dugout as I brush the dirt from my pants.

After three more innings with neither team able to score, my run turns out to be the one that helps us clinch the win.

I wish Danielle could have been here to see it, but I am still trying to give her the space she needs. I think I might call in an order for a crab cake sandwich or three from the restaurant after the game. Maybe I can catch her working. Ordering food from North Bay's only restaurant could be a reasonable excuse to see her again without looking desperate. I head to the locker room to grab my gear, but before I can get that far, someone is calling my name.

"Mikey."

I stop mid-stride because I know that voice.

"Shelley?" Turning around, I come face-to-face with my sister. "What are you doing here?"

"We came to see you, dummy." She rolls her eyes and turns her head so her gaze lands on Jordan, who is standing on the edge of the field talking to Coach. Her chin moves up and down as she watches him. "You owe him a thank you. Jordan called us. He wanted to make sure we knew about Family Night. You should have told us yourself, you coward."

Guilty.

"Who is we?"

"Mom was just right here. Oh, there she is." Shelley waves both of her arms over her head to signal where we are standing. My mom walks over and wraps me in a tight hug. Next to her is someone I definitely did not expect to see tonight.

"Dad?"

His beard is longer than the last time I saw him, and there is more gray in it. He steps forward. We're silent for a long, awkward stretch before he finally speaks.

"That was a nice hit in the sixth. You looked sharp, son."

Son.

"Um, thanks."

They are the first words we have spoken in years. The fact that they sound so normal passing between us throws me off-kilter. I brace myself for him to say something harsh and insulting, maybe criticize the at-bat in the second inning when I swung and missed twice before hitting a pop-up, but the negativity doesn't come.

"The team looked good out there."

"Yep." I rock on my heels while he puts his hands in his front pockets. The girls quietly peel off to give us more space. For what, I'm not sure. I don't miss that Shelley goes over to talk to Jordan and part of me wonders how long they've been planning this behind my back, but I have more important things to worry about right now. I have no idea what I'm supposed to say to my dad.

"Uh, the team's been gelling well."

"Good. That's good."

More nodding and awkward silence. I miss Danielle. She would be better at this than I am. She has to make small talk every day with customers at the restaurant, I'm sure she could handle pulling a few words out of my old man.

"Yeah." I take a breath and summon the courage to extend an olive branch. "It's nice that you could make it tonight. I guess you were able to take a night off from the Coffin Conference."

"Mm-hm. North Bay seems like a nice little town. You like it here." It's an observation, a statement rather than a question. He can tell I like this place. A part of me likes knowing my dad can still read me. Another part wants to stay annoyed with him and yell that I could have liked Idaho just fine if he had given me the chance to land on my feet there. I decide to let the grown-up side of me win.

"I do."

I really do. I could see myself settled here in the future. This is Danielle's home, and I want my home to be where she is. I'm not sure when that happened, but it feels true. She says she needs time, but I have to believe she will come around and we'll land on the same page.

"I have a girlfriend," I blurt, even though I'm not sure it's true.

"That's what Shelley said." Dad hooks a thumb over his shoulder in the direction of my sister. "Sounds like you really like her, from what the girls were saying." What else has Jordan been telling them?

"Danielle." Saying her name aloud brings a peace that breaks away some of the cloud of shame and uncertainty over me. My dad is here and he's talking to me. I'm going to say what I need to say while I have the chance. I need to own it. This conversation has been a long time coming. I take a breath and go for it. "I told her everything."

"That so?"

"Yeah, Dad. Look. I know you would probably rather not be here. I'm sorry Mom dragged you along. If you're still ashamed of me, I get it. But I wish you could see I am not that guy anymore."

"Ashamed of you?" He takes a step back and shakes his head. "Mikey, no. If I am ashamed of anyone, it's myself."

"What?"

Seriously, what the hell is he talking about? It takes me a second to process the fact that he is still speaking.

"I said a lot of things that a father should never say. I was angry. At first, I had a right to be. I thought cutting you off would teach you a lesson and you would come crawling back begging. But then you stepped up and turned your life around, and it turned out you didn't need me. Look at you." He uses both hands to gesture at my uniform. "You graduated from college. You're playing pro ball just like you always said you would. I watched you suffering, and I felt so angry and helpless, I didn't know what to do. But I told myself you needed some tough love. I said awful things I can't take back. Then when you got better and made it on your own without me, I felt like an even bigger failure. I knew I screwed up, but I had too much pride to admit it."

"Dad." It's all I have in response. I don't know what else to say. This does not compute. I spent years thinking this man hated every fiber of my being. "What changed?"

"I guess when you work with death every day, eventually you realize life is short, and sometimes you just have to swallow your pride and do the work to repair the wounds. I know it's going to take a while, and I should have been here sooner, but I'm here now. Anyway, I'm sorry."

I'm stunned into silence. I honestly don't know what to say to him. I've been imagining a moment like this for years, waiting for my dad to say those words, and it is surreal that this is actually happening. But the words don't dissolve the pain the way I thought they would. I'm still angry, and I wish those words were never necessary in the first place. We both could have handled things a lot better than we did. I can imagine Shelley rolling her eyes at me and saying, *"Welcome to being human, dumbass. Now go give Dad a hug,"* but my feet won't move from where I'm standing.

Dad nods and moves his hands from the front to back pockets of his jeans. "It might take us a while to find our rhythm again, son, but that's okay. I'm not going anywhere. Now that Maddy has graduated, your sisters are all old enough to handle themselves. Mom and I haven't taken a vacation for a long time, so we've decided to stay here in Virginia for a while. Shelley might stick around, too. She likes it here, and there are some good law schools in the D.C. area."

They're staying? For me? I blink slowly trying to process all of the new information overloading my brain, and I feel a heavy hand land on my shoulder. Coach Johnson takes a step around me and extends his free hand to shake with my dad.

"Mr. Miller, I'm Henry Johnson. Nice to meet you. Mike here has been a great addition to the team this year. Glad y'all could make it out for Family Night."

My dad's face beams with pride, the same way it used to when I was in high school and other parents would tell him his son just might have the talent to go all the way. He calls my mom over to meet Coach, and my sister follows. Mom makes small talk about North Bay for a few minutes and then moves the conversation to Coach Johnson's family. My mother has known the man for less than half an hour, and already she has him telling stories I haven't heard after traveling with him for months. How did I not know he has a daughter who is a junior at a private liberal arts college near Williamsburg, or that his wife just adopted two bichon puppies and they are terrorizing him daily by chewing his favorite socks?

With my parents occupied, I find Jordan hanging out with a few of the guys. He didn't have any family come today. Jordan doesn't talk much about his life before North Bay. I've been so wrapped up in my own drama I never even thought to ask if he was inviting anyone.

"Hey, Rookie. Your parents made it," he says when he sees me walking toward him.

"They did. Thanks, man. Did you ask yours to come?"

"Couldn't even if I wanted to. No idea where they are. Last I heard, my old man was serving time, and my mom hasn't had a permanent address since I was seven."

"Why didn't I know this?"

"You never asked."

"Well, that changes today."

I hold out my hand, and when he shakes it, I pull him in for a hug.

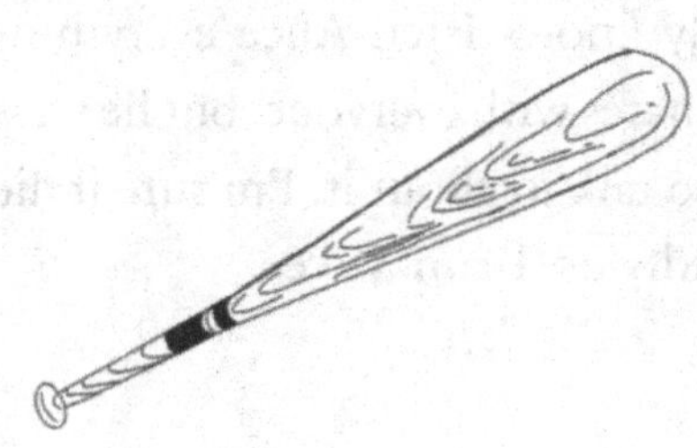

Chapter 22

Danielle

"**O**ne more time," Alice instructs me to tell her the whole story again as we carpool back to Honey's house after our last afternoon classes. There are only a few days left in the semester, and I'm ready to be done. I only groan in response, so she recaps the story herself. "He said they were Jordan's pills, and he had no idea why half of them went missing. But we weren't sure if we believed him. And we haven't spoken to him since. But now Jordan has confirmed Mike was telling the truth, and we still aren't sure how we feel?"

"Correct."

"Would we have believed him about the pills if we didn't know about the addiction? What if he hadn't poured his heart out and shared his past with you? Would this still be a big deal?"

Mike already knows I tell Alice everything. He said his past isn't something he shares with everyone, but he was glad I have a friend I am close enough to talk to about it. I'm sure it didn't hurt that Alice has always been solidly on Team Mike.

"*We* don't know," I say, making air quotes around the "we" because this is clearly a "me" problem, and her question is impossible to answer.

"On one hand, no, I would not be worried about his addiction if I didn't even know there was an addiction in the first place. That's an impossible scenario. How can you be worried about something if you don't know it exists?"

Sure, I would have believed Mike when he said the pills were Jordan's because he has never given me a reason not to trust him. Or at least I thought he hadn't. But seeing the photo and finding the pills on the same day was too much.

"On the other hand, just because I don't know about something does not mean it's not a problem."

Tons of people don't know they are being cheated on or that their partners have secret families. Although I feel like I know Mike well enough to be able to say he would never do those things, I'm sure everyone who has started a relationship with someone who turned out to be a liar felt the same way at the beginning. Plus, that doesn't change the point. Not knowing about a problem wouldn't make it go away. And I *do* know about this. I can't just pretend it never happened.

"Even if I believed him from the beginning, it wouldn't change the reality of what happened. Whether or not it was intentional, Mike is still an addict who was carrying someone else's prescription narcotics around in the glove compartment of his truck."

"That's all true," Alice concedes.

It's something I need to think long and hard about. Even Mike doesn't know for sure what would have happened if he were the one who found the bottle. If I stay with him, this won't be the only time we are around medicine. It's just a part of life. Pills are not an easy thing to avoid, especially in a career like his where people are prone to injuries.

"I can't go back in time and erase the fact that Mike told me about it, and even if I could, I don't think I would want to do that."

"Totally understandable."

I love that he trusted me enough to share the most vulnerable parts of himself. I hate that I can't seem to find that same level of trust to give back. At first, I thought I was protecting myself by not letting things get too serious between us. Now that I've had more than a week to think, I still don't know if I did the right thing after all. The Mike that I know is honest and trustworthy and kind. I want to believe that he can stay sober forever. I think I might actually even love him. But I don't know if that is because my instincts are good and Mike is The One who is going to make my fantasy future a reality, or if I just have an intense crush on a hot, troubled baseball player who is going to tear my heart to shreds if this goes any further.

"Even if we get past all of this and I somehow manage to forget about the pills, there is still the original concern that he can get drafted by another team. One way or another, he will still leave." I let out another loud groan in frustration and cover my face with my hands.

"You already know what I think about that particular concern. You can't let fears about the future rob you of the present. Do you want me to come inside with you?" Alice asks when we pull up to Honey's house.

"No, thanks."

I appreciate the way she is always here for me when I need her, but right now I need to have some space to be alone and think. Once

I'm through the door, I drop my backpack on the kitchen floor, pour myself a glass of milk, and take an entire stack of chocolate chip cookies out of the ceramic jar on the counter. Then I get a pen and a pad of paper from the junk drawer.

Thirty minutes later, I look up when I hear the floorboards creak.

"What has you scrunching your nose? That something for school?" Honey points a bright pink fingernail at the paper on the breakfast bar in front of me. I've been sitting here writing and erasing things from this pros and cons list for the past half an hour. I'm still no closer to deciding what to do. The whole world knows Honey will have an opinion. I guess at this point I might as well ask for it.

Taking a deep breath, I admit, "I really like Mike."

"Sugar, everybody can see that. The two of you can't keep your puppy dog eyes off each other when you're in the same room, not to mention your paws. But I have noticed that boy hasn't been around much. So, what's all this about then?" She nods at my list.

"Well," I start, but don't quite know how to phrase it in a way that will still respect Mike's privacy. He told me about his addiction in confidence. It's not my place to be spreading his business all over town, especially not to a known gossip like Honey. "He told me something about his past, and I'm not sure I can handle it." There. Vague, but truthful.

"I take it you don't want to share that list you're working so hard on?" Honey asks.

I shake my head. "I'd rather not."

"That's okay, don't matter much anyway. It's not telling us anything we didn't already know. Lists and charts are great for helping you make decisions with your head, but they aren't much use when it comes to matters of the heart. What's your heart saying?"

My stupid, reckless heart knows exactly what it wants. That is the problem. It would be so much easier if I didn't care. If this were a casual fling, the pills and who is taking them wouldn't matter. It does matter, though. It matters because Mike matters. He matters to me. And that is terrifying.

"I think he might be the one for me, but I don't know if I can handle that." I put my elbows on the counter and bury my face in my hands.

Honey raps her knuckles on the counter twice. "That's the thing about love, ain't it? Knocks you on your ass every time. But when you find the real thing, it's worth it, even when things get bumpy. I've been around a long time and haven't met a person yet who'd disagree."

It sounds so reasonable coming from Honey's perspective. She didn't have Pop as long as she would have liked— he was only fifty-two when he died— but from what I've heard, they were everything to each other before he passed. She's taken a lover (her words) on occasion in the years since, but never anyone serious. Honey always says no one else could hold a candle to him.

"Whatever that boy told you about his past, do you believe it will stay there? In the past, where it belongs."

"Do I think he's strong enough to move on from it, you mean?" She nods.

"I hope so. It seemed like he had, but this is the sort of thing people have to work hard to keep behind them. He's been fighting this particular demon for a long time. I'm not sure I can trust that it will stay in the past." I hate being this cryptic with her.

"Hmm." Honey nods solemnly. "When he took Jake home I wondered if that might be the case."

"You knew about that?"

She scoffs. "You think I don't know what happens in my own house? Of course I knew. The three of you weren't exactly trying to keep your voices down. I heard how Mike reacted, and I liked that he seemed slow to anger. There are a lot of men who wouldn't take too kindly to someone interrupting their date with such a disrespectful spectacle."

"Yeah, Jake was a mess that night."

"Wasn't the first time. That boy has something weighing on his heart, and he's not going to find the answers where he's been looking. But Mike seemed patient and, more importantly, he had empathy for someone at a low point. I wondered if that wasn't because he's been in a similar boat himself." She quirks an eyebrow and waits for me to confirm. I twist my lips to the side and look at the floor.

"I see," Honey says in response. "Well, I haven't known the man long, but here is what I do know about Michael Miller: He drove my granddaughter home from work, and a week later he kept her calm and got her home safe after a car wreck. He brought me flowers the first time he came around, and he doesn't want to start a relationship with a woman until he has been honest with her about the darker parts of himself. Oh, and he plays for the baseball team. That all sound about right?"

"It does."

"None of that sounds too bad to me, but you're going to have to make this decision for yourself. What I do know is that it's been quite a while since I saw you smile as much as you did while you were sitting on the couch and watching those movies next to him."

"He makes me happy," I admit. He also makes me angry, frustrated, and confused. But mostly happy.

Honey nods. "I'd say the feeling is mutual. He was wearing that same dopey grin that whole evening." She motions to my face.

I'm swept back into the memory of our movie night. Right up until that knock on the door, it truly was perfect. Watching old movies and playing games with Honey and the man I love, eating too much chocolate, giving in to our attraction and sharing an amazing first kiss. I couldn't ask for a better first/fourth date.

I know it's true now. I do love him. But this doesn't feel like the lighthearted romance in Alice's stories or the romcom movies Honey and I like to watch around the holidays. It's heavier because it is complicated and real.

I am still leery of the pills I found, but as far as I know, Mike has always been honest with me. My gut says he's telling the truth, and Jordan has confirmed it. Honey and Alice seem to think it's worth giving this relationship a chance. Maybe they're right.

Jake was right, too. Being with Mike does feel like someone turned up the volume on everything in my life, and that's a great thing, I just didn't realize it was also going to amplify my own insecurities. I should have tried to explain how I was feeling rather than throwing things he told me in confidence back in his face. I got upset and I was afraid I was going to lose him, so I ran. That wasn't fair. I don't like the way we left things between us. He deserves to know what this conversation with Honey has helped me realize. Our fight in the truck only hurt this much because I was already all-in. Now I just need to show him.

Chapter 23

Mike

Brew-Ha-Ha is packed tonight. I hold the door so Shelley and Jordan can enter in front of me. I feel Danielle before I see her, so I freeze on the threshold.

"You're here. Can we talk?" Hearing her voice again makes a dangerous surge of hope run through my veins.

Danielle motions to the grassy area between the building and the parking lot, and I follow her. She's wearing a sweatshirt that hangs loosely off one shoulder and tight black leggings that make it impossible for me not to stare. There's an adorable little nervous bounce in her walk and she fidgets with her fingernails. The fact that she wanted to see me again is encouraging. I think. Unless she called me here so she could officially end things with me in public, with witnesses. But I don't think she would have told me to bring my sister and Jordan along for that.

The text she sent earlier this week didn't give a lot of clues about where she stands. After weeks of radio silence, she reached out to say she talked to Jordan and needed more time. Then things went quiet again until she sent me two sentences.

Would you like to come to Karaoke night at Brew-Ha-Ha on Saturday? Bring anyone you want.

I know it probably seems desperate, but I responded immediately.

I'll be there.

That's all we've said to each other. Until right now.

"It's really good to see you," I tell her.

"Is it, though? After what I did to you. God, Mike I'm so sorry. I didn't know how to handle everything you told me, and then when I saw those pills, I let myself use them as an excuse not to trust you. I ran away at the first chance I got because I thought you would leave me eventually anyway. You were right about everything. You didn't deserve that." A thin sheet of water starts to cover her eyes. I want to touch her, but there are things I need to say first.

"Maybe I didn't. But I also should have fought harder for us. I just sat there and watched you walk away from me, and I didn't do anything to try to stop it. I thought I wasn't good enough for this. I'm working on owning my own shit, too. We both could have handled things differently."

I step toward her and she meets me in the middle and throws her arms around my neck. Waves of relief, joy, and pride run through me. Danielle is mine again. I wrap her in a hug and bury my face in her hair. She squeezes back tightly, then she pulls my face to hers and plants kisses all over my cheeks, nose, and forehead until Alice pops her head out of the doorway.

"You two ever plan to join us?"

Danielle takes my hand and leads me inside. Karaoke wouldn't have been my first choice, but I will gladly follow her anywhere.

I notice Honey across the room sitting with another older woman and offer a small wave to be polite. Danielle tells me the other lady is Edna, her boss from the restaurant. I start to head in their direction, but Shelley calls out from a table in the corner to the left of the stage and beckons us over. Jordan is next to her and Alice is at their table, too. Jake is on the other side of my sister, looking uncomfortable, but to his credit, he stands to shake my hand and give Danielle a hug.

I formally introduce everyone. "You may have already covered this while we were outside, but this is my sister, Shelley, and my roommate, Jordan. Shelley, Jordan, meet Danielle's friends, Jake and Alice."

This should be an interesting evening. But I told myself to be on my best behavior, and I will. I've come out on top. Danielle is still mine, and I'm not going to do anything stupid to screw it up, like gloat in front of Jake. At least I won't make it obvious. If I happen to get a little bit handsy with her in front of the guy, so sue me. He'll live.

Danielle sits down at the round table next to Alice. I take the seat between Danielle and Jake. Three high schoolers are on the stage, screeching their way through a death metal song I don't recognize.

"Have you guys been waiting long?" Danielle raises her voice over the—let's be generous and call it "music."

"Nah, we only got here a few minutes ago," Jake answers.

Alice leans in to ask, "So, what are we all singing tonight?" Danielle shoots her a look.

Do they think I will be getting on stage? Because that is not happening. Next to me, Danielle rubs her hands together and giggles.

"Blue Moon?"

"A classic, but a little slow," Alice says, while Jake sits quietly, sipping from a paper cup and listening to them speak. I try to make myself tall and not fidget in the chair next to him. As the girls get deeper into their discussion, I realize how much I have underestimated their commitment to the karaoke portion of the evening. By the time Alice turns to me, I'm already dreading her question.

"What's your favorite karaoke song, Miller?"

"Can't say I have one." I shrug and try to play it cool. I'm a terrible singer and an even worse dancer, but I know better than to show weakness in front of women like Alice and my sister. If I don't perform tonight, they will never let me forget it.

"We could always do *You've Got a Friend in Me* again," Jake offers.

That little hint of competition gives me all the courage I need. I'm not spending my first hours back with Danielle sitting here watching Jake reenact the best parts of his history with my girl. I will put my name down in all of the available time slots and spend the next hour belting out every song from *The Little Mermaid* soundtrack before I let that happen. Realizing Danielle would actually love that makes me chuckle to myself, which earns me a glare from Jake, who thinks I'm laughing at him. I lean my head to the side and stretch my neck.

"Danielle and I have been practicing our performance of *One Headlight*," I say, trying to project more confidence than I feel. I mean, we did sing it together. Once. Danielle is biting her bottom lip, trying to rein in a smile at my reference to our first road trip.

There is a feisty challenge in her eyes when she says, "I can't wait for everyone to hear it. Although, I did promise to do a song with Honey first."

Well, challenge accepted, baby. I push my chair out from the table and walk over to the sign-up sheet to add our names to the list. Jake doesn't say much else besides the occasional grunt or "uh-huh" if someone asks him a direct question, but I can feel his eyes on me for most of the night. I thought he was supposed to be away at college? Did he come home again just for this? He's at a different school, so maybe his semester ended earlier than Danielle's.

After we sit and listen through six more acts, the announcer finally calls Danielle and Honey to the stage. And, apparently, Edna? Then Alice gets up to join them, followed by my sister. What the hell is going on?

Jake conveniently excuses himself to go to the restroom. He clearly wants no part in whatever this is. I glance over at Jordan, but he shrugs like he's as clueless as I am.

There's a cardboard box on the side of the stage, and each of the women takes out a colorful feather boa and sunglasses before shuffling into a semicircle behind Danielle as she grabs microphone.

"So, um, hi everyone." There are a few murmured greetings directed back at her. Then Danielle says, "A few weeks ago, I met this really special guy, but I made a mistake, and after a misunderstanding I said some really hurtful things to him. I wish I could go back in time to take it all back. Since I can't do that, I thought a public groveling was the next best thing. I really am sorry, Mike."

The music starts and Danielle begins to sing Cher's *If I Could Turn Back Time* as low as her voice will allow her to go. I laugh along with everyone else. A second apology wasn't necessary, but I'm enjoying the show. She's ridiculous and I can't take my eyes off her. I want to take her home and peel off those leggings. Her smile gets wider and she winks at me from the stage like she can read my mind and she's thinking the same thing. I think I'm in love with this woman.

The ladies behind her perform a comically bad choreographed dance routine. Clearly, they put a lot of thought into this, even if they aren't executing it well. Their hearts are in it, but none of them have the rhythm the dance requires. There is a lot of arm pumping and hip shaking. What they lack in skill they make up for in enthusiasm. By the end of the song, Honey and Shelley are both off the stage, sharing their boas with people in the crowd and attempting to get everyone clapping along.

When the music stops, Danielle is out of breath when she leans into the microphone and says, "Mike, I promise from now on I will try to own my stuff, too."

My face is already sore from smiling so much when I stand up to clap.

The announcer joins Danielle on the stage and talks into the mic for a second.

"Speaking of these two lovebirds, it looks like they are next to perform. Stay right there, Danielle. Let's also welcome North Bay's new shortstop, Mike Miller, to the stage, please. Get on up here." He motions for me to join them, so I practically jump up onto the stage, needing to be close to my girl. Needing everyone in this room to know Danielle is mine.

"Hey." Danielle looks at me as she takes the microphone back again.

"Hey." I grin at her. There's softness in my voice that isn't usually there. Only she can bring it out of me, just like she's the only one who could ever get me to agree to sing in front of half the town like this.

We lean in to share the mic. When the music starts again, we miss the first cue. She and I are singing the lyrics at completely different times. I don't know how to match the rhythm of the music to the words lighting up on the screen in front of us, and Danielle is no better. We are terrible and off-key. None of it matters. By the end we are both laughing so hard that it is almost difficult to breathe. Danielle uses a finger to blot a tear away from her eye and smears her mascara. I reach out and cup her cheek with my hand and use my thumb to wipe the dark smudge from her face, and we stand frozen, eyes locked on each other.

"What are you waiting for? Kiss her already!" Honey's voice booms from the back of the crowd, and laughter erupts below us. Danielle's grandmother is quickly becoming my favorite wing woman. I don't hesitate to take her advice and lean in. All of the tables at Brew-Ha-Ha clap and holler for us as I kiss Danielle on stage.

When we pull apart, I whisper in her ear, "Are you ready for that dinner date now?" She knows exactly what I'm asking, and when she nods, it feels like my entire world has finally clicked back into place. As we return to our table, Jake's seat is still empty, but Alice gives us a slow clap. Jordan nods at me and raises his voice over the start of the next song. "It's about damn time."

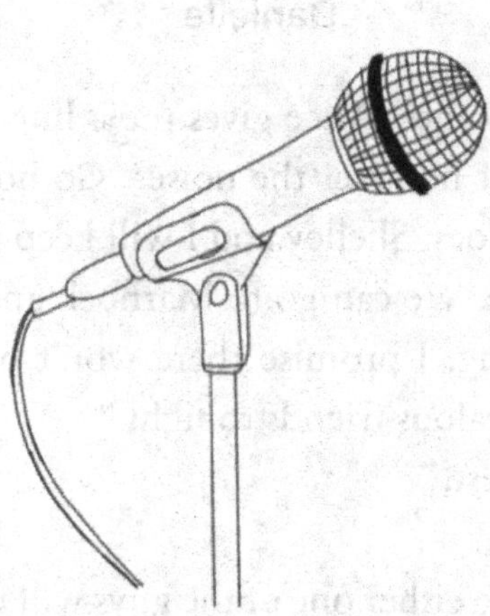

Chapter 24

Danielle

After our performance, Alice gives me a hug and speaks into my ear so I can hear her over the noise. "Go home with your man. See where the night goes. Shelley and I will keep Jake and Jordan out of your hair this time. We can go to Marnock and ride go-karts then get tacos or something. I promise there won't be any interruptions from roommates or jealous friends tonight."

"You're the best."

"I know."

I can't imagine either one of the guys will turn down her offer, so I should have plenty of privacy with Mike for the next few hours.

I do still want to talk more in detail about the issues that led to our fight, but that can wait. Tonight, I'm glad we seem ready to move on from it, and I just want to focus on this amazing man being back in my life.

"Want to get out of here?" I tilt my head up at him.

"I thought you'd never ask."

Back at Mike's apartment, I learn that he does make an impressive carbonara. He wasn't kidding, but it's hard to concentrate on the food he cooked for us when all I want to do is stare at the way his mouth moves while he eats it. Judging from the heat in his eyes when he looks at me across the small kitchen table, he feels the same way.

It's like we are picking up exactly where we left off the last time I saw him, minus the hiccup of our giant argument. The vibe tonight is the same as it was when he walked me down the pier. This is where we both wanted to end up that night. Except tonight, all the time we spent apart adds to the tension that has built up between us, and all of that pressure needs to find a release. You know what they say separation does for the heart. Apparently, it does the same thing to the rest of my body. That kiss on the stage felt like a promise of so much more to come, and I'm ready for all of it.

Mike wipes his mouth with one of the paper towels he set out as napkins. He gathers our plates and dumps them in the sink. Then he turns to face me and tells me exactly what is on his mind.

"I've missed you so much. I would really like to take you to my bedroom." Hearing the needy rasp in his voice causes my mouth to go dry. I lick my lips and swallow hard. He hasn't asked a question, but I answer anyway.

"Yes."

He chuckles and steps forward, reaching out to tuck my hair behind my ear. "Yeah?"

"Yes," I try to repeat, but I only breathe out half of the word before his mouth comes crashing down on mine. He kisses me until the room starts to spin, then breaks away to run his nose along my jaw.

"You set the pace here," he says. "Tell me how you want this to go."

"Um, what do you mean?"

He pulls back just a little bit so he can look at me. "I hope I've made it clear by now that I will always mean exactly what I say to you. I've wanted you since the minute I saw you at that crab feast. I'll be happy with anything that happens here tonight. I want to make sure you are, too. I want to make you feel good now. What do you want? Tell me what you like." His voice is so tender it is almost reverent when he adds, "I need you to talk to me. Please."

I have never had anyone ask me that so directly before. It's embarrassing to talk about, but I know he deserves to have me return the same honest vulnerability he offers so easily. This is a way to do that. I try to harness the confidence I was feeling at karaoke.

"You," I tell him. "I want you."

He smiles. "That part is a guarantee. You have me for as long as you want me." He pulls me into his body and lets me feel what our close contact is doing to him.

"Promise?"

"I do." He runs his fingertips gently down the length of my arm, causing goosebumps to rise along the trail of his touch. "But right now the question is how do you want me, Danielle? Do you want me to be gentle? Or would you prefer something firm? Hard? Or do you want to be teased? Do you like to be in control?" he asks, punctuating each option with a kiss behind my ear. My back arches involuntarily. "Talk to me. Be honest," he says it like he is begging me to share this part of myself. He needs the same level of trust he has always given me. Finally, I can do that for him.

I swallow and duck my head as I start talking against his chest, still hesitant to voice my own needs. "I do like to be teased, and I like a lot of praise. I want you to take control, but not, like, too much."

He uses one finger to lift my chin so I'm looking at him. "Got it. What else?"

"Not super rough, but not too gentle either. I guess somewhere in the middle? Also, I get overheated really easily, so can we keep the fan on?" I feel awkward and silly saying the words out loud, but Mike nods like he appreciates the direction and my confession seems to add to his confidence.

"I can definitely do that."

Judging by the way my body is reacting to just his light touch on my arm and a few kisses, I have no doubts about that. "I know you can."

"Good. The first time we met, you told me you like games. So, maybe we can play a little game to get you ready. Do you think you would like that?"

The heat I feel spreading through me tells me we are not going to need any help in the "getting Danielle ready" department, but I'm intrigued by his suggestion, so I nod. "What did you have in mind?"

"How do you feel about toys?" he asks.

"Like the ponies you bought?"

Mike laughs, but he looks at me with heat behind his eyes. "No."

"Oh." I don't use them often, but I'm not a stranger to toys in the bedroom. Alice gave me a vibrator for my birthday two years ago. When Honey found out, she bought me a gift certificate to an online boutique and shared recommendations of her own, which like I said to her, is something no one wants to hear from their grandmother. Unfortunately, I have to admit her recs were good ones. They helped me learn I need more external stimulation. But *I like the sex toys my grandma gave me* is definitely not something I want to say right now. In the spirit of honesty, I tell him, "I feel fine about small ones. As long as they only go near the front door."

"Here?" He reaches down and rubs me gently through my pants. The heel of his hand is in the perfect spot to create the friction my body is craving, and once again I don't have any control over the way my hips begin to push into him. "Tell me what you need, Danielle."

"Bed."

That's all I have to say before Mike picks me up and throws me over his shoulder. I laugh when he playfully swats at the back of my thighs then gently rubs the sting away.

He sets me down, reaches into his nightstand, and pulls out a pink bullet vibrator about the size of my thumb, then he grabs my waist and tugs me closer to him so the fronts of our bodies are touching. I can feel heat start to build low in my belly and my face feels flushed. I want this. I want him.

"I'm totally down for this, but only if you tell me that hasn't been used on someone else before, because if it has then ew," I say.

He chuckles before answering. "I ordered it after you texted me. Call it wishful thinking. It's brand new for you."

I love that he planned for this, and that he can admit he's been wanting me for a while. Bending so his head is closer, he whispers into my ear with gravel in his voice. "If you're a good girl, maybe I'll even let you keep it." That sends a shiver through me, which does not go unnoticed. "You do like that, don't you?"

I nod. Now that we've pushed past the initial awkwardness, I'm having fun.

"How do we play this game?"

"Lie down," Mike says as he guides me backward until the backs of my knees are leaning into the bed. Happy to comply, I flop onto the cool sheets, giggling. He throws the comforter on the floor and stands over me, giving instructions. "I just told you I bought you a new toy. Is there anything you'd like to say to me?" His tone is commanding, but playful.

"Thank you."

"That's better." He smirks. He looks so hot with dark jeans riding low on his hips and that signature dark tee that stretches across his pecs and highlights his well-defined biceps. I could get used to him taking control like this.

"Get naked," he demands, and I start to obey, sliding my leggings and my panties off together, then sitting up so he can help me remove my shirt. Mike hums his approval and buries his face in my neck. Being with him and seeing the way he appreciates my body gives me a newfound confidence. When I reach behind me to unclasp my black lace bra, he puts his hand over mine. "On second thought, I like you just like this for now. You look gorgeous. Spread your legs for me. Now I'm going to turn on your toy, and when I tell you to, you're going to hold it right here." He runs a finger gently over the little bundle of nerve endings that is already swollen with anticipation. "Does that sound fun?"

"Yes," I breathe.

"Good. Then I'm going to set a timer on my watch so we can start the game. You will hold it there and do whatever I tell you for five minutes. The only rules are that you can't move the vibrator away, and you can't come. If you can control yourself and wait that long, then you win. You will get to decide when, where, or *if* I come tonight."

I smile at him. The game he's made up sounds so *Mike*, ever the athlete, even bringing that competitive spirit into the bedroom, but he's met his match. I never say no to a dare. This should be fun, not to mention easy for me to win. Five minutes is nothing.

"But," he continues "if you can't control yourself and you come before time is up, then I win, and I will get to decide how I come. That means if I tell you to get on your knees for me you do it, no questions asked. Deal? Would you like that?"

I nod. It sounds like I win, no matter what happens. Either I'm going to have an orgasm in the next five minutes, or I'm going to get to do whatever I want to him for the rest of the night. It's not exactly a hardship.

"Use your words."

"Yes."

"Yes, what?"

"Please."

"That's my girl. Here you go." He turns the vibrator on and a low hum fills the space between us while he hands it to me and sets his watch.

Before we get started, I have one question. I hold the vibrator in the air and ask, "What happens if *you* go off before the timer does?"

Mike lets out a small laugh and reaches a hand into my bra. He runs his thumb over my bare skin and admits, "If you can make that happen, then you deserve to win. But I don't plan to make it that easy for you." Pulling his hand away, he taps his watch one more time to start the clock before he says, "Go."

As soon as the vibrator touches me, I realize this is going to be much harder than I thought. The ceiling fan is spinning above us, blowing cool air onto my skin, and causing goose bumps to form on my arms and my legs. It's making me extra sensitive. Seeing Mike, still fully clothed, stare down at me while I'm lying in nothing but my bra and using the toy he bought for me feels so deliciously naughty.

"Does that feel good?"

I can only moan in response. "Show me how you do this when you're alone," he encourages. "Have you been thinking of me, because I've been thinking about you. Every time." His words are turning me on just as much as the vibrations between my legs. Wanting to win, I continue to hold the vibrator in place with my right hand, then slide my left hand down my belly and over my thigh before dipping it between my legs. All of my senses are heightened. I'm barely touching myself, but it feels like I'm on fire. With one finger, I stroke lightly.

"I'm so ready for you."

"I know, baby." Mike puts his arms on either side of me and leans down in a push-up position over my body. "You're doing such a good job. I'm so proud of you." His words make me whimper. He places gentle, barely-there kisses on my forehead and my nose.

"I wish it was your hand," I admit.

He hums a low note. "That can be arranged. We didn't set any rules that said I couldn't touch you." And suddenly his fingers are replacing my own. I can feel his warm breath next to my ear. "Tell me what else you want."

"You." I don't care about the game anymore. I need to feel him.

My eyes are closed, but I can hear his smile when he answers. "Patience. We'll get to that." He slides one finger into me, then another, in long, slow strokes that are making me suck in short breaths as my chest rises and falls.

"I changed my mind. Take off your bra," he orders as he continues his relentlessly perfect torture, holding the vibrator in place for me while I prop myself up on my elbows to remove my last article of clothing and toss it aside, fully exposing my body for him. When he curves his fingers and finds the perfect spot as the toy continues to buzz against me, my back arches involuntarily and I grind greedily into his hand.

"Please. I need you."

"It's hot when you beg me, baby, but your time isn't up yet." That's the second time he's called me baby in the past five minutes, and I love it. His fingers are still stroking in that rhythm I hope he never changes. I wish I could lie here like this forever, but…

"I'm going to come," I whine in a way that would be embarrassing if I could bring myself to care about anything except the way he's touching me.

"Good. I want to feel it." He smiles and nips at my lower lip.

This playfully dominant side of him is driving me into a frenzy. My thoughts are so cloudy and incoherent that I'm not sure I could spell my own name correctly. I can't take it anymore, and my body explodes onto his fingers at the same time that his watch starts to beep.

"Look at that. It's a tie. We both win." He chuckles and takes the vibrator from my hand before switching it off and tossing it on the bed.

"Great," I pant. "Now take your clothes off and get over here."

"Yes, ma'am."

Mike stands and reaches behind his head to pull his shirt off from the back. Then he drops his pants and boxers in one motion, leaving all of his clothing in a pile on the bedroom floor. His body is insane, like a marble statue. The only imperfection is the small scar on his left shoulder.

"Can I touch you?" I ask, still struggling to catch my breath.

"Of course. You can do whatever you want. You earned it," he teases.

I pull myself onto my knees on the bed while he stands in front of me. Kissing him hard, I reach down to touch him at the same time that my tongue explores his mouth. He moans and grabs my thighs.

I pull away just far enough away to ask, "If you'd won the game, what were you going to do to me?"

"That's an excellent question. Why don't you let me show you?"

"I think I'd like that." I smile.

The nightstand drawer is still open and he reaches in again to retrieve a condom. The rest of the night is a blur, but by the morning two more foil wrappers have joined the first, all sitting empty next to a discarded water bottle.

Chapter 25

Danielle

As the early morning sun sneaks in through the sliver of space between the blackout curtains, we lie together trading lazy kisses. We are both exhausted after being up for most of the night. Mike pauses to take a shaky breath. He touches his forehead to mine and closes his eyes when he speaks. "We still need to talk about it."

I know he's not talking about last night. That was wild, fun, and it unlocked a part of me that I did not know existed, a part with no inhibitions that could ask for what I want and take charge of my own pleasure. I've never felt more like myself or more completely accepted by anyone. But that is not what we need to say.

He means our first fight and all of my questions and accusations that are still hanging in the air. It's true. We need to talk. If this addiction is something he still struggles with, I need to know what I can do to help him in those situations. And I need to know I can talk to him about my own fears. Would he steal medicine from Honey if she gets sick? I don't know how to trust him unless we can both be honest about this.

"You're right. We do. If you're ready to share it, I'd really like to know your whole story."

Mike swallows and nods. When he speaks, it's in a quiet voice, just barely above a whisper.

"I think I already told you, but when I was using, my dad wanted nothing to do with me. My mom and my sisters kept in touch. They would let me into the house when my dad wasn't home. He didn't want me around unless I got clean, and I just couldn't do it. I was couch surfing at friends' houses and doing whatever I could to find pills. I stole a lot of money from my mom while she was trying to support me. It caused a ton of issues in my parents' marriage."

When he looks into my eyes, shame radiates off of him. I nod and silently bring my hand to his chest to encourage him to keep going.

"The thing is, outside of my house, it was so easy to hide the fact that I had a problem. The pills made me feel good. I had a lot of energy. I was actually doing well in school, I showed up for the team, and I had friends. My professors didn't notice. My friends just thought I liked to party. Some of them even bought pills from me on the weekends. No one, including me, realized things were getting worse."

"Weren't you worried about drug tests?" I thought that was a big thing in college sports.

"Not really," he admits. "The NCAA allows exceptions for prescription narcotics. I figured it would be easy enough to claim a medical reason if I got caught, but I never did. Not until the crash."

Mike rubs both of his hands on his face then folds them on his stomach. He swallows hard and looks away from me.

"Mike?" I reach out and touch the same spot on his cheek he was rubbing. "Tell me what happened. You said there was an accident." I didn't let him get to that part of the story the first time we talked about this, but I know it must still weigh on him because of the way he stresses over everyone's safety.

When he finally looks back at me, his eyes are glistening.

"I was with my friend, John." Mike's voice breaks and he clears his throat. After one long blink, he continues. "We were on the baseball team together, but he was a few years older. It was a Saturday night and we were getting ready to go to a party. John was about to graduate, so he and his friends were partying pretty hard. I brought out some of my stash and took a few, and John asked if he could have some. I didn't realize how much he had already been drinking. I gave him the pills, and then he drove us to the party."

"He drove after you gave him the pills?"

Mike nods solemnly. "We never made it to the party. John passed out and crashed into a tree. I woke up in the hospital with a few nasty bruises and a concussion, but other than the fact that I have a bit of a hang-up about people I care about driving at night now, I was fine." He looks at me. I stroke his cheek and snuggle closer into him while he continues his story. "Thankfully we didn't hurt anyone else, but John did break a few bones, and he also got arrested for driving under the influence. He didn't rat me out, but he never spoke to me again. My parents were so upset after learning about the accident and the results of my blood tests that Mom went to my coach. My dad wanted me kicked off the team, but my mom and my coach thought it was a better plan to get professional help. They worked with the hospital to get me into a treatment program. The first two times it didn't stick, but the third time it did."

"So, you don't feel like you need pills anymore?"

"I'm not going to lie to you, Danielle. I'm always going to be an addict. It's really hard to be in situations where I have to be around narcotics, like if I'm visiting someone in a hospital. Or I might be tempted to sneak into the medicine cabinet at someone's house. But I've been in recovery for years, and so far I've been able to work through those moments. That doesn't mean it doesn't hurt. It just means I know from experience the pain caused by doing it is worse than the pain of not doing it." He pauses as if he's trying to figure out the best way to explain what he wants to say. I hold his hand and give it a light squeeze.

He sighs. "I wake up and choose the lesser pain. It's still hard, and I'm still worried I'll fail and disappoint you and myself. But I'm not afraid of hard work, and I will do everything I can to avoid that. I did not take Jordan's pills. I drove him to the pharmacy, and then he stashed them in the glove box when we went out to dinner. He forgot they were there. I swear that's the truth."

"I know. I trust you," I reassure him, running my hand lightly over his chest. "You've always been honest with me. It took a lot of courage for you to share all of that," I say because it's true and I don't know how else to respond to the weight of what he just hung in the air between us. He's waiting to see what I'm going to do with all of this heavy new information.

"It didn't feel like I had a choice. I need you to know." There's a long pause before he sighs, resigned. "I love you," he confesses, but the words are laced with sadness. He's still carrying so much shame, and the surprise of hearing those words in this context steals the air right out of my lungs. "Don't say anything," he tells me quickly, and I can tell he's terrified of what my response might be.

In truth, so am I, because I know what I need to do now and it's scary.

"Take some time. Being with me is always going to mean being with an addict. You need to know that."

"I don't need more time to know I love you, too."

His mouth turns up in half of a sad smile before it meets mine for another tender kiss.

Chapter 26

Mike

The weight I've been carrying for years has lifted a bit after telling Danielle about my past. For the first time in a long time, I feel like I am worth something. All I want to do is cling to her so she can't run away again. Danielle is the first woman outside of my family to tell me she loves me back. The ball of anxiety in me is slowly starting to unfurl, but it's still there.

"It's hard for me to believe I deserve it," I admit, running my fingers down her back.

"I love you, Mike," she repeats. The second time stings less than the first, like jumping back into a pool after you are already wet. My body is more willing to accept her words. "Whatever happened in the past, you're not that guy anymore, and I should never have implied you were. I'm sorry I made you doubt yourself."

"No more apologies today. Just truth. Deal?" I kiss the tip of her nose. All I want to do is put this conversation behind us, pull her on top of me, and carry on where we left off last night. But what happens now isn't completely up to me. I need to follow her lead.

"The truth is I love you so much." The words leave her mouth for the third time, healing a little piece of me every time I hear her repeat them. "But it scares me." She lays her head on my chest and I put my arm around her.

This time there are tears on her cheeks, and the lump forming in my throat feels like it might be big enough to choke me. I understand why loving me could be scary. I'll put in the work every day to prove to her that what we have is worth it, but that will take time.

"Don't cry, baby. Please," I beg.

She doesn't try to stop the tears, just swipes a hand down her cheek to brush them away. "This is a lot to think about. I'm still nervous about your career stealing you away from here," she whispers. I squeeze her gently with the arm I have wrapped around her body.

"To be honest, so am I. I don't know where I'll be playing in a year or two." I can't offer her that stability.

"I was going to ask if we could take it slow, but clearly I don't want to." She lets out a little laugh and points to the position we are in right now, naked in my bed.

"We still can if that's what you want. Whatever you need."

"That's not what I want."

It would be reasonable. We haven't known each other long, and it's true that I may still get called away. I won't push for more than she is ready to give. But I don't need to go slow either. I'm already hers.

"What I want is you," she says.

"Well, good. Because same." I kiss her one more time before I change the subject. "Now that we have that settled, tell me more about my girlfriend."

"What do you want to know?"

"Everything. If you could only eat one food for the rest of your life, what would it be? Oh, and what's your favorite dinosaur? Think carefully because your answers will absolutely be held against you." I put my hands behind my head, elbows out, and attempt to lighten the mood with a series of silly questions. It doesn't take her long to decide she likes chocolate croissants and Pteranodons. I go for the more obvious T-Rex and a burrito bowl, because one: it's a T-Rex, and two: if I have to live on something for that long, it should probably be balanced enough that I won't lose muscle mass. She giggles and tells me that sounds like a smart plan.

My eyes are closed while she runs her hands through my hair and her nails lightly scratch my scalp. "What else do you want to know?" She asks.

"Hmm. If you could be anything, what would you be?"

"Anything?"

"Yep. Anything."

"And I have to be honest?"

"Those are the rules, so yeah."

"The answer is so silly, it hardly seems worth telling you. It's not like it will ever happen." She takes her hands out of my hair and folds them on her stomach.

I open my eyes again to stare at her. "Try me. I literally play my favorite game for a living."

"Okay. In that case, I would own a book van," she says, curling into me.

"What's that?"

"You know how everyone would get so excited for the book fair when we were kids? It would be like that, but for all ages. I would sell books out of the window, like the ice cream man or a food truck."

"Only this would be food for your imagination?"

"Exactly. But I know it's dumb." She shrugs.

"Why do you think it's dumb? I think it sounds like a great idea." I turn to her, propping myself up on one bent arm, and using my other hand to twirl her hair around my finger.

"Really?" She brightens. I could listen to her talk about her dream all day.

She says she has never told anyone about the idea before, but she thinks about it a lot. How cool it would be to drive around to other towns like ours where there are no book stores and the library is twenty miles away. She could visit hospitals, nursing homes, and schools or offer mobile story times, book clubs, and talk about her recommendations with people all over Virginia. Maybe other states too. She could see a little bit of the world and travel when she wants, just like she used to do with her mom, but still have a home base here in North Bay with Honey. Sharing all of this with me seems to ignite her spirit in a new way, a way that makes it seem like the silly little idea that has been tugging at her brain might not be so silly after all. Of course it's not. It sounds great. Maybe when I get a higher-paying contract I could even help her make it happen. The idea of making one of her dreams come true warms my chest.

"A book van could be a fun thing to have at the stadium," I say. This is new, dreaming with someone about the future and its possibilities.

"Hmm," she purrs. "Maybe that could be our thing. The Book Lady and her Baseball Guy."

I laugh. "That sounds like a bedtime story."

"It should be," she yawns. "And the book van should definitely also sell M&M's." I pull her closer, and when she is settled in the crook of my arm, I use a soft tone to lull her to sleep while I weave the story together.

"Once upon a time, there was a beautiful princess who wanted to deliver books to all the people of the land. She just so happened to be betrothed to a very handsome, talented, athletic, funny..." That's as far as I get before I feel her body relax and she slips back to sleep for another hour.

Chapter 27

Danielle

When I finally drag myself out of Mike's bed, there is coffee brewing on the counter. Next to the pot I see a new mug with the Blue Crabs team logo on it. My favorite brand of chai concentrate and a half-gallon of milk sit beside it.

Mike is leaning back against the closed refrigerator, sipping his own mug slowly, and looking at me over the rim.

"For me?" I ask.

"I may have taken a peek in Honey's fridge to see what you like." Mike shrugs like it's no big deal, and maybe it's not, but what I'm learning about falling for this man is that it's the small things like this that are actually the biggest reason I love him. That still feels weird to admit, even privately to myself. While I'm mixing my morning drink, Jordan comes out of his room to join us. He must have come in late last night. The team has another game this afternoon, and the guys need to leave soon to make their warm-up.

As Jordan pours himself a bowl of cereal, he looks from Mike to me and takes the opportunity to apologize once again, now that we are all in the same room.

"I really am sorry about the pills. I wouldn't have done that to my man on purpose."

"No one thought you did." Mike blows over the edge of his steaming cup and motions for Jordan to hand him the cereal box. He is not accusing me of jumping to conclusions, but the guilt makes me wince anyway, because until I came to my senses that is exactly what I thought.

"I'm the one who needs to apologize. To both of you. I made a lot of assumptions when I found those pills, and that wasn't fair. Then I did the same thing I blamed you for doing and left Mike alone with those meds. I'm sorry." It shouldn't have taken me this long to say this to Jordan, but it is true. Jordan nods his acceptance. Mike walks over to me and gives me another kiss. Then he leans into my ear and whispers, "I thought I told you to stop apologizing to me about this." He swats my butt lightly. I look at him with wide eyes and motion to Jordan, but I can't help smiling. Mike laughs and shrugs. Jordan is already too absorbed by his breakfast to care what we are doing.

The guys pivot to talking about their strategy for today's game while they eat their cereal. I guess we are all moving on.

"Will we see you at the ballpark today?" Jordan asks me between bites.

"Sorry, but I have another shift. I can bring dinner over later, though. Jackson makes a pretty good crab cake."

They exchange a look I don't understand, then Mike smiles as he sets his mug in the sink, right along with our other dishes from last night. He walks by me, pausing to kiss the top of my head on the way to his room to grab his gear.

"He's eaten a lot of crab cakes this month," Jordan says. "I think getting food from The Blue Crab reminded him of you."

I hold back a grin because I know the feeling. I now stop in Major Dollar almost every day to pick up a pack of M&M's, but I keep that to myself. When Mike comes back into the room, I wish the guys a good game and we all walk out together. I need to go home to shower and change before work.

I haven't been back for long when I get a Facetime call. The on-site internet must finally be working for Mom and Bob. I hit accept and my mother's face appears on my phone screen.

"Dani. There you are. It's been too long."

"Hi, Mom. How's everything going there? How's Bob?"

"We're doing just fine, but I want to hear about everything going on in North Bay. I finally got access to my emails, so I think I'm mostly caught-up. It sounds like you went to a dance with Jake last month, and then you started dating a baseball player, but now you might be broken up?"

"That was accurate until last night. Mike and I are officially back together. There was some strategic karaoke groveling involved."

"That sounds like a fun story. As long as you're happy, I'm happy."

"I am happy," I say, and I realize it's true. Even though it's complicated and the future isn't promised, being with Mike makes me happy. Maybe, for now, that's all I need to know.

"Good, I'm glad. There was one other thing I wanted to talk to you about. Shelia has been emailing me, too. And her last few letters were concerning. She says things have been rocky since March. Is Jake okay?"

"As far as I know. Why?"

Mom and Mrs. Gibson might be complete opposites, but they have been friends since before Jake and I were born. I wonder what she wrote in those emails? March was back before the gala. It must not have anything to do with me.

"Well, maybe you could go pay him a visit soon. It seems like he could use a friend."

"Sure. I'll go over there when we hang up. But first tell me about Haiti."

Mom tells me about the weather and the animals she's encountered, and all of the fantastic people she's met. Then we chat for a while about Bob and the work they're doing, and I tell her the latest gossip Honey has collected. Eventually, though, the connection starts to break and we need to wish each other a hasty goodbye.

"Love you, sweetie."

"You, too. Bye mom."

After we hang up, I get showered and dressed for work, but as promised, I stop at Jake's house before heading to the restaurant. His parents are at a marriage retreat this weekend, so Jake is alone when he answers the door.

"Hey, Dan-Dan. What's up?"

"You tell me. Apparently, both of our moms have been worried about you since March. Do you know what that's about?"

"Oh. Um..." He motions for me to come inside and closes the door behind me. "Probably the fact that I failed three classes, lost my scholarship, and dropped out of school."

"What?"

Seriously, what? I was at school with him less than a month ago and everything seemed fine. Well, it didn't exactly seem fine, but I selfishly assumed it was all about me. This is Jake. Straight A's, computer nerd, so-crazy-talented-it's-borderline-annoying Jake.

"Things got out of hand. I'm handling it, but my parents are less than thrilled with me at the moment."

I'm guessing that's the understatement of the century, knowing his dad. This is why he's been around so much more lately. He moved back home.

"Jake. Why didn't you tell me?"

"I guess I didn't want you to think less of me. Besides, don't take this the wrong way, but what were you going to do about it?"

"What do you mean?"

"You've been a little preoccupied."

"You listen here, Jacob Gibson." I poke his chest with my index finger. He tilts his head and looks down at me, amused. "I don't care who I am dating. You are my best friend, and I am your best friend, and best friends don't keep secrets this big from each other. Now let me be here for you, dammit."

He laughs. "Okay. If it means that much to you, the next time I'm ashamed of myself for failing out of school, you'll be the first one I call."

"Thank you, that's all I ask. Now come here, you big oaf." I hug him. "I'm sorry you went through all of that alone."

"Who said I'm alone?" Jake smirks. I look back toward his bedroom.

"Do you have someone here?"

"I wouldn't be much of a gentleman if I answered that."

"Oh my god, is it the red head? No, don't tell me. I don't want to know. I'm leaving. I'm leaving. Sorry to hear about the school thing. That sucks. We'll talk more later. Have fun with your mystery person. I'm going to work."

"Bye, Dan-Dan."

Chapter 28

Danielle

It's been two weeks since Mike and I made up. We finally made it out to Marnock for a real date last Saturday. Tonight, Honey is in the kitchen with him steaming the crabs for dinner. Mike's parents are bringing Shelley, and they are all coming to our house to share a meal. Honey wanted to give them a taste of our North Bay culture, so we're having crabs and corn on the cob. Honey's special chocolate snowball dessert is already in the freezer for later. I suggested just ordering in from the restaurant, but Honey insisted on cooking for our company herself.

I can hear pieces of her conversation with Mike drifting through the open window as I sit in a rocking chair on the front porch, shucking the corn and tossing the silk into the small trash can I'm holding between my knees.

"That's right," Honey says to my boyfriend. "Yep, go ahead and add the mustard seed to the water now. This recipe calls for a cup of beer, just for flavor. Will that be all right? The alcohol cooks off. You know what? Never mind. Forget I said that. We'll use apple cider vinegar instead."

"Wait. Why are they scratching? These crabs are still alive?" Mike sounds apprehensive.

"They're still kicking, just stunned from being put on ice. Don't let them get you. Oh, there goes that one."

I hear a high-pitched scream that seems to come from Mike, followed by a clatter.

"Get back here, you little twerp," Honey yells at the crab. "Gotcha." Then to Mike she says, "You might not be quite ready for this part. Why don't you go find my granddaughter and help her with the corn? You probably had plenty of that in Idaho. Maybe you can teach her a few tricks for how to clean it faster. She's been out on that porch for hours."

"I can hear you," I call out.

"Haven't said nothing that wasn't true," Honey shouts back.

The door opens and Mike steps onto the porch wearing the World's Sassiest Grandma apron I gave Honey for Mother's Day last year. I laugh and motion to the rocking chair next to me, then put the trash can between us.

Handing over half a dozen ears of corn, I tell him, "That looks good on you."

"Thanks." Mike takes the corn and sits down to shuck it, but he's too distracted to get much accomplished. Every few seconds his eyes dart to the road, searching for his parents' rental car. He's nervous, and if I'm being honest, so am I. They have come to the restaurant a few times with Mike while I was working, but we haven't had much time alone with his family, and they have yet to meet Honey. It's no secret that she doesn't always make the best first impression.

"Hey." I put my hand on his knee and try to sound convincing for both our sakes. "Everything is going to be great tonight."

Mercifully, it isn't much longer before we hear the muffled sound of a car engine and see a minivan turn at Major Dollar and head our way. Before the car has fully stopped, the door flies open and Mike's firecracker of a sister is sprinting toward us. Mike stands to greet her, and she hugs him quickly before turning to me and reaching out with both hands. She pulls me up out of my rocking chair and wraps her arms around me tightly.

"So great to see you again," she says.

"You, too."

Their parents walk up the porch steps to join us. His mom has the same dark blonde hair and gray eyes that Mike and Shelley do, and Mr. Miller is round and bald with a graying beard. They are both smiling.

"Hi, Danielle," he says.

"Nice to see you. Come on in, I'll introduce you to my grandmother. Everyone calls her Honey." I carry a bucket filled with the newly-shucked corn into the house and lead them inside.

Once the crabs and corn are finished cooking, we all sit around the table on Honey's screened-in back patio. Mike is sitting between both of his parents and Honey and I are across from them. Shelley has a chair at the end of the table.

"I've never eaten steamed crabs before. I'm so curious to learn." Mrs. Miller tucks a paper towel into the neck of her blouse like a bib.

"It's a little weird at first, but you get used to it," Mike tells his mom.

"Jordan showed me the other day," Shelley says. "I think I remember."

"Well, go ahead, son. Let's see what this town has taught you." Mr. Miller turns to Mike to get a better view of his demonstration.

"Okay." Mike picks up a crab. "This is controversial, but we like to start with this area here. It's called the apron." I smile while Mike tells his parents my mom's silly anecdote about crabs with a wider apron having a ticket to the White House.

"Seems like you've learned a lot about this."

"Yeah, well, I had an excellent teacher." He winks at me from across the table, and I fall just a little bit harder in love as I reach for the salt for my corn.

"Oh, Mike. I almost forgot. Dolores over at the library gave me a copy of the paperwork for you," Honey says.

"Paperwork?"

"Oh, um, yeah. Thanks." Mike dips his chin and looks down as though he's intensely focused on his crab.

"Mike?"

"It's nothing, really. I just figured North Bay should have some in-person NA and AA meetings."

"That's not nothing. That's great. Good job, Mikey." Mrs. Miller rubs Mike's back while she smiles up at him. When she realizes she is getting crab seasoning on his shirt, she tries to wipe it away, but only makes it worse.

"It's cause for celebration, is what it is. Save some room for dessert," Honey reminds everyone. "I made chocolate snowball."

"That sounds amazing," Mike tells her. Then in a shyer tone he says, "As long as we're celebrating, I also got some news from Coach that I wanted to share."

"Oh." His mom clasps her hands together in anticipation. My heart is suddenly in my throat. It sounds like whatever he is about to say will be good for his career, but it could mean he will be leaving North Bay even sooner than we thought. I brace myself for the news.

"My contract has been extended, and they're making me the starting shortstop on the Blue Crabs next year." It's not exactly a promotion for him because, with Davis on the way out, Mike has already been starting in most of their recent games, but this is great news. He gets to continue doing what he loves, his coach has recognized his talent, and he gets to stay in North Bay with me, at least for now.

"That's fantastic. The position and the meetings. Both of them." I scramble from the table to his side. He stands up to meet me and catches me as I leap into his arms.

"That's my boy," Mr. Miller says.

I am not processing much beyond my own happy squeals and Mike's low chuckle at the base of my neck, but I know Mike's mom tells him, "It looks like you are fitting right in here in North Bay."

That's the truth. We overanalyzed and overcomplicated things until they all fell apart and we had to put them back together again, but in the end it was simple. This is where he belongs. Right here with me.

Epilogue

One Year Later

Danielle

"**Y**ou look breathtaking, sweetie."

My mom smooths a few flyaway hairs into place for me while Alice finishes fastening the back of my trumpet-cut gown. I can't believe it's finally here. In less than an hour, it will be official. Mike and I are creating our own family.

He had a great season, and last month he signed with the Foxhounds. There is finally a Major League Baseball team coming to Virginia, and Mike has been recruited to join them. We used his signing bonus to buy Honey's house. It was Mike's idea. He knew how much I wanted to stay connected to my life here. Honey will continue to live in the house with us so we can care for her as she gets older, and she no longer has to worry about the burden of the increasing property taxes or bills. She can relax and enjoy her retirement. Not that she wasn't doing that before. Of course, Mike will still need to travel with the team. I'll go with him whenever I can, but our home will always be in North Bay.

There's a soft knock on the door, and we hear Jake ask, "Is everybody decent in there?"

"We're all dressed, if that's what you mean, but you'll never hear me promise to be decent," Honey answers from our side.

Jake laughs as he opens the door. He stops in his tracks the moment he sees me.

"Danielle," he says my name in an awed whisper.

"It's just a dress. Still me in here under all of this fabric. Call me Dan-Dan. It will make this all feel more normal."

"I can do that." He nods as he starts walking toward me again. "Mike asked me to give you these?" Jake takes a package of peanut M&M's from his pocket. Honey cackles from her chair in the corner.

"Always with the candy, that one."

I feel a blush rising to my cheeks. If they only knew. My mind drifts to the night last week when Mike brought strawberries with melted chocolate into the bedroom.

"I'll just set them down here." Jake puts the candy next to my purse on an empty chair. "Are you ready?"

"As much as I'll ever be."

We walk outside as a group, and Alice holds up the train of my dress while we cross the driveway and round the Gibsons' house to get to their backyard. A hundred white folding chairs are set up in rows on either side of a wide grass aisle, and everyone stands and turns to face me when Rodriguez starts to strum Ed Sheeran's *Perfect*.

Emily goes first, tossing white rose petals from her wicker flower girl basket before she joins Regina in the front row next to Bob.

Then Jake escorts Alice down the center aisle. Those two are actually managing to get along, for once. They walk down to the pier, where Mike is already waiting with Jordan standing next to him as his best man. Edna Plum is positioned in the center, under a floral arch at the end of the pier, ready to act as our officiant. I hold my bouquet of flowering dogwood in front of me and stick out my elbows so that Mom and Honey can each take an arm.

"Let's get my granddaughter married."

And that's exactly what we do.

This day is better than I could have ever imagined. I especially love the end, when I get to drive away with my new husband in my freshly decorated book van, with the words "Just Married" written in chalk paint on the back window.

Want to know what happened when Alice and Jake went go-karting? Who was in Jake's bed? Turn the page for a sneak peek of **Right as Rain**, Book 2 in the North Bay Series.

Right as Rain

Alice

Jordan was supposed to be our buffer, but he left a few minutes ago with his roommate's sister. So now I'm buckled into a go-kart getting helmet hair while I chase Jacob Gibson in circles around an indoor track. When your best friend has a different best friend who is not you, things can get awkward. I thought I could handle one night, for Danielle's sake. I thought wrong.

I promised my BFF I would keep those two occupied tonight so she can finally get some alone time with her boyfriend. There have been weeks of drama, but from the way sparks were flying at karaoke earlier, it looks like things between Danielle and Mike are about to get spicy. The least I can do is keep our friends out of their way. Well, Jordan's our friend. Jake is Danielle's best friend and my worst frenemy. Driving out of town to occupy them with a game of laser tag and some go-kart racing seemed like such a good idea two hours ago.

The go-karts roll to a stop and we awkwardly climb out of the harnesses. Just as I step out of the car, a little boy exits his own go-kart and runs toward his parents. He's only about eight years old, but because I am barely five feet tall, we're almost the same height.

"Mom, mom, mom, did you see me? Can we get ice cream now?" He's barreling ahead at full speed, and with the go-kart blocking the other side, I have nowhere to go when he crashes into me.

"Oof." I fall back into my car as the boy sprawls onto the track, scraping his knee. He looks up at me and glares.

"Watch where you're going, lady. Mooom. This lady was in the way and I fell down. And she has a weird thing in her nose. Gross, it looks like a metal booger." He's pointing at me, even though we are only inches apart.

"I see that. I'm so sorry, baby. Grown-ups should pay closer attention. Let's get you some ice cream." His mother comes through the gate to scoop him up in her arms and she carries him away. She shoots me a dirty look in the process, like I wasn't minding my own business when her little cherub knocked into me. I can hear her muttering under her breath about my pink hair and piercings, as if the way I look has anything to do with what happened.

I roll my eyes and try to pull myself out of the car again, but it's a struggle this time, with my butt firmly wedged between the seat and the steering wheel. There's a throbbing on my hip that will probably bruise tomorrow, and my right ankle is burning because I twisted it on the way down. A hand appears and yanks me out by the arm.

"You good, Louse?"

Yep. Jake calls me Louse, as in the singular form of head lice, because in the seventh grade he thought it was hysterical that Alice spells "a lice." Ten years later, not much has changed.

"I think so," I say as he stands me up. "Although, as always, I would be even better if you weren't touching me."

"Then maybe try learning how to avoid collisions with small children."

"Shut up. It was his fault. And I'm fine."

But when I try to walk, pain shoots up my ankle and I wince. Ugh. I do not need to deal with this right now. Not in front of Jake. Jerk kid, this is all his fault. This is exactly why I'm never having any little crotch goblins of my own. Well, it's part of the reason. I suck in a deep breath and try to walk again.

"Ouch." This time a small yelp escapes on its own.

"Okay, tough guy, just sit back down. I'll go get some ice," Jake tells me. But I don't want to take orders from him, and I hate that now there are so many eyes on me as the next round of wannabe drivers are impatiently waiting for their turn.

"First of all, I'm a tough *girl.* No, not girl. Woman. And can you just—" I don't mean to sound so angry, but I do because I'm embarrassed and in pain, and I hate having all of this attention on me. I'm not actually sure what I want him to do, so I let the sentence hang. Jake is biting his cheek and trying not to laugh at me. I'm sure I sound ridiculous. He must see something in my face that makes him take pity on me because he rolls his eyes and scoops me up so I'm lying across both of his annoyingly strong, tattooed arms. Instinctively, I start to wrap my arms around his neck, but then I think better of it and cross them over my chest. He chuckles.

"Glad you're finding this amusing," I snap.

He doesn't respond to that, just sets me down in a chair by the snack bar and asks the teenagers behind the counter for a cup of ice. He puts a lid on it and wraps it in a handful of napkins from the dispenser before handing it to me.

"Here. Give me your keys. I'm driving your car home."

God, he's so bossy. I hate that looking up at him from this angle makes me notice the way his Pokémon t-shirt stretches across his pecs.

"You wish I'd let you touch Bertie." It took me years to save up for my vintage Volkswagen Beetle, and I am very protective of her.

"Guess we're spending the night here then, because you couldn't even walk the twenty feet from the track to the snack bar just now. You really think you're going to be able to drive on that foot?"

I hate that he has a point. His dark hair is falling into his face, and when he brushes it away it's hard not to notice the veins popping on his arms. I would rather die than let anyone catch me ogling Jacob Gibson. He would never let me hear the end of it. But it's not my fault he's filled out so much this year and finally grown into his formerly lanky body. He must be spending a lot more time in the gym.

I want to argue, but I truly can't put any weight on my foot, so I don't know how I would be able to use the pedals. Reluctantly, I let him scoop me up again and carry me to my own car, then I bend down to hold the ice to my ankle.

"Do you want to go over to the Urgent Care and get an X-ray while we're in Marnock?" he asks as we pull out of the crowded parking lot. We drove for forty minutes to get here tonight, which means we are closer to health care. North Bay, our home town, is too small to have its own 24-hour access to a medical center, but there is one another half an hour away from here. "We're more than halfway there already."

"No, I think I just rolled it. It will probably be better in a day or two." I don't know if that's true, but either way I can't afford to be taking on any medical bills for small things like this. Admission to the go-karts and money for the gas to get out here was a little bit of a stretch as it is, but an X-ray will cost hundreds. Then if they send me to the Emergency Room for more tests or a cast, it could add up to thousands of dollars I don't have. "Um, thanks for the ice. Do you think you can just take me to Honey's house?" I look straight ahead, not wanting to make eye contact. He already knows why I don't want to go home.

It's no secret that my house is a miserable place to be. Everybody in North Bay knows Earl Caulfield is a hot mess. Thankfully, Jake doesn't say anything about it.

"Yeah. Honey's." Jake clears his throat, and I think I see his grip on the steering wheel tighten just a bit before he reaches over to fool with the radio. Before we leave Marnock, he pulls into the gas station. "I'm going in to grab a soda, you want one?"

"No. I'm fine." I wince, holding the dripping ice cup against my skin and watch him walk away. When did he get so freaking hot? It's really unfair. He was our valedictorian in high school, and he's been away at college for three years. He's only home because the semester just ended. People who come from rich families shouldn't be allowed to also be smart and good-looking. Especially when they have obnoxious personalities.

When Jake comes back, he opens the driver's side door and puts two Cokes in the cupholders between us because he bought me one anyway, then turns around and starts pumping gas into my car.

"What are you doing? I said I didn't want one. I have a job. I can buy my own drinks," I yell through the open door. I might be tight on cash sometimes, but I can pay my own way. I don't need a rich boy to buy me sodas or gasoline. I take care of myself.

Jake bends to stick his head through the doorframe and speaks in an exaggerated calm tone meant to highlight how ridiculous he thinks I am.

"Relax, Lousy. You drove out here. I'll cover the gas to get us home. It's hardly charity. This is how normal people function. I realize that might be a new concept for you." He taps the hood of the car twice, dismissing me like he's a middle-aged dad and I'm a kid he's sending off to summer camp.

"Whatever. Just take me to Honey's." I twist the cap off my soda bottle, no sense in wasting it. I attempt to take a sip, but it bubbles over and erupts, getting all over me.

"Ugh!" I screech. "Did you do this on purpose?"

Jake laughs diabolically as he gets back in the car and twists the cap off his own drink. His hardly fizzes at all and he takes a long drag from the bottle before looking at me.

"I did not. Although I can't say shaking yours up a little didn't cross my mind, this time it was pure karma. And it was exactly as hilarious as I thought it would be. The universe agrees with me, you need to lighten up a little."

"Easy for you to say when you aren't the one whose lap is completely soaked."

His expression changes for a brief second, and I could swear there is a flash of heat in his eyes, but it disappears just as quickly. He reaches into my cluttered back seat and hands me one of my own crumpled t-shirts to use as a towel. Then he produces a small pack of peanuts he must have purchased when he went inside and uses his teeth to tear them open. He pours half the package into his soda and offers the rest to me, but I ignore the offer. I turn in my seat to face away from him and look out the window for the rest of the ride.

Unfortunately, thirty minutes later we find out that my best friend's grandmother isn't home. I try to call her, but her cell phone goes straight to voicemail. Who knows where Honey disappeared to after we saw her at karaoke earlier? That woman has always been a wild card. And there is no way either Jake or I are interrupting Danielle tonight to get her to let us into Honey's house.

"Come on." Jake motions to his parents' huge waterfront house, which is directly across the street from Honey's much more modest rancher. He and Danielle grew up neighbors, whereas my family was on the other side of town. They rode the bus together every day, but I lived close enough to ride my bike to school.

"What? No. I'm not going home with you." Although, I don't want to go back to my house either. Being around my dad when I can't get out of his way quickly isn't the best idea. It's not that I think he would hurt me on purpose, but when he gets in one of his moods, he might break things or start yelling, and I just can't deal with that right now.

"I'm not seeing a lot of options here, Lousy." Jake must notice me looking at my car and formulating my plan because he is already protesting. "Absolutely not. No way am I agreeing to let you sleep in your car right in front of my perfectly decent house." The largest waterfront property in North Bay is a lot more than "perfectly decent." It's intimidating, and it's a reminder of how different our lives really are.

"Well, good thing you have no say in how I spend my nights. I'll be fine."

I mean, it wouldn't be the first time I've slept in my car to avoid my dad, but I don't think anyone knows that. North Bay is a safe neighborhood. We only have three police officers, and we share them with the neighboring towns. I've lived here for my entire life, and in those twenty-one years, I can't remember ever hearing of a serious crime. Occasionally, a teenager might try to shoplift a tube of mascara from Major Dollar, and once a tourist family walked out of the Blue Crab restaurant without paying their tab, but that turned out to be an accident and they came back the next day to square up with Edna. Honestly, I'm surprised Honey even locked her doors. I wish she hadn't, because then we could have avoided this whole predicament. Besides, my ankle is already starting to feel better. Kind of. Maybe. Okay, fine. It still hurts a lot.

Jake rolls his head in a slow circle, stretching out some of the tension from the car ride. It seems like his patience with me is wearing thin. Well, bro, same.

"Don't fight me on this, Lousy. It's getting late, your clothes are sticky, and this has been a crazy long day. We're going over to my place. It's right there. My parents aren't home, they're at some marriage retreat near the beach. I'll take their room and you can sleep in mine. Besides, I still have your keys. So, actually, I do have a say in this."

He holds the keys over my head and laughs while I try to reach up and grab them. I'm in no state to jump, but even if I could, Jake is a full foot taller than I am, so it is pointless trying to fight him on this.

There might have been a time before everything that happened in high school when sleeping in Jacob Gibson's bed would have seemed like a dream come true. Now it's just an inconvenience that I don't seem to be able to avoid tonight. It probably would be a good idea to elevate my foot and get more ice, and that's going to be hard to do in the car. Plus, these damp, sticky clothes really are uncomfortable.

"Come on," he says, pocketing my keys again. "You can see Hazel."

That seals my fate. As annoying as I find her owner, I love that sweet fifteen-year-old bulldog. It will be worth putting up with Jake tonight if I can convince Hazel to sleep snuggled up with me.

"Fine." I huff out a breath. I realize he has been pretty helpful tonight and I sound like an ungrateful brat, so I try to rein it in because I refuse to let him have the upper hand when it comes to matters of civility. "Thank you."

"Aw, that must have been really hard for you. Was it? Was it hard to admit you need me right now?" He has the easy laugh of someone who doesn't know what it means to struggle.

I want to wipe that smirk off his face, but instead I just hobble behind him and cross the street.

◆◆◆

See more of Jake and Alice's story in *Right as Rain.*

Author's Note

Thank you for visiting North Bay with me. You are the reason I get to bring these characters to life and continue doing what I love. Thank you for indulging my dreams. I would love it if you could leave a review on Amazon or Goodreads or post on social media about this book. Your reviews and shares help independent authors so much! If you want to see more of Mike, Danielle, Alice, Jake, and Honey make sure to visit my website http://stephaniegiese.com and sign up for my newsletter. You'll have exclusive access to deleted scenes and be among the first to know when new books are released. Sign up today to learn how Mike earned his new nickname from the team!

Scan the below QR code to leave your review on Amazon.

Acknowledgements

It takes a lot of people to make a book happen. Thank you to my family for all your unwavering support during the hours I ignore you to spend time with my imaginary friends in a fantasy world of my own creation. My amazing husband, Eddie, and our children: Nick, Donny, Abigail, Ana, and Penny, you are my real world. Special thanks to my mom, Teresa Wilkins, for her proofreading skills, and my daughter Abigail for her original artwork.

Tabatha, Meredith, and Veronica, you are the best alpha readers a girl could ask for and incredible friends as well. Thank you for wading through half-finished scenes and offering insightful feedback before the story even made sense. This book is better because you cared enough to tell the truth. Matthew, I appreciate having a critique partner as committed as you are to forcing me to answer hard questions, finish the things I start, and take myself seriously. I would probably still be neck-deep in incomplete manuscript files if not for you.

My editor, Denise Drapeau, it was an honor working on this book with you. I learned so much, and I am excited to see where we can take these characters next. My cover designer, Rachel Howard, thank you for bringing these characters and their world to life.

To all my beta and ARC readers, I appreciate your time, feedback, and enthusiasm.

I am so lucky to have you all on my team.

About The Author

Stephanie Giese is an indie author and freelance writer. She lives in an overflowing house in Florida with her husband, five teenagers, her mom, and one very naughty beagle.

www.ingramcontent.com/pod-product-compliance
Lightning Source LLC
Chambersburg PA
CBHW011033190726
48290CB00011B/2821